W9-ASR-116

The MIGHTY Miss MALONE

Also by Christopher Paul Curtis

Mr. Chickee's Messy Mission

Mr. Chickee's Funny Money

Bucking the Sarge

Bud, Not Buddy

The Watsons Go to Birmingham—1963

The MIGHTY Miss MALONE

Christopher Paul Curtis

This is a work of fiction. Names, characters, places, and incidents either are the product of the author's imagination or are used fictitiously. Any resemblance to actual persons, living or dead, events, or locales is entirely coincidental.

Visit us on the Web! randomhouse.com/kids

Educators and librarians, for a variety of teaching tools, visit us at randomhouse.com/teachers

Library of Congress Cataloging-in-Publication Data is available upon request.

ISBN 978-0-385-73491-2 (trade)
ISBN 978-0-385-90487-2 (lib. bdg.)
ISBN 978-0-375-89736-8 (ebook)

The text of this book is set in 12-point Goudy.

Book design by Kathleen Gartner

Printed in the United States of America

10 9 8 7 6 5 4 3 2 1

First Edition

Random House Children's Books supports the First Amendment and celebrates the right to read.

In memory of three of my heroes:
my uncle,
George Taylor.
Tuskegee Airman. Congressional Gold Medal winner.
Hero. 1914–2008.
My friend
Harrison Edward Patrick. Hero. 1949–2010.
And
my brother,
Herman David Curtis. Hero. 1957–2011.

DEDICATION

There is a small archipelago off the eastern coast of Africa whose name escapes me at the moment. The name isn't the important part; the important part is the group of people who have inhabited these islands for millennia and developed a unique and thriving culture. Unfortunately, I can't recall what these people are called either, but once again that's not really important.

What is important is the language these kind, peaceful people have developed. Linguists have noted that unlike other languages, which have developed out of practical necessity, this language is based on the description of emotions. The one word in this language that I want to focus on is the word for a Pavlovian type of behavior found in humans in which one action inevitably causes the same reaction. That word is *aharuf*, and it is translated as meaning the process by which the sight or thought of a particular person, place or object triggers an instantaneous lowering of the *gnar* (a concept most like blood pressure), a sharp rise in the *Qarlo* (most closely related to our understanding of endorphins) and an unavoidable beaming grin like that of the upper-paradise squink (a horselike quadruped very similar to the common American jackass).

After a long journey, I have found my *aharuf*, two people whom I cannot think about without splitting my face in a joyous smile. No matter what is going on around me, all I have to do is bring them to mind and I'm transported to a better place. They are my wife, Habon, and my daughter, Ayaan.

This book is dedicated to Habon and Ayaan in, as Miss Malone might say, *internal*, undying gratitude for bringing me joy and guaranteeing that at the end of each day my cheeks will be sore from far too much smiling.

Part One

". . . Gang Aft A-Gley . . ."
Late May 1936
Gary, Indiana

Chapter One

Journey to Wonderful

"Once upon a time . . ."

If I could get away with it, that's how I'd begin every essay I write.

Those are the four best words to use when you start telling about yourself because anything that begins that way always, *always* finishes with another four words, ". . . they lived happily everafter."

And that's a good ending for any story.

I shut my dictionary and thesaurus and went back over my essay for the last time.

The best teacher in the world, Mrs. Karen Needham, had given us a assignment to write about our families. I knew, just like always, she was going to love mine. She'd only asked for two pages but this was our last essay for the year, so I wrote six.

Once upon a time . . . in Gary, Indiana, lived a family of three very special, very happy and uniquely talented people. I am the fourth member of that family and much too modest to include myself in such a grandiose description of their exalted number. But many people say I am of the same ilk and for that I remain internally grateful.

My mother, Mrs. Margaret "Peggy" Sutphen Malone, was born here in Gary, Indiana. She is willowy and radiant and spell-blindingly beautiful. She is also very intelligent. She has a great job cleaning for the Carsdale family. Yes, that Carsdale family! The family whose patriarch is the president of the Gary Citizens' Bank.

Her most endearing trait is that she is the glue holding this family together.

"Deza?"

I jumped and my pencil flew out of my hand.

When I'm writing or reading a book, everything else around me disappears. Father says it's because I've settled into what I'm doing, the same way my brother Jimmie does when he's singing.

"*Jimmie!* I told you not to sneak up on me like that when I'm writing!"

He handed me the pencil. "I couldn't help it, sis, you were so far gone. What're you writing?"

"My last essay for Mrs. Needham."

"You know, a lot of people are saying her not coming back to teach is the best thing that ever happened at Lincoln Woods School."

"James Malone, if I ever give one-half a hoot what a lot of

people are saying, you have my permission to slap me silly. Mrs. Needham is the best teacher in the world. Now, if you don't mind. I never bother you when you're singing, don't bother me when I'm writing."

"But lots of people love listening to me sing, Deza, seems to me like only you, that little pest Clarice Anne Johnson and Mrs. Needham like reading what you write."

Jimmie is one of those people who can say something that might sound mean at first, but when he smiles and makes his eyebrows jump up and down you can't help smiling. He gets this deep, deep dimple in his right cheek and you end up laughing right along with him.

My dearest friend, Clarice Anne Johnson, has a horrible and completely un-understandable crush on Jimmie. She says she bets you could pour cornflakes in his dimple and eat them out with a spoon.

I'm hoping Clarice's taste in boys improves as she gets older.

"Jimmie, please."

"Sorry, sis. I'm heading out, can I do anything for you before I split?"

"No, thanks. Just make sure you're back for supper."

I looked at Mrs. Needham's instructions again. "What is the most annoying trait of some of your family members?"

That was easy to come up with for Father and Jimmie, but I couldn't think of a single annoying trait for Mother. I wrote:

Mother's pet peeve is that she hates the way a lot of people are mean to Jimmie for no reason.

Her dreams are to see Father get a job where he doesn't always get laid off, for Jimmie to start growing again and be happy and to watch me graduate from college and be a teacher.

My father, Mr. Roscoe Malone, was born in a village in Michigan called Flint, which is geologically located 250 miles northeast of Gary. For some reason that none of us can understand he is very proud of this. He is tall and strikingly handsome, he's also intelligent and well-read.

He toils and labors mostly for the Company doing work in a horribly hot furnace and sometimes being a janitor.

His most annoying trait is the way he uses alliteration every chance he has.

I looked up from my paper. That is so true, but I wondered for a minute if I should put it in the essay. It isn't like he can help himself.

He always calls me his Darling Daughter Deza, and I'm supposed to answer that he is my Dearest Delightful Daddy. He calls Jimmie the Genuine, Gentle Jumpin' Giant, and Jimmie's supposed to call him his Fine Friendly Father Figure. Father also calls Mother the Marvelous Mammalian Matriarch, but she says she won't respond because she refuses to play silly word games with such a "hardheaded husband who hasn't heard how horrible he is."

Mother told me, "Such nonsense is in the blood of the Malones and you should be happy that so far it looks like you haven't inherited any of it."

She says Jimmie is a different story.

I tapped the pencil on my teeth. I know it's rude and

disloyal to discuss family business with other people, but Mrs. Needham says good writing is *always* about telling the truth.

Father's most endearing trait is that he is the best storyteller and poet in the world. He can come up with a poem at the most inappropriate times. His pet peeve is that even though he's smart it's very hard to find a job.

His dream is to do what he was trained to do in Flint, being a carpenter.

The oldest child in our family, Mr. James Edward Malone, is fifteen years old and has been blessed with the singing voice of a angel.

Jimmie's most annoying trait is that he has what Mother says is a napoleon complex. That means Jimmie is not as tall or robust as most boys his age and tries to make up for it by being as loud and full of braggadocio as he can. He also gets in lots of fights.

Jimmie's most endearing trait is that he loves me more than any big brother has loved a little sister since time immoral.

Jimmie *is* the best big brother in the world.

On my last birthday we had just finished eating and I could barely sit still because after supper the birthday person gets something special.

It was my turn to clear the dishes and I stalled around in the kitchen to give them lots of time to get my surprise ready, then walked back into the dining room.

There were two cupcakes with a candle in the middle of them sitting at my and Jimmie's spots! A chocolate frosted one for me and a vanilla frosted one for Jimmie!

I was speechless.

Jimmie said, "Wow, Ma, these are store-bought!"

Mother must've been putting pennies aside for a long time to buy two such beautiful little cakes.

Father said, "James, please do the honors."

Jimmie closed his eyes, then settled into singing "Happy Birthday."

I got chills. I wasn't sure if it was because of Jimmie's voice or because I was so excited.

Mother and Father joined in on the last chorus.

When they were done I smiled so hard it felt like my cheekbones were crushing my eyeballs!

Jimmie said, "I got you two gifts. One, I'll wash *and* dry dishes for a week, and two . . ."

He looked at Father and they walked into the other room.

When they came back each one of them was carrying a heavy package wrapped in newspapers.

They set them down in front of me.

I said, "Flint style or Gary style?"

Father always tells us Mother opens packages and envelopes Gary style. He says we Gary people pry and poke and pull the envelope so carefully and daintily and take so long doing it that we might as well be doing brain surgery. He says we do it that way because Indiana people are so cheap that we want to use the same envelope over and over.

"Word has it," he said once, "that there've only been two envelopes used in the whole state of Indiana since the War of 1812."

Then he showed us what he called opening something

Flint style. It was a race to see how quick you could get what was inside the envelope or package out.

"To be officially Flint style," Father says, "the envelope or the wrapping paper has to be shredded into at least six different pieces. It's got to look like confetti."

I glanced at Mother.

She shook her head and said, "I suppose you can't fight the fact that half of your blood is from Flint."

I tore into the newspaper on the first present and was shocked!

It was old and tired and I had used it a million times before. How did Jimmie get this?

Jimmie said, "The library was selling books they didn't want anymore. Here's the receipt for these two."

He handed me a piece of paper.

He'd paid three cents for the dictionary and two cents for a thesaurus.

Inside the first page of the dictionary someone had stamped in red ink WITHDRAWN.

Jimmie had written underneath that, *Febarery 14, 1935, happy twelve brithday sis.*

The dictionary and the thesaurus are the best birthday presents I will ever get. The best "brithday" presents too.

I looked back over my essay.

Jimmie's pet peeve is when people call him Shorty, Little Fella, or worst of all, Pee-Wee.

His dream is to start growing again until he is a six-foot-tall man who is covered with bumpy muscles. Jimmie's other dream is to be the first boy to drive a rocket ship to the moon. He is very disillusional.

The youngest Malone child, your devoted author of this essay, Deza, is twelve years old, which makes me the third-oldest child in my class. I didn't flunk, but two years ago I had to sit out a year of school because Mother was struck down by a horrible disease called Tic Do La Roo. That is a French word that means "Pain of the Devil." Her face felt like it was on fire and she needed a very responsible person to look after her all day. I did it. My teachers said I could skip fourth grade to stay with my class but being a year behind meant I could be in class with the dearest friend anyone's ever had, Miss Clarice Anne Johnson. I fought to stay. And I won.

I am neither very intelligent nor very tall. I also have not been blessed with a beautiful singing voice. I have a pleasingly even disposition unless it's one of those times that I become very angry or scared and have embarrassing wishes to hurt someone real bad.

In the next part of the essay I was supposed to tell about *my* most annoying trait. I really did try, but I couldn't think of even one. I thought about making one up, but even with my good imagination nothing came to mind that anyone with a whit of sense would believe.

Clarice and I had been walking home. "What do you think is my most annoying trait, Clarice?"

She said, "Ooh, Deza, you're not done with the essay yet?"

"I was just having trouble with that part."

"You know that I don't think you have any annoying traits, Deza, but . . ."

She stopped.

"But what?"

"But maybe you could use some of the things other people say about you behind your back."

I don't pay a bit of attention to anything people say behind my back, but Mother tells me and Jimmie that we can learn something from anybody, even from a big idiot.

I said, "What do they say?"

"Well . . ."

I thought Clarice might have a problem coming up with something, but she held up a finger. "First, they think you're too friendly with teachers. . . ."

Her next finger went up.

"Second, they say you think you're so smart. . . ."

Another finger came up.

"Third, they say you think your family is so great. . . ."

Another finger.

"Fourth, they say you talk too much and that you talk all proper. . . ."

Her thumb came up.

"Fifth, they think you've got your nose stuck up in a book most of the time. . . ."

Clarice raised a finger on her left hand. "Sixth . . ."

I stopped her before we had to sit so she could take off her shoes and start counting on her toes. I said, "Maybe I do talk a little too much."

At home I put in my essay:

My most annoying trait is that some of the time I might talk a little too much, I can be very verbose. I also exaggerate but that is because I come from a family of great storytellers which is not the same as great liars.

My most endearing trait, and being as modest as I am I had to ask my brother Jimmie for this, is that I have the heart of a champion, am steady as a rock and can be counted on to do what is required. Jimmie also said I am the smartest kid he has ever met, but my all-encompassing and pervasive humility prevents me from putting that on this list.

My first pet peeve is when people don't pronounce my name right. They'll say Dee-za instead of Dez-uh, just like the first syllable of a desert, like the Sahara, which is geologically a arid, huge part of Africa. And they do it on purpose. My second pet peeve is that the Gary Iron-Head Dogs, the best baseball team in the world, have been cursed and will never win the Negro Leagues championship.

My dream is to read every book in the Gary Public Library and to be a teacher who has the reputation for being tough but fair. Just like Mrs. Needham.

I had the perfect ending for the essay.

In summation and conclusion, the Malone family has four members who are very bright, very good-looking and uniquely talented, just not all in one person at the same time. We are the only family in the world, in my ken, that has a motto of our own! That motto is "We are a family on a journey to a place called Wonderful."

I can't wait until we get there!

Chapter Two

The Pie Thief

Jimmie said, "So, what's for dessert, Ma?"

We had just finished supper and Chiefs' and Children's Chow Chat, something Father had made up where we told each other what our day had been like.

Mother's eyes locked on Jimmie's. She saw he was serious. "Well, Master Malone, this evening the chef has prepared for your dessert a lovely stack of dishes which Deza will wash and you will dry."

Jimmie said, "How 'bout tonight we just let those dishes drip themselves dry?"

Mother said, "How 'bout tonight, just like every other night, we let 'em be dried by a little drip?"

Jimmie was still smiling. Most times if any of us forgot and called him anything that had the word "little" in it he'd get pouty and would quit talking.

"Can I be excused for a second?"

Mother nodded and Jimmie went into the living room.

Father said, "Dessert? Where did that come from?"

From the porch Jimmie yelled, "Hey!"

He walked back through the dining room and into the kitchen holding something behind his back.

A second later he came back smiling like a Cheshire cat, still with his hands behind his back.

He said, "Ma, I'ma give you one more chance. What would have to happen for me to take a month or two off from drying the dishes?"

Mother said, "What's this all about, Jimmie? You can get a couple of months off doing the dishes if lightning strikes either one of us."

Jimmie put his hand to his ear. "Wait! Was that the roll of thunder I just heard? *Ta-da!*" He showed us a pie tin holding a half a gorgeous apple pie!

It was thicker and bigger than any pie I'd ever seen. The crust was the same light-brown goldy color as the wood floor in the kitchen. There were strips of dough on it in a criss-cross way and some of the juices had bubbled up and oozed out.

Father said, "Where did you get that pie?"

Jimmie said, "You don't know, and you don't want to know."

I had to shake my head. Jimmie loves talking about rocket ships and outer space and I figure that's because he comes from a different planet than the rest of the Malones.

And most other people who live on Earth too.

He was smiling and making his eyebrows go up and down. He was hopping from one foot to the other. All he needed was a green hat and some pointy shoes with big silver buckles to look like a little brown leprechaun holding on to a pot of gold.

I shook my head. Jimmie had broken our deal.

Our deal was that if I was going to do anything that wasn't about school or books or studying, stuff he calls "regular living," I'd ask him for his advice. I said I'd do it if he promised when he made plans that were about anything more than breathing, he'd ask for *my* advice.

I would've told him that popping up in front of us with this pie for dessert was a terrible idea.

Mother is a pretty good baker and she couldn't ever make a pie like this one. And we all knew there was no way the Malones could afford such a pie. It was something you'd think the Carsdales would eat.

Mother said, "Where . . . did . . . you . . . get . . . that?"

Jimmie looked at Mother and Father.

I had to stop him before he lied. "Jimmie! Tell the truth. Just tell the truth."

"Uh . . . I kind of took it off of a lady's windowsill. But I paid her for it."

Father pushed his chair back and stood up. "OK, let's go."

"Go? Where?"

"You're returning this pie. Who ate the rest of it with you?"

Jimmie looked to the side, a sure sign that what he was going to say wasn't all the way true.

"No one, Pa. It was like that when I found it."

Father said, "*Found?* James Malone, you *stole* that pie."

When Mother is upset her face gives a warning. The skin between her eyebrows folds and you can tell how much trouble you're in by counting the lines that pop up there. If it looks like a 1, you're OK. If it looks like 1-1-1-1-1, watch out!

She was at 1-1-1. "Hold on, Roscoe. Jimmie, this is extremely important—did you steal that pie from a white neighborhood?"

"No, ma'am. I got it over by the park."

She dropped down to 1. "Thank God."

Father said, "Let's go."

Jimmie got nervous. And that was strange.

Living on Earth had made Jimmie very tough, and something like returning a pie shouldn't bother him this much. Then I saw what it was. He'd be humiliated to death if any of his criminal friends saw him being dragged down the street by his father like a five-year-old kid.

Father's tone changed. "Move it. Now."

Jimmie's eyes went from Father to the front door. He was going to make a break for it!

I stood up, took the pie and said, "I'll take him back. We'll return the woman's pie. Jimmie, promise them right now you'll come and won't give me any lip and will do everything I say."

Jimmie's eyes went from me to the door. I stamped my foot. "You apologize right now! Tell them you'll work for the woman for as long as she wants until the pie's paid off. Do it!"

Jimmie waited a heartbeat. "I'm sorry. I'll do everything Deza says."

Father wasn't buying it. "Too late. Let's go."

I caught Mother's eye and she said, "Hold on, Roscoe. Come into the kitchen for a minute."

Father told Jimmie, "Don't you move."

They left us standing there.

I slapped Jimmie's arm. "We had a deal! You're supposed to come to me before you do anything like this."

Jimmie looked down. "Aw, sis, I'm sorry. I feel like I'm the only one not pulling his weight around here. I wasn't looking to steal nothing, all I wanted to do was help."

"What are you talking about? You help all the time. You don't get in as much trouble as you used to, you always bring something for supper, you sing for us whenever we ask—that helps."

"But I wanted to do something special. I only wanted you all to be proud of me."

"By stealing?"

"It wasn't stealing, I left the woman some money."

"Jimmie, you only make things worse by lying all the—"

Mother and Father came back.

Father had the kitchen clock in his hand. "How far off does this woman live?"

Jimmie said, "Just past the park."

Father set the clock on the table. "Deza, you've got forty-five minutes."

"We'll be back in time."

I got a clean dishrag to cover the pie and we left.

When we walked Jimmie tried to trick me into getting in a conversation, but I kept strong and scowled.

It was a good thing it was me walking with Jimmie instead

of Father. Every friend Jimmie ever had was sitting on their porches or walking down Gary's streets.

Jimmie started that funny walk he and his friends do. He put the thumb of his right hand in his front belt loop and swung his left arm far out in front, then far out behind. He dragged one of his legs and hopped more than walked. Mother thinks this is a scream. She says it's just a nonsense walk some young men use to draw attention to themselves. Rooster-strutting, she calls it.

"Jim-Jim," one rooster-strutter yelled, "what's shaking?"

"Ain't nothing going on but the rent, baby."

"Where you headed, pops?"

"Just taking baby sis over to the park to lay this pie on some po' folks."

"We po', baby."

Jimmie laughed. "Ain't that the truth! Catch y'all later."

I could tell we were close to the woman's house. Jimmie started walking like a normal person and the nervous look came back to his face.

He stopped. "Sis, I gotta tell you the truth about something."

"You don't have to say a word, I know you didn't pay anybody for this pie."

"I *did* pay! But it was a whole pie when I first got it. I hid it under a porch chair before I brought it in and when I got outside a rotten stray dog was chomping on it like a old bone. He ran off the porch with it in his mouth but dropped it on the sidewalk and—"

"Jimmie! You were going to let us eat a pie that a dog had dropped out of its mouth? On the ground?"

"Deza! Stop interrupting, please. I cut the chewed-on parts off and wiped the dog's slob off the rest. I said, 'God kissed it, devil missed it,' and it wasn't on the ground long enough to pick up any germs."

He pointed at a beautiful house across the street. "It was that place there. Is there any way you and me could eat the rest and let Ma and Pa think we give it back? We could leave the tin on the porch."

"Are you crazy?"

"I had to give it a try. Come on, let's get this over with."

"We're not going to give that poor woman a pie that was dropped on the ground and that a dog has been licking! We've got to get rid of it."

He said, "I'll drop it in the sewer. I bet the rats won't mind a little dog slob."

I started to hand the pie to Jimmie, then stopped.

What he said made me think.

It *was* such a beautiful pie that it did seem a shame to waste. But there was no way me and Jimmie would eat it. The Malones shouldn't get anything good from something that Jimmie stole.

I pulled the tin back. "No. Come on."

Some poor people *do* live in the park. They sleep in huts and tents in the woods. We should give human beings first choice to see if they wanted this pie.

Except for the big baseball diamond and stands, the park

isn't really much of a park. It's just four swing sets and three or four picnic benches next to some woods.

As me and Jimmie walked between the trees we could see three saggy, sad little wood and cardboard huts with a group of women and children sitting in front of each one.

I walked over to the hut with the most children.

A woman looked up. "Hello, dear."

"Hello, ma'am. My name is Deza Malone and my brother made a mistake and took a pie from someone and we were going to return it to the woman but I found out at the last minute that half of the pie had got chewed on by a dog. Jimmie cut all the doggy parts off of the pie and wiped the dog's spit from the rest. It's the most beautiful pie I've ever seen and I thought it would be a shame to throw it away. I was wondering if you and your kids might like to have it instead?"

I took the dishrag off and the woman said, "Now, that's a pie! Sweetheart, thank you very much! We'd love to have it."

She laughed. "A little dog slob could never ruin a fine pie like this. Besides, do you know how many times we've had to fight dogs off of something we were gonna eat?"

She dipped her finger in the juices and closed her eyes. "My, my, my! Whoever baked this knew what she was doing."

She pulled a piece of apple out of the pie and reached it to me.

She said, "I think if you ate one little bit it wouldn't hurt. We won't let the thief have any if that makes you feel better."

Jimmie said, "I paid her some money."

The woman said, "Boy, hush!"

It's rude to refuse food if someone offers it. Even if it tastes terrible and makes you want to gag, you still have to tell them how much you appreciate it.

"Thank you, ma'am." I put the piece of apple in my mouth.

Eating this pie must be what it feels like to read the greatest book ever at the same time you're sitting in a bathtub full of soapy bubbles like a rich white woman in a magazine!

The woman called out, "Roslyn, Coleen, come here and bring a sharp knife. This child has gone to heaven and brought a little piece back for us."

She said, "Can y'all stay for supper? The men should be back with some catfish."

"Thank you, ma'am, but we have to get this pie tin back."

She slid the pie onto a piece of cardboard and looked at Jimmie. "Son, you're so young, you need to learn not to thieve folks' food, cut it out."

Jimmie said, "I'm fifteen."

She looked surprised. "I don't care how old you are. What kind of example you setting for this here girl?"

Jimmie said, "I know it was a mistake. I said I was gonna 'pologize."

"Fine, but before you do, could the two of you do me a favor? Whilst you're at the pie lady's house could you distract her so the thief here could stuff a couple of 'em under his shirt for me?"

Even Jimmie laughed. I said, "Thank you, ma'am, we've got to be going."

She said, "No, sweetheart, thank *you*!" I wiped the tin with the dishrag as we headed toward the house of the best baker in the world.

Chapter Three

The Pie Lady's Revenge

We stepped onto the porch. Jimmie grabbed my arm before I could knock.

"This was my fault, Deza, there ain't no shame or blame in your game. Give me the tin."

I rolled my eyes. This was more of Jimmie's jazz-musician talk.

"Besides," he said, "what if she comes out shooting?"

He knocked.

A very pretty, very tall and distinctive-looking woman with a glorious mane of pulled-back silver-and-black hair and tiny glasses on her nose opened the door.

"Hello, may I help you?"

"Excuse me, ma'am. My name is Jimmie Malone and it was me who took your pie."

The woman looked over her little glasses and put her hand on her hip. "Oh, really?"

"Yes, ma'am, I come to apologize, give you your tin back, and see what I gotta do to make it up to you."

She came out on the porch. She was dressed like a rich lady in a very nice blue dress and a lovely pair of brown sandals.

"What do you propose?"

Jimmie said, "I can do all kinds of odd jobs until you tell me to stop, ma'am."

The woman looked at me. "You're his big sister?"

Oh, boy.

"No, ma'am, Jimmie's my older brother. I'm kind of big for my age."

She said, "You two ate that whole pie all by yourselves?"

Jimmie said, "No, ma'am, she didn't have nothing to do with it. A rotten mutt ate half the pie and I was gonna bring the other half back but Deza told me giving you a pie that a dog had been licking on wasn't right, so we give it to some folks in the park who are down on their luck."

"Oh, I see. You steal from the rich and give to the poor."

Jimmie thought for a second, then smiled. "Yeah. That's what I did. I took from the rich and gave to the poor." He said it like he was very humble and proud at the same time.

"Only problem with your epiphany is I don't believe there's a rich person within ten miles of here. All right, Robin Hood, how much did you eat?"

I'd have to look "epiphany" up in my dictionary.

Jimmie said, "I just ate the scraps I cut off that the dog didn't finish."

She said, "How was it?"

Jimmie said, "Ma'am, the parts I ate had some dog slob on 'em and were a little crunchy from the dirt but it still was the best thing I ever ate."

She looked at me. "Did you eat any?"

"Well, ma'am, Mother tells us it's a grand and kind gesture when someone offers you food and it's the height of rudeness to turn them down. The lady in the park handed me some so I ate one slice of apple."

"What did you think?"

"It was heavenly."

She pointed at Jimmie. "Robin Hood, sit on that top step. Miss Malone, come inside with me."

Jimmie sat and I said, "Ma'am, we're not allowed to go into strangers' houses."

She smiled. "Good girl. Make sure the thief doesn't take it on the lam. I'll be right back."

I pulled up all the sarcasm I had. "Thanks a bunch, Jimmie. I don't know if I'll ever speak to you again. You better not ever steal another thing in your life."

"I know, I know."

The woman came back with a tray and two glasses rimming with milk and two pieces of apple pie!

She set it on a table between two porch chairs.

"What was your name again, young lady?"

"Deza. Deza Malone, ma'am."

"My name is Dr. Bracy. Please join me for some pie. And I know you won't turn me down, because I'm making the sort of grand gesture which, as your mother has taught you, is rude to refuse."

Doctor?

Maybe she could tell us why Jimmie had stopped growing three years ago.

"Thank you very much, Dr. Bracy." I sat and she handed me a paper napkin and a fork.

My feet dangled in the chair, but I crossed my ankles and spread the napkin on my lap.

She said, "Why do I suspect you do well in school, Deza?"

"I don't know, ma'am, but I really do."

"How about Pretty Boy Floyd there?"

"He works very hard."

She knew I was exaggerating. "Really? Look what he left me."

She passed me a folded-up piece of paper.

The note read, *do not call the polees I promes to brink the tin back hears 8 cens*.

No punctuation, no word over four letters spelled right, and a run-on sentence. Jimmie's work for sure. He'd written his name at the end of the note but scratched it out. With one measly line.

At least he hadn't lied about paying her, but eight cents?

I sighed and handed Dr. Bracy the note.

She gave me a piece of pie and said to Jimmie, "You look strong. You know how to chop wood?"

"Sure I do, ma'am."

"Fine. First, even though you left me eight cents, you stole my pie. Do we agree?"

"Yes, ma'am."

"Now tell me where you got eight cents. Did you steal that too?"

"I wouldn't never take no one's money. I worked all day cleaning out boxcars at the yard."

"And they paid you eight cents?"

Jimmie's eyes cut to the side. "Really they give me a dime, ma'am, but on the way home I saw a starving old blind lady crying in a wheelchair and I give her two cents of it."

I was mortifried.

Dr. Bracy laughed and picked up the other piece of pie. "Miss Malone, I was thinking about giving him this piece of pie, but now I'll enjoy it myself. It must be quite the experience living with this one!"

She asked Jimmie, "Has school finished this year?"

"We've only got two more days."

"So here's what you're going to do, Mr. Malone. I've got a field in the back that needs clearing, and there's some wood that needs chopping and stacking. Once you're done with that I've got something else in mind.

"Deza, do you think it would do any good for your brother to come here every night and work on his spelling and grammar?"

It was Jimmie's turn to look mortifried.

We had tried to help Jimmie but nothing seemed to stick. Mother says that different people are good at different things, and while being good at schooling is important, being a good singer is very important too.

Not really, but that is a kind thing to say to someone who's a good singer.

"You can tutor him only if you want to torture him, ma'am."

"Fine, we'll see how he does around here. Jimmie, I'll expect to see you at eight sharp Saturday morning."

While Jimmie sat on the top step and pouted, Dr. Bracy and me ate our pie and chatted.

She was a most delightful conversationalist.

I told her all about my essay and how Clarice Anne Johnson and me were going to read every book in the Gary Public Library.

She told me how she wasn't the kind of doctor who worked on sick people, but was the kind who had gone to college for a hundred years to study all about books and writing!

Me and Jimmie both jumped when a bell rang inside her house.

"You've got a telephone right in your house?"

She smiled. "Excuse me for a moment."

When she came back I hopped out of the chair. "Thank you very much for the pie, Dr. Bracy. Our father gave us forty-five minutes to return the dish and we have to get going."

We waved as she started piling things on the tray.

We were about half a block away when I heard, "Deza, could you come here for a moment?"

I ran back.

"I can't seem to find your napkin, Miss Malone."

I felt my face get hot. I looked at my shoes.

She said, "I don't mind as long as you give whatever is left of your pie to Clarice and not to Jimmie. We can't encourage that kind of behavior, can we?"

"No, ma'am. I'm sorry."

"Deza, you're a good girl. Next time, think things through."

Alliteration!

Going to school for a hundred years must really be worth it.

* * *

When I got home I asked Mother how to spell "epiphany," then looked it up in my dictionary.

> *Sudden intuitive perception of or insight into the reality or essential meaning of something, usually initiated by some simple, commonplace occurrence or experience.*

That's the only bad thing about dictionaries. You start by looking up one word and end up having to look up seven others to understand the first one.

I lugged the dictionary to Mother and Father. They were sitting at the kitchen table talking.

I plopped it down. "Translate, please."

Father pulled the dictionary to him. "What's the word?"

"'Epiphany.'"

He didn't even look. He closed the book and said, "Think of a light going on. An epiphany is being surrounded by darkness and bumping around. Something happens or is said that causes a light to be switched on and everything becomes clear. It's when you suddenly understand something. The moment you *really* get it."

So that was what Dr. Bracy meant. She'd said something about Robin Hood and it was like a light came on for Jimmie.

A dim light, but that's probably the best you could expect from a pie thief.

Chapter Four

Stabbed in the Back

Mrs. Needham returns our work by calling each student to her desk in the reverse order of how good you did. Getting called last is the best.

Dolly Peaches, who is a roughneck, a hoodlum and a boy, even with a name like that, has been called first every single time this year.

I have been called last for every paper and test all of sixth grade! It's like what we say on the playground,

First is the worst, second is the same, last is the best in any old game.

Mrs. Needham picked up our final essays. "I enjoyed learning about your families. We've had a slight change in our usual rankings today.

"Mr. Peaches, keep trying. Hope springs eternal."

Dolly slouched up to her desk.

It was a very short walk because Mrs. Needham keeps Dolly Peaches and Benny Cobb exactly one yardstick and one stretched-out arm away from her.

She said, "Young man, stand straight and pick up your feet when you walk or I will leave you with a memory that will extend well into the summer."

Benny Cobb was next and the roll call went on until it was down to me and my loving friend, Clarice Anne Johnson.

We looked across the room at each other and smiled. We each held up two fingers, touched our cheeks, then held up one finger and put our hands on our chests, like we were getting ready to say the pledge to allegiance. But we weren't. It's secret sign language for our motto I thought up: *Two girls, one heart.*

Mrs. Needham said, "As usual, we're left with the ladies!"

I tried to look humble while I waited for Clarice to walk up and get second place.

Which is really just about as good as first place. Just about.

Well, not really, but that *is* a kind and comforting thing to say to second-place people.

Then I remembered what Mrs. Needham said about a change!

No. I'd worked extra hard on this essay.

I watched her mouth, scared that something horrible was about to cross her lips.

She said, "And with an A minus . . ."

I fought the feeling that my whole world was about to collapse in a smoking heap.

". . . another excellent piece of work by . . ."

I prayed, Oh, please say Clarice, please! She's used to second place.

". . . Miss Deza Malone."

The shame!

I looked back over at Clarice and had to quickly turn my eyes away.

It was bad enough that I hadn't gotten my usual grade, but it was even worse to see the crazy look on my loving friend's face when she knew that it was her, and not me, who did the best on the last assignment of the year.

Clarice's mouth and eyes were wide open. She was being eaten alive by guilt already.

I knew just how bad things had got when my second brain started talking to me.

I'm different from most people and one of the main reasons is, I think I might have two brains. Whenever I get nervous or mad or scared or very upset, I have thoughts that are so different from my normal thoughts that there isn't any way they could be coming from just one brain.

My first brain decides it doesn't want to know about what is happening and stops working. Then my second brain takes over.

And that brain is always looking to start trouble, to hurt someone or break something.

I felt myself rise out of my seat like a prisoner on her way to Old Sparky, the electric chair. I had to bravely make that long walk to Mrs. Needham's desk, a walk once bright with sunshine and hope but now choked with thunder, despair and crabgrass.

"Buck up, kiddo," the second brain said, "she won't be expecting a thing!"

Ooh! One of the main reasons I hate this second brain is that it always calls me kiddo!

"Smile, kiddo," the bad brain said. "Get as close as we can."

Clarice had covered her mouth with both hands. It was easy to see that she was grief-struck that something this terrible could happen on the next-to-last day of school.

"Okay, kiddo, when she hands the paper to you, snatch her arm! We'll get two or three bites in before she can slap us off or call for help!"

I stopped in front of Mrs. Needham's desk.

I held my breath, giving her one last chance to say, "Dear me, Miss Malone, I'm so sorry, I've made a terrible mistake, I should have called Clarice."

Mrs. Needham looked right in my eyes, held my essay out and said, "Very good job, Deza."

Thank goodness that woke my first brain up. It stopped me before anyone got bit.

Very good job?

Was she playing a joke on me? I looked at what was written in red on the top of my paper. There was a big "A-" sitting there!

My grade is supposed to be a A *plus*!

How could Mrs. Needham, who I used to love like a grandmother, be so rude and uncaring to tell me "very good job" when I didn't even get a A?

I floated back toward my seat. Most times I pretend I'm reading the back of the last page of my essay while I'm walking to my desk. That way my classmates get a chance to see my grade and maybe will want to try harder the next time.

This paper was a crinkled ball in my fist.

Dolly Peaches, who's got enough teeth cramped into his mouth for a crocodile, a shark and two regular full-grown people, whispered, "You ain't smart as you think, huh? How's it feel to be number two?"

Benny Cobb snickeled, "Deeza's a number two!"

"Okay, kiddo. Jump real high and drop a quick elbow into Dolly's left eye, then do a sharp uppercut to Benny's jaw. They'll never see it coming!"

All there was left for me to do was quietly and with a bunch of dignity walk to my desk.

I told myself, Stop being silly. Keep your chin up.

But as soon as I sat down, my arms folded on my desk and my head thunked down.

Mrs. Needham said, "And we close this year with another A for Miss Clarice Anne Johnson."

I couldn't bear to look. Clarice would be unconsolable.

I raised my head when I heard Clarice's gut-wretching yips and yaps.

I am so proud of that girl!

Clarice had decided to pretend she was excited by jumping up and down. She hopped like a bunny to the front and gave our traitor teacher a huge hug! Clarice is such a champion! She was making sure our classmates took their mocking eyes off of me and put them on her by waving her paper in the air and braying like a donkey.

I loved her even more than I already had.

"Well, kiddo . . ."

I clenched my teeth so hard that the back ones started

hurting. That's the only way to make that second brain quit talking. When it shut up I laid my head back down on my desk.

I'll probably be pondering what went wrong until I'm weak and weary.

Chapter Five

Maid of the Mist

I didn't even hear the bell ring or notice that my horrid classmates were gone.

I could feel Clarice rubbing my shoulder. Mrs. Needham called from way, way off, "Miss Johnson, wait outside. Miss Malone. Sit up. Are you all right?"

I wanted to say, "Other than having my life destroyed by your A minus, I'm fine, thank you," but I raised my head. "No, ma'am."

"What did you think about my comments?"

I sniffled, smoothed my essay on my desk and looked down to see what she'd written.

We have discussed this many times before, Miss Malone*. In the future, give your thesaurus a break. One more session like this and* *that poor book will burst into flames. Good writing is simple and communicates naturally. Your past work has shown this is something you can easily do. I appreciate that you are not digressing as much. As for this essay, when I ask for two pages that's all I will accept. I'm aware how upsetting this will be. A point is being made, and this shouldn't be a complete surprise. This will be the most important paper you have ever written. Please see me after class.*

Mrs. Needham said, "Well?"

I wiped my eyes on the back of my hand.

"You said this is the most important paper I've ever written."

"Depending upon how you react, I believe it could be."

I looked at the red minus sign that looked like a tiny bloody slash cut into my work and my soul by a razor of hate.

"But I worked so long and hard. Why did I get a A minus?"

"Deza, come here."

This day was getting stranger and stranger. She had never called any of us by our first name.

Mrs. Needham sat at Benny Cobb's desk. "Have a seat, Deza."

I started to sit next to her but she said, "No, there," and pointed at the chair behind her desk.

"Really?"

"Miss Malone, sit."

The old saying that every cloud has a silver lining is true!

I'd pretended a million times that I was sitting here and giving my unappreciative, hardheaded students a lesson. I had even lifted buckets of rocks at home a couple of times with Jimmie to build muscles so I could call Dolly Peaches and Benny Cobb to the front of the class, then mercilessly beat them into bloody pulps with a yardstick for embarrassing and bullying their classmates and not trying hard enough on their work.

I'd imagined that many years from now, I'd pick one of my favorite students, maybe it would be Clarice's daughter, to work a problem on the blackboard.

The chair had burgundy leather and buttons and was cool and smooth on the back of my legs. I looked at the classroom and forgot all about that red grade.

Well, pretty much forgot.

Mrs. Needham said, "I know being a teacher is your ambition, Deza, and a fine one it is. But I can see you as a professor or, if we can pry the dictionary out of your hands, even as a writer."

I wiggled and the chair swiveled from side to side! Only the tips of my toes were touching the floor but it felt perfect!

"Deza, I have been teaching longer than you could imagine, and I've always had the dream any teacher worth her salt has. I had thought, prior to this year, that I would have to be satisfied in coming close to the dream once, before, alas, 'the best-laid schemes of mice and men gang aft a-gley. . . .'

"The dream is the gift of having one student, just one, who is capable of making a real contribution. One child who'd have no choice but to make a difference for our people.

"Out of the thousands of students I've had in the thousands of years I've been teaching, I've suspected for quite a while who the child I've been waiting for is."

All I could think was, I love her like a sister, but *please*, just don't say Clarice!

"Miss Malone, you are that child."

I stopped wiggling.

"That's why I gave you that A minus, Deza, and it won't be the last if you're not up on your p's and q's. Any more grandstanding in your writing, there might even be a B or two down the road. Remember, much is required of her to whom much has been given."

My heart flew like a rocket ship!

"These are trying times for the whole country, Miss Malone, and I'm aware that you have been dealt a pretty rough hand, but, child, with your gifts, you are the richest person I have ever had the honor of teaching.

"I believe from the bottom of my heart that if we lose you, we've lost this country. If we can't get *you* to your true path, it's the failure of everyone from President Roosevelt right down to me.

"And while President Roosevelt is far too busy to give a hoot, I have nothing but time on my hands. I will not sit idly by and see you fall.

"I understand that *you* are the reason I've taught for all these years. We are both in the right spot at the right time."

Goose bumps danced all over my arms!

"Oh, Mrs. Needham, I can do whatever needs to be done. Jimmie's always saying if I read one more book or study one more minute my brain will explode out of my eyes, but I can work harder! Your words are like manna produced from heaven to me!"

I hope I pronounced "manna" the right way.

Mrs. Needham's eyes rolled. "Oh, for the love of Pete! The first thing I have to do is wrench that dictionary and thesaurus out of your hands. And we're going to have to work on the way you react to bad news. You have to toughen up, missy, but we'll get by."

"Yes, ma'am!"

"As you know, the board is forcing me to retire this year. So what I'd like to do is have you come to my home every day after school and weekends for private tutoring. The work here is not challenging enough for you, but I'll take care of that."

It was like she was reading my mind when she said, "We'll include Clarice if you'd like."

Mrs. Needham almost smiled!

My eyes swelled with tears. I wanted to run around the desk and give her a hug, but she'd looked like she'd eaten a piece of bad fish when Clarice hugged her.

"Oh, thank you! Clarice will be just as happy as me! But could I ask you what does the thing you said earlier about gangs mean?"

"Gangs? Oh, it was 'gang aft a-gley.' That's from Burns, my favorite Scottish poet. We'll be studying him later. The poem is called 'To a Mouse.'"

Mrs. Needham closed her eyes.

"The best-laid schemes o' mice an' men
Gang aft a-gley
And leave us nought but grief and pain
For promised joy."

I didn't understand a bit of it.

Mrs. Needham said, "Mr. Burns wrote this after he was

plowing his field and accidentally destroyed a mouse's nest. He tells the mouse that even though its home is ruined, it's still better off than most humans because the mouse only looks at the present, while people look to the past and end up being sad, or look to the future and end up worrying. No matter how well a mouse, or a human being, plans for the future, those plans 'gang aft a-gley.' In other words, no matter how well you think something through, many times schemes simply will not work out. They will go astray."

I already knew this, but I could never have said it like a poem. This sounded like something Father would say.

"By the way, a former student of mine is graduating from Meharry dental school and plans on returning to Gary. I have prevailed upon him to take you on in September once he's officially a dentist and starts practicing."

"A dentist? But my teeth don't bother me." Not too much.

Mrs. Needham looked at me long enough to make me a little nervous. "A thorough checkup won't hurt."

I wondered how she knew that my teeth *can* be a little sore some of the time, especially the back ones that are all hollowed out by cavities.

She'd said this new dentist was just starting to *practice*. I'd rather wait until he started working for real. But I said, "Thank you very much, ma'am."

"You're quite welcome, Deza. Now open the right bottom drawer of my desk and remove the bag, please."

I put a crumply brown paper sack on her desk.

"Take out what's inside, please."

Inside the bag there was a beautiful pair of new patent

leather shoes and some folded-up clothes. Mother says it's rude to set shoes on anything but the floor so that's where I put them.

"Do you wear a size five?"

"I'm not sure."

"Try them on."

I picked up the first shoe. There were some socks rolled up in it.

"Should I put on the socks too?"

"Yes."

I was glad I was behind her desk and she couldn't see my shoes and socks. My shoes are quite tired and my socks have been darned a million times. Jimmie says our socks and clothes are very religious because they are so holey.

My hands were shaking, but I pulled the new socks on and slipped my feet into the shoes. I knew just how Cinderella felt! They were a little big, but maybe that was because mine were so tight. I sat on my socks so Mrs. Needham wouldn't see them.

She said, "My niece from Cleveland spent the summer with me a while ago and left a few things. I thought they might fit you."

Did Mrs. Needham really mean these shoes were for me?

I walked out from behind the desk so she could see her niece's shoes. I'd never felt this tall!

The right-hand heel on my old shoes had fallen off. Jimmie tried to put it back on but it wouldn't stay. He ended up pulling the left heel off so I wouldn't walk with a limp.

Mrs. Needham said, "What do you think?"

"I've never *seen* such a beautiful pair of shoes, not even in a store window! Are you really going to let me have these?"

"They may as well be put to good use."

"I'm going to save them until seventh grade!"

"You don't need to save them. My niece left a few pairs of shoes and I'll give them to you as needed. Take them off and ask your parents if it's all right for you to accept them."

"Yes, ma'am!"

This horrible day was turning into the best day anybody ever had!

"Empty the bag, Miss Malone."

I pulled out two brand-new half-slips and three pairs of blue underpants.

The last thing I pulled out was even more beautiful and special than the shoes!

I read this book about a place called Niagara Falls, which is a waterfall geologically located between the United States and Canada. The last thing in the bag made me think of it.

The book said you could ride a boat called the *Maid of the Mist* right underneath these huge waterfalls and get covered with a cool mist the water made when it splashed on rocks. The last thing in the bag was just like the mist. It was a lovely, soft blue gingham dress! I ran my hand over the dress. This was what it must feel like to ride the *Maid of the Mist* under the falls.

I pressed my face into the gingham and found out how new smelled. I must have dreamed about this dress, it was so familiar.

"Hold it up and see if it fits."

I squeezed it to me, then quickly pulled it back. It made my regular one look really, really old.

There was a little piece of paper held onto the dress by a string and a safety pin. My hands were shaking like a leaf and I read, HIMELHOCH'S FINE APPAREL FOR LADIES AND GENTLEMEN.

Then I remembered. I *had* seen this dress before!

Himelhoch's is a rich people's clothes store me and Clarice walk by every day on the way home. We'd seen a dress just like this one in the big front window on one of those little white dummy girl statues! I fell in love with it and Clarice fell in love with the green-and-gray dress that the dummy sister of my statue was wearing.

Every day we passed Himelhoch's we'd imagine where we'd wear the two dresses.

Once it was for going to a real restaurant and asking a stranger to cook us some food, once for our graduating from college and once for Clarice's wedding, where I was her maid of honor.

The best thing we imagined was wearing them to Benny and Dolly's funeral! We'd wear veils so people would think we were crying, but we'd secretly be laughing about how rich and happy we looked while those hoodlums were put six feet under.

The dresses disappeared from the windows in April and we hated what took their place.

I held the piece of paper. Mrs. Needham's brow wrinkled. "Dear me. Bring that here!"

She undid the safety pin. "That silly child. Wore this all summer and never took the tags off."

"Thank you, thank you so much, Mrs. Needham. . . ." My throat betrayed me again.

"Be sure to ask your parents, Deza. They may contact me if

there are any questions. Tell absolutely no one, not even Clarice, about my niece's clothes. Use that explosive imagination of yours to come up with a story. Now, be prepared for September. I can't wait!"

My hands were shaking even harder when I put my brand-new clothes back in the sack.

I went to my desk, collected my books and smoothed out my essay even more. The A- wasn't so bad after all. I headed to the door, then turned back. "Mrs. Needham, you'll never know—"

"Deza Malone! One more peep out of you and I will mail those clothes right back to Cleveland. Pull yourself together and go!"

I would have gone, but she held up two fingers, touched her cheek, held up one finger and put her hand on her chest.

Like she was saying the pledge to allegiance.

And she smiled!

I knew I was risking my new clothes but I dropped everything and ran back. She jumped up and made a face, but I wrapped my arms around her and held on tight.

"Mrs. Needham, I've always dreamed that one day I'd have the same heart as you, but I thought I'd have to wait until I got to be real old too!"

She let me cry before she got me arm's length away. "Fine, Deza. Now please go home."

I grabbed Mrs. Needham one more time.

The only thing that the best teacher in the world could say was "Oh, for the love of Pete!"

Chapter Six

Hershey's Kisses and Lockjaw

I walked into the hallway. My path was lit up with sunshine and happiness and bright flowers. To make it even more perfect, Clarice was sitting on the floor right under the picture of President Roosevelt with tears rimming out of her eyes.

She jumped up. "Oh, Deza, please! I'm really, really sorry I acted that way, I was so surprised and happy and I lost my mind for a minute. Will you ever forgive me?"

"You don't even need to ask."

We hooked arms and started our walk home.

"What did Mrs. Needham tell you? She wouldn't change your grade, would she?" Clarice put her hand to my ear. "Don't tell anyone, but I have an uncle in Indianapolis who got tried for murder. He got away with it, Deza. If I write to him he can give us a plan for rubbing Mrs. Needham out without getting caught!"

"No, Clarice. Second place was to teach me a lesson. I won't even mind if Mrs. Needham gives me a B plus or two. I'm sure your essay was much better."

Clarice stopped and looked at me. "Deza Malone. Thank you very much!"

I pulled her along, anxious to get home and talk to Mother.

"What's in the bag?"

I wanted so much to tell Clarice everything and show her the beautiful clothes, but I *had* promised.

"Oh, this. It's just some papers and a few things that—"

Thank goodness we were walking past Himelhoch's. Clarice pointed at the window and said, "That dress is so horrible I wouldn't even wear it to a stoning of Dolly Peaches."

Maybe Mother would let me give Clarice my other dress, the one I wear to church. It has a lot less patches than the one Clarice wears now.

We reached Clarice's house and hugged.

She said, "Only one more day, Deza. I'm really going to miss school and Mrs. Needham. Even if she gave you the wrong grade."

I had to tell Clarice, "Mrs. Needham said she's going to tutor us after school and on weekends next year!"

Clarice said, "*Really!*"

I said, "Really."

Clarice walked up on her porch and turned around to wave.

At the same time, we both held up two fingers and made our special sign.

Still two girls sharing one heart.

I ran the rest of the way home.

* * *

"Mother! Mother!"

"Hey, sis. You forget it's the end of the month?"

I *had* forgotten, Mother would be waiting in line for the food they gave away at the mission.

Jimmie was sitting on the couch with a pencil and a couple of pieces of paper.

"What are you doing?"

"This? Just drawing the fight. And making plans."

Jimmie's plans were mostly about murdering whoever was the latest bully in his life. It's lucky he's kind of lazy. If he followed through with any of these plans I'd get to wear the new dress and shoes to watch Jimmie take that long walk to Old Sparky.

I stuck out my hand. "Let me see."

As good a singer as Jimmie is, he's just as bad a picture drawer.

The first page showed a man in shorts with boxing gloves on. He had "MS GERM" written across his chest. By his feet was a head that was frowning. Next to him was a man with "JOE" written across his chest. He had a huge smile and was holding his arms above his head. He was wearing boxing gloves and was waving a flag that was probably a American flag, even though it only had two stars and three stripes.

Jimmie said, "See, that's what's going to happen on the seventeenth. Joe Louis is gonna knock Max Smelling's head off."

I rolled my eyes. If I heard one more thing about that ridiculous, worthless fight I'd lose my mind.

I looked at the other drawing. This plan was just as horrible. This picture showed three people and what looked like the biggest Hershey's Kiss in the world. For some reason there was a big cloud raining down on the kiss.

The first person in the plan was a boy with his arms spread wide. I knew it was Jimmie. In his pictures he always draws himself as big, and bumpy with muscles. In his hand was a box of something that had "NITULS" written across the front of it. He'd drawn lines from the nituls that pointed at the giant Hershey's Kiss.

On the other side of the Hershey's Kiss was a boy who was standing with *his* arms spread. This had to be Dolly Peaches because of all the teeth the boy had.

The third person in the plan was me. I was holding something with "BIG BOOK" written on it and had a gigantic toe.

I'm usually the only one who can figure out what Jimmie's plans mean, but not this one.

I said, "OK, it's you, Dolly Peaches and me, right?"

"Yeah."

"And Dolly's standing up but he's dead, right?"

"Oh, yeah! That's a picture of the exact second Dolly starts pushing up daisies!"

I pointed at the huge Hershey's Kiss. "Why is this chocolate here?"

"Naw, sis, that ain't chocolate, that's a haystack."

He said it like *I* was the one who was crazy.

"And why is my toe so . . . ?"

A light went on in my head. A epiphany!

When I was littler I used to have accidents all the time. Jimmie joked that even if it hadn't snowed for years I'd find something as small as a puddle of frozen bird pee and would slip on it and spring my ankle. And my feet were like magnets for every rusty nail, broken bottle or jaggedy tin can lid in Gary.

I had been six years old and remember Father holding my ankle tight. Mother's reading specs were on his eyes and a straight pin was between his thumb and pointy finger.

Jimmie was squeezing my hand and had given me a folded-up washrag to bite down on. He'd seen that in a Western movie when someone was digging a bullet out of a white cowboy who got plugged by a Indian. I didn't have a bullet in me, just another splinter.

Father said, "Deza Malone, looks to me like you're doing something that only a few of the smartest professors at a few of the best colleges have ever done."

A little pinch of pain made me squinch my eyes shut.

"Sorry," Father said. "That's right, you're going to be responsible for a change in the King's English. Another archaic saying is doomed to bite the dust due to Daddy's Darling Daughter, Deza!"

He dug the straight pin around in my foot to make the sliver show its head so he could tweezer it out.

I pulled out the washrag for a second and said, "How could I change the language?"

"Well," he said, grabbing the tip of the splinter with the tweezers, "because of you that old saying that something is as hard to find as a needle in a haystack won't be used anymore, it will become moot.

"Folks will learn if they want to find that needle all they need to do is have you stand within thirty feet of the haystack. That needle will come flying out of the hay at you like it was an arrow shot out of an itsy-bitsy bow and your rusty old foot was the bull's-eye!"

I felt the sliver slide out.

Father said, "Wow, that's a beauty even for you, Dar Dawt!" That was what he called me when he didn't feel like saying "Darling Daughter Deza" all the way out.

Jimmie's plan was to trick Dolly Peaches into standing by a haystack where my crazy brother had emptied two big boxes of needles, which Jimmie spelled "N-I-T-U-L-S." Then I'd walk to the haystack until I was close enough for the needles to shoot out at my big toe. They'd come so fast and hard that Dolly would be run through by a hundred needles and would drop dead.

I said, "I get most of it, but why's it raining in only one spot?"

Jimmie said, "Pa told me about this thing called lockjaw or tendunus, it's where if you step on something rusty you might think you're OK once the wound heals up, but you aren't. The rust puts a bunch of germs in you and they come out later and make it so your jaw gets locked shut, then you starve to death."

"So?"

"So? It's raining so the needles will get rusty. Then, once they go through Dolly Peaches, they will kill him in a couple of weeks when the lockjaw germs get strong."

I gave the drawing back to him. "If you studied as hard as you plot murders you'd get all As."

"Sure, sis. What's in the bag, goose?"

I showed him my dress and shoes.

"Wow! Are you going to show Ma?"

"Of course I am."

Jimmie said, "Hold on, Deza."

I wish I could rewrite my essay about my family, 'cause there's a trait that Jimmie has that's even more annoying than his napoleon complex. It's when he imitates Father.

He always pretends he's smoking a pipe even though Father has a little asthma and has never smoked anything. But Jimmie's voice and acting *are* a whole lot like Father's.

Jimmie pointed the invisible pipe at me and said, "Let's look at this clearly."

He crossed his legs and looked off over my shoulder, something Father does when he's thinking hard about what he's going to say.

"You've already fallen in love with this dress and these shoes, right?"

"I do like them a awful lot."

Jimmie/Father put the invisible pipe back in his mouth, nodded and said, "We'll say that's close enough to love to be worried. So we have to look at the cons-or-quenches of what you want to do. Let's say you show 'em to your mother and she decides you have to give 'em back, what then? You've lost your new clothes, just like that." He snapped his fingers.

I hadn't thought of that.

Jimmie uncrossed his legs, leaned forward and flicked ashes from his pipe onto the floor.

He's such a good actor that I almost yelled at him for messing up the floor that I'd swept.

He waved the pipe in front of himself. "My suggestion, Darling Daughter Deza, is to decide which of the two things you like the most and show Mother the other one. That way, if she says take it back, you've only lost one and can sneak around with the other."

"Thank you, Jimmie, or Father—whoever you are. That sounds like a good idea."

Not really, but that is a kind thing to say to someone who's a great singer, a good imitator and full of more baloney than Mr. Schwartz's butcher shop.

* * *

I sat on my bed upstairs. I'd spread the dress next to me and set the shoes on the floor. They were so beautiful!

I wished I hadn't told Jimmie. Before I'd talked to him I'd thought I'd just run into my bedroom, secretly put the clothes on and show Mother my special new dress and the magic clickity-clackity shoes.

Mother would say something like, "Oh, Deza! You are so beautiful!"

If Jimmie wasn't around she'd even say, "And look how tall you are in those new shoes!"

As I smoothed my fingers over the dress I started having worries. Maybe I *should* show her only my shoes . . . no, maybe only my dress. . . .

My other brain said, "He's right, you know, kiddo. . . ."

And just like that, I *did* know. If the bad brain was agreeing with him then Jimmie was wrong.

I gave myself a good soapy wash and smoothed my hair back with a little Vaseline. I put baking soda in my palm and brushed my teeth. I rubbed some more of the Vaseline into my legs and arms till they were nice and shiny. I put on the new slip, the socks and shoes. Then, being extra careful not to get any Vaseline on it, I slid the most beautiful piece of blue gingham clothes ever made over my head.

The mirror in the bathroom is really tiny so I reached up on my tiptoes, pulled it off the nail above the washbasin and moved it up and down so I could see every part of me.

The dress was gorgeous!

I walked back to my room on my tiptoes so the shoes wouldn't click-clack and ruin my surprise. I picked up *Great Expectations*, sat on the bed, smoothed my dress, crossed my ankles and started reading.

I hadn't read five pages when I heard the screen door open downstairs and Mother said, "Hello, James, how was school?"

My heart beat so loud I didn't hear Jimmie's answer. I opened my door and clacked down the steps.

Mother said, "What is that sound . . . ?"

I stepped into the living room.

Mother stumbled back till her legs hit the couch and she crashed down on it. One of the paper sacks she'd been carrying split open. A big loaf of cheese and a box of powdered milk bounced off of the couch.

Her hand covered her mouth and she said, "Deza! Turn around . . . ," and I knew by the happy look on her face that she wasn't going to take my new clothes away!

I spun until my dress blossomed and became a beautiful blue-and-white rose!

Jimmie started clapping and whistling.

I finally fell on the couch next to Mother. I told her how Mrs. Needham said she'd been waiting a thousand years for me to be her student and how she was going to tutor me next year.

Mother said, "I'm not the least bit surprised, your father and I always tell both of you how talented you are. It feels like Christmas in July when someone else agrees, especially someone as wise as Mrs. Needham!"

I told her about Mrs. Needham's niece and the clothes. "Can I keep them?"

Mother said, "Stand up again."

I stood up and something about the dress and shoes made me go right back into a spin.

Mother laughed. "Deza Malone, that dress and those shoes were *meant* for you. The only time you've looked more beautiful was when they handed you to me on the day you were born.

"Help me get these groceries into the kitchen, then we'll both start working on our thank-you notes to that wonderful woman."

As I picked up the welfare food Jimmie said, "You lucked up."

I slapped his head. "No, Jimmie Malone, the truth is always the best way."

He said, "Not in real life, Deza. Let's be *truthful* and admit it, you just lucked up. I gotta tell you, though, Ma was right, that getup was made for you. You're one sharp bit of calico."

Me, the cheese, the milk and the ruined paper sack twirled into the kitchen.

I couldn't wait for Father to get home. Even if he hadn't found work, this dress would cheer up the saddest person in the world!

Chapter Seven

The Mysterious Smile of the Man on the Quaker Oats Box

The next morning I woke up and wiggled my toes.

My feet felt heavy and horrible. Then I remembered. I'd worn Mrs. Needham's niece's shoes to bed.

I took them off and got up and started getting ready for school.

When I was dressed, I must have tried six times to go downstairs wearing my new shoes.

Mrs. Needham said I shouldn't save them, and Mother *had* told me it was OK to put them on, but something wouldn't let me take more than two tappity-tap steps to head downstairs.

I sat on the bed and picked up my old no-heel shoes. Since this was the last day of school, I could wear them one more time. And I could go barefoot all summer long. I put my regular shoes back on. I'd never noticed before how much they cramped up my toes.

By the time I got downstairs my feet were back to being used to them.

Father was on the couch reading a newspaper and Jimmie had his head on the arm of the couch and his feet tucked under Father's legs.

This is a bad habit Jimmie picked up from Mother. She's always complaining that her feet are cold and when she's laying on the couch reading she'll ask me or Jimmie or Father to sit on her feet so they'll warm up. She's turned us into a bunch of brood hens.

I gave each of them their good morning kiss, then went into the kitchen and kissed Mother.

I reached into the cabinet and pulled out the big new box of oatmeal.

Mother said, "Wait, Deza, there's the open box, it must have something left."

What was I thinking? I put the new box back and got the open one. I turned the box until the strange-looking white man was smiling at me. The man was what Mother says we should call big-boned. He was wearing a black cowboy hat, had long gray hair like a very old white woman and must have been getting ready to eat his supper because he had stuffed a fluffy white napkin down into the front of his shirt.

Father came into the kitchen.

It's funny how something can look so normal to you one day, and then all of a sudden it can look so strange. I wonder if that's because as you get smarter and older you look at things with different eyes, even things you've seen a million times before.

I stared at the man on the Quaker Oats box. "Mother, Father, who is this man?"

Father took the box. "Well, Deza, I don't think anyone knows. The way he's skinning and grinning, though, he must've just heard some very good news."

"What do you think the news was?"

Father looked at Mother. "Peg, what would good news for a Quaker be?"

Mother said, "All I know is the Quakers have a reputation for being very honest. And they helped a lot of our people get North on the Underground Railroad during slavery."

Father clapped his hands. "There you go! Our happy Caucasian friend here has been so busy waiting for another escaped slave that he hasn't had a chance to read a newspaper for the last . . . how long have we been free?"

Father did the math in his head. "Seventy-three years. Wow, it was only seventy-three years ago that Lincoln freed the slaves. So, Dar Dawt, this guy's so happy because he *just* heard about the Emancipation Proclamation! He's overjoyed because he can quit fighting for freedom and get back to quaking."

I pulled the round cardboard top off of the oatmeal box and stuck my face over the opening. The smell of the oatmeal was lovely. I closed the box and shook it. Shaking made little bits of powder float around inside the box.

When I pulled the lid off again I dropped the box and screamed.

Mother and Father jumped and Jimmie came running into the kitchen.

I pointed at the floor. There, along with the spilled cereal, was a army of teeny-weeny, wiggling-squiggling, wormy-looking bugs and beetles trying to hide under the flakes of oatmeal.

Mother said, "Deza Malone, do you have any idea how much a box of oatmeal costs? Sweep that cereal back into the box this instant."

I don't know what was a bigger surprise, the bugs and worms, or Mother telling me to sweep them back.

Father smiled at me. "Deza, those are only some harmless beetles that hitched a ride."

I couldn't believe I was having to point out something so obvious to Father. Most times he was very quick to understand. I crossed my arms. "But they're bugs. Bugs in the food?"

He crouched down so he was looking me square in the eye, something that made me feel big and important and small and silly at the same time.

"Deza, times are hard, we can't waste a thing."

I stamped my foot. "Father, they're *bugs*!"

He went from crouching to sitting on the floor with his legs crossed in front of him.

"My Mighty Miss Malone. You know I haven't worked regular for months now. We're going to have to be very careful until I can find work. That might be a while."

He reached over and pinched a bunch of the spilled oatmeal into his hand. A couple of bugs scurried around in his palm, ducking between flakes like they were hiding under a umbrella.

"The bugs are harmless."

Father smiled and tossed the oatmeal, bugs and all, into his mouth!

Jimmie yelled, "Holy mack-a-rollee!"

He scooped up a pinch of bugs and cereal and threw them into his mouth.

Mother said, "Roscoe! James! Neither one of you knows when to stop. Deza, before I cook the oatmeal I always sift any of those beetles out, and the boiling water kills any germs."

The news was getting worse! Mother had used buggy oatmeal before! I felt my stomach clenching and twisting, just like I'd eaten another bad piece of fish.

Mother said, "The last time I checked, Deza, your birth certificate said 'Malone' and not 'Rockefeller.' We just can't afford to throw any kind of food out, my dear."

Father got up and started out of the kitchen.

Jimmie said, "Hey, Pa, how come you quit talking?"

Father had been quiet since he'd put the buggy oatmeal in his mouth. Jimmie grabbed his arm. "What's wrong, Pa, cat got your tongue?"

Father had tried to teach me a lesson but the lesson wasn't going to go as far as chewing or swallowing the wiggling worms.

Father slapped the back of Jimmie's head and when Jimmie said, "Hey!" and ducked, Father spit the oatmeal into his other hand. "What, Jimmie? I didn't quite hear what you said."

* * *

All the way to school Jimmie couldn't quit talking about how him and Father had ate some bugs.

"Wait till I tell everyone!"

I rolled my eyes. That was all he needed to do, give people more ammunition to shoot at him on the last day of school, but with Jimmie it's best to come at things sideways.

"Jimmie, don't tell anyone, you know we're not supposed to talk with anyone about what happens at home."

Jimmie said, "Yeah, that means we can't talk about family *business*. This ain't business, this is something funny."

Me and Jimmie look at the world in different ways. While Jimmie was bragging about eating buggy cereal, I was promising myself that I was through with oatmeal for the rest of my life.

Chapter Eight

Jimmie Gets a Free Train Ride

Just before the last bell rang on the last day of school, Mrs. Needham passed out our report cards. Worst first. It was a true relief that everything was back to normal. When Dolly Peaches's name was called he said, "I sure will enjoy not seeing you every weekday."

The whole class went, "Ooooh!" and waited for Mrs. Needham to beat him into a bloody pulp, but she just called, "Benny Cobb."

Right after the kindest, most loving friend in the world, Miss Clarice Anne Johnson, picked up her report card, my name was called.

Last!

Instead of holding it so the rest of them could see, I folded it and walked back to my seat.

Mrs. Needham leaned on the front of her desk. "Well, students, another year has come to an end. I hope all of you have a good summer. And let's all keep our fingers crossed for Mr. Joseph Louis Barrow, the Brown Bomber."

Cheers came from everywhere!

Mrs. Needham said, "It won't be long before he and that horrible German will be fighting. Normally I am opposed to violence of any kind, but this fight is something special and Joe needs all of our support, so let's remember him any way we can."

She timed her speech perfect, the bell rang and even though everyone was wound tight as a spring waiting to get into the summer, nobody moved. Mrs. Needham said, "Enjoy your vacation. Class dismissed," and students shot out of the room like lava out of a volcano.

Me and Clarice helped her load her things into boxes and waved to her as we left. "See you in September!"

* * *

Three blocks from school, in a vacant lot, there was a big circle of children screaming and laughing and punching their fists in the air.

Every Friday after school the hooligans get even with each other and meet to fight. Since this was the last Friday of the year there was a lot of getting even to do; the fight circle was two times bigger than usual.

Me and Clarice Anne Johnson hooked arms, leaned our

heads into one another and walked by. Right after we passed the crowd Clarice stopped. "Deza! Did you hear that?"

I said, "Yes, I'm sure it's a swearword, but I'm going to ignore those little hoodlums and you should too."

She shushed me. "Listen!"

The crowd was singing,

> ***"Pee-Wee Jimmie Malone,***
> ***Same size as a chicken bone!***
> ***Kill him, kill him all the way home!"***

I dropped my books and ran back to the pack of yelling kids, pushing and clawing people aside until I got to the center.

My heart broke in two. Jimmie was curled in a ball with splashes of blood all over his shirt and that monster Dolly Peaches standing over him with his fists balled up and a grin that would make any alligator or dinosaur proud.

I heard a scream that didn't sound human and was so loud that I bet people in China, which is geologically exactly on the other side of the Earth from Gary, could hear it.

I slapped my hands over my ears and didn't know who was wailing until Clarice Anne Johnson said right in my ear, "Deza! Stop screaming! Let's get Mrs. Needham."

She yelled real loud, "Let's get Mrs. Needham . . . *and the police!*"

That only got the crowd more excited. They bunched around us tighter and tighter. Me and Clarice were trapped in a wall made out of evil and meanness.

Dolly Peaches looked right at me. "If it ain't another circus act from the broke-butt, poorhouse Malones. It's Pee-Wee's show-off, crybaby, stank-mouth sister, Number Two!"

He pointed at me. "Here's one 'n'em limparisk poems you can run and tell that old cow Needham."

He crunched his foot down on Jimmie's back.

I heard that horrible scream again and Clarice held my waist even tighter.

Dolly Peaches sang,

"Little Jimmie Malone asked his mommy for
some hugs,
'Cause he found out that his daddy ate some
bugs.
Jimmie never got no taller,
Just got smaller and smaller,
And now he has to sleep under someone's
stinky rugs."

When his foot went up again I remembered what Father had told Jimmie when he was teaching him how to box. "Twist your hips when you throw a punch. You have to shift all of your weight into it, and the only way to do that is to twist your hips. It's physics.

"It's just like hitting a baseball, if you use only your arms you aren't going to hit the ball far, but put your hips into it and. . . POW! . . . you'll knock that baby clean out of the park."

He showed us how to throw punches with our waists. Then, "Don't be a headhunter. Punching someone in the head is a good way to break your hand. Go for the belly, it'll get their attention just as surely as a pop to the head."

Dolly brought his foot down on Jimmie again. I tore away from Clarice and shoved Dolly as hard as I could from behind. He stumbled and would have fallen if the circle of kids hadn't held him up.

He turned to see who had nerve enough to push him, and gave me one of his alligator smiles.

Everyone let out a long "Oooh . . . !" Clarice Anne Johnson threw her hands over her ears and looked shell-shocked.

Dolly stepped over Jimmie and stood in my face. He pinched his nose between his thumb and finger like he was smelling a pile of garbage.

"So, Stank-Bug, you think just 'cause you's smart and a girl I won't knock you out too? I ain't no gentleman. I'm gonna show you exactly how Joe Louis is gonna crush Max Smelling."

Dolly took a step back and spit in each hand. "Dee-za, get ready to meet your midget brother. I got him a one-way ticket to the city of Kicked-Your-Butt, U.S.A., and I'm buying you one too!"

Dolly swung his right hand hard and caught me in the neck and the jaw.

It felt like I swallowed a firecracker.

Red light and white pain came out of my back teeth on the left. I felt something loose in my mouth and thought I'd lost a tooth, but as my tongue turned it over in my cheek I knew it was one of the pieces of camphor-soaked cotton I keep in my back teeth to stop them from hurting.

He'd hit me his hardest, but hadn't twisted his waist. He didn't even knock me down.

The crowd roared. He raised his hands over his head and I put my fists up like Father showed us.

Dolly said, "Hey, Pee-Wee, old Number Two can take a punch better than you!"

More laughs.

"But if she don't go down with this one y'all can call me Dolly-Girl Peaches."

He showed his teeth and reached his right hand back as far as he could. And threw another arm punch.

I heard, "Well, kiddo, here's our chance. . . ."

I planted my feet and threw all my weight into a uppercut aimed at Dolly's belly.

He ran right into it.

If his spine hadn't gotten in the way, my fist would've poked a hole clean through his back! He grabbed his stomach and dropped. First his knees, then the rest of him fell like a mighty oak. He rolled onto his back.

Father also told us, "Press the advantage. One good punch doesn't mean the fight is over. A wounded animal is more dangerous than any other kind."

I sat on Dolly's chest and grabbed his hair. "Dolly Peaches, I'll stay here until you apologize for everything." I looked at Clarice. "Keep track of how many times he has to apologize."

I dug my fingers into Dolly's hair. "First you will apologize for hurting my brother, then you're going to apologize for talking about my father, who did actually eat some bugs but did it for a very selfless and noble reason, then for calling Mrs. Needham a cow, then for mispronouncing my name on purpose, then for that horrible poem, which wasn't anything close to being a *limerick*."

Clarice held up five fingers. "What about for calling you Number Two?"

I said, "That's too immature to even think about. Five will do."

Dolly's eyes were rimmed with tears and his nose streamed a disgusting river. His mouth opened and shut, just like one of those out-of-luck, soon-to-be-fried catfish Father used to bring home from the river. He tried to say something over the mocking laughs from the crowd.

I raised my arm over my head. "Hush!"

And they listened! The crowd turned into a pack of librarians as the "Shhhs" started at the front row and washed back.

I leaned close so I could hear Dolly Peaches. He half-gasped, "Sorry . . . sorry . . . sorry . . . sorry . . . sorry." Five times!

Then he whispered, "Oh, please, get me a am-bo-lamps, sweet baby Jesus, I'm dying here."

Jimmie stood up. The blood of the Malones was pouring from a cut on his forehead. His face got tighter and tighter and he was just as angry as he'd been scared a second before. He looked right at me. "Why, Deza? *Why?*" He pushed his way through the crowd and disappeared.

Clarice said, "Deza! Let's go! Looks like Dolly-Girl here has had enough."

I love that girl!

She dragged me through the crowd to go pick up my books.

As soon as we were far enough away she whispered, "Oh, Deza! Did you see the look on Dolly's face? He *is* close to dying. We'll just have to go on the lam! I hear there's a place just outside of town where we can hop a freight train and be in California in two weeks."

She looked around to make sure no one was listening. "I have a cousin in San Diego who was tried for murder and got off, I'm sure he'll help us to—"

"Clarice Anne Johnson! Would you be still for a minute, please! Dolly isn't going to die, he's just like all the other bullies, a big nothing. Besides, I can't for the life of me understand how a boy would have the nerve to be a bully when he's been forced to go through life with a name like Dolly Peaches! What on earth was his mother thinking? And Clarice, why have so many of your relatives been charged with murder?"

She ignored my question. "Oh, Deza, you were so brave! You must have been terrified! Look, your hands are still shaking. And you're crying!"

She grabbed my right hand and I noticed how terribly it trembled.

The real reason I was shaking dawned on me like a cold, lonely sun coming up on a frozen February Gary morning. This wasn't something new. This didn't have a thing to do with being scared. This was the same way I felt when I'd get to the end of a really good book. I was shaking now because I *really*, *really* liked what had just happened!

I *loved* how I had raised my arm like I was carrying a magical sword and all the little thugs got quiet. They parted for me and Clarice like the Red Sea did for Moses! But most of all I *loved* knowing that when something was happening to someone, I could do more than wring my hands, I could strike back!

I loved those feelings at the same time I hated them.

Fighting is wrong and very unladylike, but worse than that, by gut-punching the biggest bully at Lincoln Woods School I had humiliated Jimmie. And even though I'd stopped him from being hurt and maybe even murdered, I now saw a very scary side of myself.

Brain number two was starting to take over.

All I could hope was that Jimmie would understand that I was trying to rescue him.

All I could hope was that the crown of being biggest bully wouldn't automatically come to me, because, even though I had *really* enjoyed beating that million-tooth monster, that crown would rest uneasy on my head.

We stopped at the library, then left, too worried and excited to sit and read. I walked Clarice to her house, we did our motto, then I ran to see if Jimmie had made it home.

* * *

Jimmie was sitting on the couch with a pencil and piece of paper. He raised the paper to cover his face. This was something I wasn't going to put up with.

"Look, I'm sorry if I did anything wrong, but I just couldn't stand there and watch. Who knows what Dolly Peaches would have done to you? Besides, it was just a lucky punch, I'll bet you anything the next time I see him he's going to pulverize me."

Jimmie sounded very serious and rough. "He'll have to go through me first."

I covered my mouth but a laugh slipped out anyway.

Jimmie said from behind the paper, "Yeah, by the time he finishes pounding me into the ground he'll be too tired to fight and you can give him another ticket to Kicked-Your-Butt, U.S.A."

We both laughed. Jimmie had forgiven me.

I pulled the paper away from his face. He had stuck a piece of tape on the place where Dolly Peaches had cut his forehead.

"Here, let me see that." There was a one-inch gash on his forehead that ran down into his left eyebrow.

"Jimmie, you didn't cover the whole cut, it's not going to heal right, it'll leave a big scar."

"Really?"

Jimmie thinks scars make him look older and tougher. I went to the bathroom to get the tape, the gauze, and the five-hundred-year-old brownish-red bottle of Mercurochrome.

I gently pulled at one corner of the tape. He twisted his face. "Naw, sis, that's too slow. When you're 'bout to do something that hurts, do it fast. Get it over with. Give it a good snatch."

I said, "I'm going to count to three, then pull it, OK? One, two . . ." I closed my eyes and yanked the piece of tape before I got to three. It held on way too long.

There was so much eyebrow on the tape that it looked like a furry white-and-red caterpillar with a million skinny black legs sticking out of it. I hid it behind me and looked at my poor brother.

The cut was zigging off in a new direction. Fresh blood was pooling up and trickling down around his eye.

"Well, Mr. James Edward Malone, you're always praying for horrible scars, and now you've got one. That's going to need stitches for sure."

He forgot to deepen his voice and almost squeaked, "Nah, sis, just tape it up, I'll be fine."

"This is going to sting. Should I bring a washrag for you to bite on?"

"That's only for white cowboys. I'm from Gary, I'm tougher than that."

I dabbed a little of the Mercurochrome into a piece of gauze and pressed it onto Jimmie's cut. He made a sound like a cat having its tail stepped on. I cut ten skinny strips of tape and pulled both sides of the cut together. By the time I finished, Jimmie was breathing like he'd run a mile. The cut looked a lot better.

He went into the bathroom to see what I'd done. A normal person would've been very mad at the new upside-down V that ran into their eyebrow and up on their forehead.

He came back grinning. "Wow! This looks great, Deza! Thanks a million!" He hugged me.

"You're welcome."

Which is probably not the right thing to say to someone who you just scarred for life.

Chapter Nine

The Gary Iron-Head Dogs Meet the Chicky-Bar Giants

I was on the couch trying to read, sitting so I could keep my eye on the clock in the kitchen. So many good things were going to happen today. It was the first day of vacation and our baseball team, the Gary Iron-Head Dogs, was playing a team from Michigan for first place in the Negro American League! The knock I'd been waiting for came from the screen door.

She was right on time.

"Come in, Clarice!"

We hugged.

"Oh, Deza, have you been outside? It's a beautiful day for the game!"

"I know, I can't wait! Jimmie says Pedro T.wo-Toes' arm is OK and he might pitch!"

"Then we really don't need to go to the game, do we? That's a guaranteed win!"

"Clarice, I wouldn't miss this game for the world! Let's go."

We hooked arms and started toward the library. We would read until quarter to noon, then leave for the park. The game was at one and we'd have to be early if we wanted good seats.

Clarice said, "So, is Jimmie going to the game too?"

Thinking about poor Clarice's crush on Jimmie made my skin twitch like a horse's when a fly lands on it. I love my brother, but ick! "His face looks like he got run over by a train!"

She gasped. "Oh, no! That's not going to stop him from coming, is it?"

I rolled my eyes. "No, Clarice, Jimmie said they asked him to sing before the game."

She said, "Oh, I hope he's OK, the poor dear."

I thought the same thing about her. I know you're supposed to love and accept your friends and family the way they are, and not give them a whole bunch of suggestions to make them better, even if they need a ton of help. But this summer I'd make Clarice see how crazy it is to look at Jimmie that way.

Yuck!

* * *

The wall at the entrance to the library had a huge new sign on it.

GOD BLESS THE PRIDE OF AMERICA,
THE BROWN BOMBER, JOE LOUIS!

One of the librarians had painted a big picture of the boxer. He was in his underpants saluting a American flag with a hundred white people waving and carrying signs around him.

A pair of boxing gloves hung from a hook on one side of the painting. On the other side was a American flag. Underneath was a gold crown and: OUR CHAMPION OF THE WORLD!

Clarice said, "Boxing gloves? In the library?"

I said, "I'm mortifried too."

Mrs. Ashton, the friendliest white librarian, pushed a cart by us. "Good morning, Deza, Clarice. Isn't it exciting?"

We said, "Hello, Mrs. Ashton, how are you?"

She said, "I'm about to explode! You two must be very proud."

Clarice said, "Ma'am?"

"Oh, yes, you need to be very proud. Joe Louis is such a credit to your race."

Clarice said, "Any new good books, Mrs. Ashton?"

"Stop by my desk, I have something for each of you."

"Thank you, ma'am."

Mrs. Ashton said, "Woo-hoo! Go, Brown Bomber!"

Once Mrs. Ashton pushed her cart into the next room Clarice said, "Oh, Deza, I'll die if she's got books about boxing for us."

There was no escaping that doggone fight.

Every single table in the library had a one-foot-tall cardboard cutout of Joe Louis standing in the middle of it. At his feet were the words WE LOVE YOU, JOE! A little pair of red boxing gloves was tied to each cutout.

"Ugh! Let's go to the chairs in the stacks."

Even there a banner read, GIVE HIM HECK, JOE!

I said, "Heck? In the library?"

* * *

Maybe it was because this was the fourth time I was reading *Huckleberry Finn*, but my eyes kept going up to the little cutout paper doll Joe Louis.

In every picture I'd seen he looked like such a unhappy man. He must be wishing this fight was over as much as me and Clarice. He must be very nervous. I looked at the tiny boxing gloves.

I whispered, "*Clarice?*"

She was settled into her book.

"*Clarice?*"

She looked up. "Huh?"

I whispered, "*Why do they call these things boxing gloves? Every glove I've ever seen has five fingers, the only thing that has just a thumb is a mitten!*"

Clarice giggled very quietly into her hand, but a woman two tables away said, "Shhh!"

She sounded like a steam radiator starting up.

I whispered, "*Boxing is such a stupid sport that they don't even give things the right name. Those things they call shorts look just like my brother's underdrawers!*"

Clarice covered my lips with her hand and I covered hers with mine, but our laughs squeezed out of the sides of our mouths.

The shushing woman slammed her book shut, got up and walked toward the front desk.

I said, "We better go."

When we walked by the front desk, the woman pointed. "That's them!"

Mrs. Ashton said, "Oh, those two! They're just giddy with excitement about the fight!"

Outside, Clarice turned around and hollered back into the library, "Go, Brown Bomber!"

Someone inside hollered back, "Whip that Nazi good! We love you, Joe!"

A bunch of whoops and hollers came from the library. Even Mrs. Ashton yelled again.

We ran all the way to the park, laughing so hard that our one heart almost exploded!

* * *

We were at the park almost two hours early and half of the bleacher seats were already taken! People were even starting to line up along the outfield fences. It was like a carnival!

Clarice said, "My goodness, Deza, everyone looks so nice! We should've worn our church dresses."

We climbed into the bleachers and found seats in the very top row, nice and high. I went back down to where people were getting scorecards. Some of the time they're free and some of the time they charge for them.

I asked a man who was walking away from the line, "Excuse me, sir, are the scorecards free?"

"No, sweetheart, it's a penny for a card and a pencil."

I said, "Thank you," and started back to Clarice.

He said, "Wait a minute, ain't you Roscoe's daughter?"

"Yes, sir."

"I didn't recognize you at first 'cause you ain't got a book tucked under your arm."

I knew the man. Father used to play horseshoes with him.

I smiled. "I'm sorry I didn't recognize you, Mr. Dukes."

"Here, I've got a spare card you can have, and a pencil too."

"Thank you, Mr. Dukes!" He got back in the line.

The scorecard said that the other team was from Grand Rapids, Michigan, a city geologically located a hundred miles northeast from Gary. As I climbed back to the top of the bleachers both teams came out on the field.

I handed Clarice the card. "Pedro Two-Toes Torres is pitching. Grand Rapids has some southpaw named Lewis."

Clarice said, "Mr. Two-Toes's arm is really better?"

The man next to us said, "According to him it is, but you can't believe a word he says."

A woman in front of us said, "That's the truth. I grew up with him back in Mississippi. Back when he was Peter Thompson, before he *discovered* he was a Cuban and changed his name."

People all around us laughed.

The players from Grand Rapids and Gary too were leaning against the fence along the first-base line, looking out into the crowd.

People in the bleachers started standing up and looking back.

Clarice shouted, "It's Jimmie!" She leaned into me. "Oh, Deza, he's so good-looking!"

I nearly choked.

Jimmie was standing on a picnic table in the center of a growing circle of people.

Clarice said to the man next to us, "Sir, could you watch our books and save our seats for us?"

"I sure will."

She pulled me down the bleachers and we headed to where Jimmie stood above the crowd. His eyes were closed. There were so many people standing around the table we couldn't get very close.

Clarice hopped up and down, waving and yelling, "Jimmie! Yoo-hoo! Over here!"

I knew Jimmie couldn't hear her. He was settling into his song.

He cleared his throat, took three deep breaths, held the last one, then sang,

> ***"Oh, say, can you see . . ."***

I'm not sure what's more surprising about the first notes of any song Jimmie sings—what it does to me, or the changes it brings in Jimmie.

I have to close my eyes, just like he does. I can't tolerate anything that would interfere with hearing his voice.

Listening to Jimmie brings to mind how Father used to

swing me around and around by my wrists until everything became a blur, and even though I knew he was holding me, I felt like if I didn't hang on as tight as I could I'd fly off into the sky like a arrow.

And it seems like Jimmie makes himself larger and larger as he sings. If I opened my eyes I'd see he'd grown so much that he was filling every square inch of the park. No room would be able to hold him, chairs and rugs would get crowded up against the walls.

His voice always stayed light and high-pitched and soft, but it was strong in a way that let on that there were stories behind each word.

"By the dawn's early light . . ."

It felt like those words were asking you something and telling you something and blaming you for something, all at the same time.

"What so proudly we hailed
At the twilight's last gleaming . . ."

He finished the anthem,

". . . And the home of the brave."

There was no sound from the baseball diamond or the bleachers or the people bunched around the picnic table. Then a explosion of cheers and a huge throwing-up of hands.

Clarice was back to hopping. "Yoo-hoo, Jimmie! It's us! Over here!"

But so were a bunch of other bad-taste girls and he couldn't hear her.

People started yelling, "Sing us one about how Joe's gonna clean that Nazi's clock, Little Jimmie!"

"Yeah, Little Jimmie, sing something about Joe!"

Jimmie laughed, raised his arms and started singing.

Everyone but me and Clarice knew the song and sang the chorus.

> ***"Oh, no! Joe! Don't you kill that boy!***
> ***Bust his head, then send him back!***
> ***Oh, no! Joe! Don't you kill that boy!***
> ***Hit him hard as the grille***
> ***On my pa's Cadillac!"***

They sang that two more times before Jimmie stepped off of the table and disappeared in a forest of adults patting his back and shaking his hand.

On the way back to the bleachers, everyone was buzzing about Jimmie.

I was proud and embarrassed at the same time at the way Clarice was blurting out, "She's his sister! For real!"

We got back to the top of the bleachers just as the umpire shouted, "Play ball!"

The man we were sitting next to had been right, you couldn't believe a word that Two-Toes Peter Thompson said. His arm was shot.

The first two batters he faced sent the ball sailing out of the park and me and Clarice and the rest of the crowd booed Mr. Two-Toes with all our might.

The woman in front of us said, "Don't worry, he settles down after while."

By the time he did, the Chicky-Bar Giants had scored four runs and their lefty pitcher hadn't allowed one.

Four to nothing. We'd been shut out.

As we walked down the bleachers men were handing out flyers and saying, "Small cover, food will be served. Bring the family, brand-new RCA Victor."

Clarice took one of the flyers, then said, "Yuck!"

The fight!

A million places around Gary were having fight parties, where you could listen to the fight on the radio. Some were charging money.

Father's friend Mr. Bobbin, the barber, had invited us to his shop to listen. We didn't have to pay, just bring a dish. Jimmie'd already picked a ton of wild greens and Mother had got a perfectly good piece of meat that the Carsdales were throwing out to season those greens extra special. Clarice was going to come with us.

I have to admit I was a little excited about getting together with a bunch of people and talking and sharing food.

We got to my house and we held up two fingers, pointed at our cheeks, then held up one finger and put our hands on our hearts.

I opened the screen door. Mother called from the kitchen, "Deza?"

"Yes, Mother?"

"So?"

"Oh, Mother! It was a disaster, the Iron-Head Dogs were shut out!"

* * *

That evening, during Chow Chat, Father said, "And you, my Dar Dawt, how was your day? Anything new?"

Where to begin? Jimmie singing in the park? No, that was his story. The Iron-Head Dogs getting shut out? No, I bet Father already knew. Besides, he hadn't found work, so that was enough bad news for the night.

I remembered what I wanted to ask. "What does it mean when someone says you're a credit to your race?"

Mother and Father shot each other a glance.

Jimmie said, "It means some white person's grateful that you left them in peace, that you didn't stab 'em or shoot 'em or rob 'em."

Mother said, "Jimmie, please. Give us the context, Deza."

I told about Mrs. Ashton and Joe Louis and the library.

Father said, "It has to do with intentions. Usually when people say that, they have good intentions, they think they're giving you a compliment, but when you look at it . . ."

Jimmie said, "It's a insult."

"I can't deny that, Jimmie," Mother said, "but you learn you have to make allowances. You have to know which battles are worth fighting."

Father said, "And 'credit to your race' and a lot of other sayings you'll be running into are things that give you a warning about whoever it is who's saying them."

I said, "How's that, Father?"

"Think about a strange dog, Deza. They let you know if they're friendly or not, right?"

"Yes."

"Unless they're rabid they give you signals that if you get any closer you'll end up hurt. Their ears will go back, their fur will stand up, they'll show their teeth."

Jimmie said, "They'll growl."

"Right, think of 'credit to your race' as that first growl. Just be aware that that person is letting you know you need to keep an even sharper-than-normal eye on them. But be grateful too, because they're letting you know exactly who they are."

Mother said, "What did you say when Mrs. Ashton told you that?"

"Clarice changed the subject."

Mother smiled. "That girl has such a good head on her shoulders."

I don't like to be unhumble, but anyone could see I have great taste in picking my friends!

Chapter Ten

A Taste for Perch

Most of the time I wake up in bits and pieces. First my legs wake up and stretch out as far as they can, then my toes wiggle to make sure they're there. Next my arms and fingers do the same thing, then I yawn, stretch and open my eyes.

There was something different about the second day of summer vacation. I sat straight up in bed and felt like I'd been wide awake for hours.

I wasn't scared, I just knew something was different. I couldn't tell if it was late at night or early in the morning, but something about the way shadows were laying around my room let me know this wasn't a time that I was usually awake.

I heard bumpity sounds coming from downstairs. I undid the straps on my new shoes and went to see who was up. Father was humming and boiling water.

"Deza! Was I being that loud?" He gave me a hug and a kiss.

"I don't think so, Father, I was just awake for no reason. What time is it?"

Mother must've followed right behind me. She was squeezing her housecoat shut in front of her. "It's a little before four o'clock, Deza, and you need to get back in bed. And so does your hardheaded daddy."

Father hugged Mother. "Morning, Peg."

I said, "Why are we all up so early?"

Father laughed. "Well, Dar Dawt, I have a taste for perch."

"Perch?"

"Yup, I'm going fishing with a couple of the guys I used to work with. Tonight you'll be eating the fruit of Lake Michigan."

Mother said, "Lake Michigan! I thought you were going down to the river."

Father said, "Uh-uh. Steel Lung's treating me, Hank and Carlos to a fishing trip on the lake."

Mother near shouted, "*What!* You didn't say anything about going out on that lake!"

"Well, that's where the perch are, Mrs. Malone."

"There are perch in the river too."

"True, but Steel Lung knows a spot where they're practically jumping into the boat."

"Roscoe Malone, I know you are not seriously thinking of going out on that lake in a boat."

"Peg—"

"'Peg,' my foot! You never said anything about a boat. Coming from a landlocked place like Flint, you can't even dream what these Great Lakes are capable of. Storms on Lake Michigan have sunk ships that were six city blocks long."

Father gasped, "*Really?*" He nudged me in the side and said, "It's a good thing we're not going out in anything that big. Steel Lung's rowboat is only about twelve *feet* long."

I had to laugh.

He nudged Mother too. She didn't laugh or smile at all so I wiped mine off my face.

Father said, "Steel Lung promised we're staying right in sight of shore. He's even got life preservers."

All the steam had gone out of Mother. "I don't like this one bit."

Father hugged her and Mother dodged out of the way of his kiss.

Mother gave him a look. "Let me put something together for your lunch."

Before she could even get a loaf out of the bread box there was a soft tap at the front door.

Father kissed me and Mother on the cheek and said, "That's Steel Lung. Gotta go."

Mr. Steel Lung Henderson was the only black man in Gary who kept a job with the Company year-round. There were only two jobs that Negro or Mexican men could have in the steel mill. One was janitor and the other was worse.

Once a month the furnaces at the steel mill would have to be repaired on the inside, but the bosses couldn't let the furnaces cool all the way down 'cause it took too much time for them to heat back up again. That was the only time people who weren't white got to do regular work. They'd have to go into the hot furnace and pull out the bricks that had been cracked and damaged by the heat. Then they'd put new ones in.

Father said the bosses put wood planks on the floor of the furnace so your shoes wouldn't get burned, but lots of times the planks themselves would get so hot that they'd catch afire. The men would stay in the furnace pulling and replacing bricks as long as they could before the heat made them so woozy that they were about to pass out. Mr. Steel Lung got his name because he could stay in the furnace longer than anyone else.

Me and Mother followed Father into the living room to say hello to him. The smell of his work boots made me remember when Father used to do that furnace job. He did it for three months and I was so happy when they finally said he'd have to get laid off because his asthma meant he couldn't stay in the furnace very long. That meant a lot less money coming in, but once Father got laid off, his breathing started getting better and better.

Mother and Father's bedroom is right next to mine upstairs and the walls are so thin that I used to have to pull the pillow tight over my ears when he'd cough and try to get the phlegm out of his chest all night long. That stopped as soon as he quit going into that hot furnace.

Mr. Steel Lung promised to bring Father back in one piece.

We followed them out onto the porch. It was so cold that I huddled into Mother's housecoat. It was so cold that smoke was coming out of their mouths when they talked.

Father and Mr. Steel Lung slammed the doors of the old pickup truck and it started with a cough and a roar. Father waved and a big cloud of smoke came out of the rear of the truck.

Mother said, "Deza, run in and get your daddy his coat, quick!" She hollered at the truck, "Roscoe! Wait!"

I ran to the closet but by the time I got back all I could see were the two round red taillights of that truck getting smaller and smaller, going down Wilbur Place leaving a trail of smoke.

The truck made that grindy, gracky sound when Mr. Steel Lung shifted gears and slowed down to turn the corner on Fifth. Then they were gone.

Mother said, "Go back to bed, sweetheart."

I walked upstairs and got in bed to finish my last good night of sleep for a long, long time.

Chapter Eleven

Pulling Myself Together

We were in the kitchen working on supper. Even if Father showed up now there wouldn't be time to clean and cook the perch, so we started making our regular Sunday meal, just in case.

Mother had said that perch would make a fine Monday meal. I shouldn't've said anything, but I told her I had a bad feeling about Father not being home.

"I wouldn't worry, sweetheart. Your father can take care of himself." She rolled her eyes. "He is from Flint, after all. He'll be home soon. Let's give him another hour or two. Then, if it'll make you feel better, we'll walk over to the Hendersons'."

I watched her very close, trying to see if she really wasn't worried or was just trying to keep me from getting scared. There weren't any 1-1-1 lines showing and the way she cut the onions and hummed I knew she wasn't pretending, so I relaxed.

I still couldn't keep my eyes from looking at the clock: 5:41.

Five minutes later the knock came.

I slammed my knife down and ran to the front door, ready to give Father I-don't-know-what for making us worry like this.

Well, for making *me* worry.

A second before I got to the door I thought, Wait, why would Father knock? I opened the door.

"Good evening, Deza, is your father here?"

My stomach started slowly folding. "No, Mrs. Henderson, he's not home yet, Mother's in the—"

Mother was behind me, wiping her hands on a dishcloth. "Helen! Come in, what's wrong?"

Mrs. Henderson said, "Hello, Margaret, Roscoe's not home? Did Steve come by here?" Steve is Mr. Steel Lung's real name.

A look flashed in Mother's eyes. "No, what time were you expecting him?"

"He said they wouldn't be out past noon, that's when the fish quit biting."

Mother and Mrs. Henderson sat on the couch. I was frozen in the doorway.

Mother said, "What about Hank and Carlos, did you—"

"Yes, yes. Hank's kids hadn't seen him and Carlos's wife hadn't heard anything either."

Mother leaned back on the couch. "Oh, dear. Deza, go take the pot off the stove."

The screen door slammed behind me and Mother didn't even notice.

Mrs. Henderson said, "Peg, do you know anyone with a car? I've got a little money for gas and I know where Steve parks when he goes fishing, we could see if his truck is still there."

Mother said, "I can see if Mr. Rhymes is home. Deza! What did I tell you? Turn off the stove and wait here for Jimmie. Don't tell him anything, he'd go out looking on his own and that's all we need, two Malone men wandering around."

She squeezed my cheek, leaving the damp smell of onions and soap on my face.

Mother's voice was scaring me to death. It was far too calm. I ran to turn off the stove. By the time I got back they were gone.

I picked the dish towel off the floor where Mother had dropped it. She had been twisting it so hard that it was like a piece of soft blue and pink and white rope.

I unwound the towel and snapped it a couple of times before I hung it back next to the stove. I took the kitchen clock with me and sat on the porch, hoping Mr. Steel Lung would drop Father off and we'd all laugh about how scared we were. I'd point at the clock and say to Father, "Do you have any idea how late it is?"

About a hundred hours later, at six-fifty, a car stopped in front of our house and the back door came open. Mother ran from the car. "Any word from your father?"

"No, Mother."

"Is Jimmie home yet?"

"No."

"We won't be long." She got back in the car.

Mr. Rhymes's car turned left onto Fifth Street and disappeared.

Mother always says, "A watched pot never boils," and I can tell you that a watched clock never moves. A million hours later, at eight o'clock and starting to get dark, Mr. Rhymes's car turned back onto our street.

I ran off the porch and prayed, "Let Mother be giving Father a good piece of her mind for worrying us like this!"

The back door of the car opened. Mother stepped out and said something to Mr. Rhymes.

Not only did Father *not* get out of the car, but Mother saw me standing on the sidewalk, leaned her head back into the automobile and wiped at her eyes. She'd been crying!

My legs gave out and I fell on my knees.

Hot tears started boiling out of my eyes, but I couldn't make a sound.

Mother had me in her arms in a second.

If she started any sentence with "Deza, I'm sorry . . ." I'd die right on the spot.

But she just held me.

I heard Mr. Rhymes get out of his car. He walked up to us. "Peg, if you need anything send your boy and I can be here in no time."

Mother said, "Thank you, John, thank you very much." She squeezed my arms hard. "Deza, you have to listen to me."

Her eyes were bloodshot and the lines between them were at 1-1-1-1-1.

"Oh, Mother, I'm ready. Tell me what happened."

"We don't know yet. The truck was still parked by the lake. We figure they got lost, a huge fog bank came in while they were out there. We'll just have to wait and see."

"He's not . . ."

"No, Deza, they're just missing. We made a report at the police station. We have to be patient and wait. The police said six other fishermen have gone missing in the fog. This has happened before, it's not as bad as it might seem."

She wiped at my tears and kissed my cheek.

The onion-and-soap smell was gone.

"Deza, think how worried Jimmie will be if he sees you crying like this. You've got to pull yourself together."

Pull yourself together. This was the second time in three days I'd been told that.

As Mother wrapped her arms around me and led me into the house I wondered if my second brain was starting to get smarter and trickier because instead of thinking about where Father was and if he was safe or if he was hurt or if he was scared, like my first brain would, all I was thinking about was how perfect words can be.

Mrs. Needham and Mother had both told me, "Deza, you have to pull yourself together."

And as I sat on the couch wrapped in Mother's arms, I felt big hunks falling off of me and thumping to the ground. This must be how a tree feels in autumn when it watches the leaves that have been covering it all summer start to be blown away.

It must feel this hopeless and lonely.

I knew I really had to reach out and pick up the fallen pieces and pull them back.

Mother said, "Let's not tell Jimmie anything until we know more, Deza. Can you manage?"

"You know how Jimmie can read me, I'll just stay away from him, it won't be long, will it?"

"Deza, you know I can't tell you that. We'll have to endure."

"Can I sleep with you until Father comes home?"

Mother hugged me tighter. "You read my mind, I was going to ask if you would."

"Thank you, Mother."

"Please, Miss Malone, thank *you*."

Mother had pulled herself together.

She sniffled and said, "But there are two conditions. First, you've got to promise to tell me all about Mrs. Needham again and again and again, I'll never get tired of hearing that!"

"OK."

"And second, you cannot wear those patent leather shoes to bed, my shins would look like ground beef the way you toss and turn."

* * *

I thought I knew what it meant to be really scared. I thought Jimmie had given me enough practice so that nothing would ever bother me. When we were younger he'd sneak up on me and go "Boo!" or would jump out showing his teeth and growling, anything to try to make me cry. Mother explained that he was a boy and couldn't help himself.

Then one day it didn't work anymore. I figured all the scaredness in me had got used up.

I've never been more wrong about anything in my whole life.

There is nothing more terrifying than waking up and not being sure where you are and hearing your mother scream from a long way off. If there is, I don't want to know.

I jumped out of bed and flew down the stairs.

Mother was on the floor, halfway in the front door, being held by our neighbor Mrs. Kenworthy and howling.

I froze.

Mrs. Kenworthy said, "Peg, they don't know for sure. Mr. Rhymes is outside." She looked up, saw me and said, "Oh, Deza. Peg, Deza is here."

Mother took a huge breath, stood up, wiped her eyes and told me, "Sweetheart, I'm going to have to go out for a minute, don't wake Jimmie."

She ran past me to go get dressed.

Mrs. Kenworthy said, "Hello, Deza, how are . . ." She stopped and walked to where I was standing. She ran her hand over my head.

"Is Father . . ."

She said, "No, no. We don't know anything yet. Mr. Rhymes is carrying us to the hospital."

"The hospital? That's good, right? He's just hurt? That's not a funeral place or anything, right?"

She said, "It's not good news, but it's not bad news either. We simply have to wait."

Mother was back. "I won't leave you and Jimmie alone for long." She kissed my cheek and ran out, letting the screen door slam.

I walked to Jimmie's bedroom door and tapped. If he was awake he'd sing for me. I tapped again, then opened the door. He had pulled his pillow tight over his head.

I sat on the floor next to his bed and waited.

I would have found a more comfortable place if I'd've known how long it would be before we heard what happened to my poor father.

Chapter Twelve

Mother and the Hobo

I was back in the porch chair when Mr. Rhymes's car stopped in front of our house.

I ran out to the street. The car door opened and I stopped breathing. Grandma Sutphen, Mother's mother, got out of the car. Then I saw it was *Mother*, looking like she'd got fifty years older at the hospital.

She thanked Mr. Rhymes, smiled at me and said, "Come inside, Deza. Get Jimmie up."

I wanted to ask what happened, but she would've told me if there was bad news, wouldn't she? But why did she want to talk to me and Jimmie together? That's what you do if you're about to say something so horrid you can't bear to say it twice.

I ran to Jimmie's room. "Come quick, Mother wants to talk to us."

"Tell her I just need a couple more—"

I snatched the covers off. "Get up now!"

"OK, OK, sis."

"Hurry up!"

I sat next to Mother on the couch. It was a good sign that instead of hugging me she just smiled. A sad and puny smile, but it was a smile.

Jimmie came in rubbing his eyes. "What's wrong?"

Mother patted the couch next to her. "Sit here, dear."

Jimmie didn't move. "What's wrong?"

I said, "Please Jimmie, it's about Father."

He sat next to Mother. "What?"

Mother told him about the fishing trip and how Father hadn't come home yet. Then, "Mrs. Kenworthy came by earlier and told me they'd found two Negro men."

My head started spinning.

Mother squeezed my knee. "It wasn't your father. Hank Williams was found in the lake by some fishermen and Carlos Coulter was found on shore."

Jimmie said, "Found? Does that mean they're . . ."

Mother took his hand. "Yes."

Jimmie jerked his hand away and stood up. "What are you saying? How do you know Pa went out with them? He probably didn't even go with those men."

"James—"

"No! Pa ain't dead! I can't believe you think he was! I'd know if he was and he ain't!"

He ran to his room and slammed the door. He yelled, "Daddy's all right! I'ma show you!"

Me and Mother melted together and it wasn't two minutes later that Jimmie whipped his bedroom door open and ran out of the house.

I yelled, "Jimmie!" and started off the couch to catch him but Mother held me tight.

"No, Deza, let him go. We've each got to learn how to handle this. If burning off energy searching for your daddy is what Jimmie has to do, we'll let him."

I eased back into her arms.

"So what will *you* do, Mother, and what about me, what do I do?"

Mother covered her face with both hands. "Oh, Deza, I don't know, I just don't know."

We sat on the couch stuck together for the longest time.

* * *

We handled the next week by being in a daze. Time crawled by and nothing seemed changed and nothing seemed the same. The only good thing was that no policemen knocked on our door with news of someone else being found.

Every morning Mother would go to work and Jimmie would go out looking for Father.

Mr. Steel Lung's wife, Mrs. Henderson, doesn't have any family in Gary and her mother was coming from California to be with her so she spent her days at our house.

Me and Mother let her think she was looking after me, but Mother really didn't want her to be alone. Me neither. Clarice was a true champ and came and sat with me most days.

Mrs. Henderson started teaching us how to knit. On the

seventh day Father was gone I was learning what the saying "a stitch in time saves nine" means and was unraveling what I'd done.

Jimmie came in and slumped down beside me.

"Hey, sis. Hello, Mrs. Henderson."

"Good afternoon, James."

Jimmie asked me, "How come you're tearing up that—"

There were heavy footsteps on the front porch, then lightning hit me when I heard Mother sounding horrible and strange and weak. "Jimmie! Deza!"

Jimmie threw himself on the floor and curled into a ball with his fists against his ears.

Me and Mrs. Henderson jumped bolt up. Her yarn fell from her lap and bounced across the floor until it bumped into Jimmie.

Mother's cry came again.

Jimmie kept his fists in his ears. "No, no, no . . ."

I ran to open the door and saw Mother looking like she'd completely lost her mind.

Her arms were wrapped around a man. A very poor, very raggedy man.

She said, "Deza, sweetheart! Jimmie was right! Look, darling! Look!"

I looked at the man.

"It's your daddy!"

Then I understood, this was just another nightmare. It wasn't Father at all. I looked down to make sure I *was* dreaming, to make sure I was still in bed with my patent leather shoes on.

But all I saw was ten toes on the wooden front porch.

Oh, no! This was real. This was real.

I kept my eyes down and looked at this man's feet.

He was wearing blue cloth slippers. His legs were gray and ashy, like they hadn't been near a jar of Vaseline in a hundred years. He had on too-big blue jeans and one of those white hospital shirts.

I looked at Mother and got even scareder. Her heart was so broken that she'd found some poor hobo from the park and had brought him home thinking he was Father.

The man said in a hoarse voice, "My Darling Daughter Detha, don't you recognithe your Deareth Delightful Daddy?"

I looked again.

The man's voice was rough and hacky, like Father's after a long night of coughing, but Father never had such a bad lisp.

He was too small to be my father. He was bony and scraggly-looking.

His hair was snarled and he had a stubbly beard.

The skin around his eyes was dark and bruised like he'd been in a fight. There were big clumps of dried white stuff in their corners and trails of gray running down his cheeks.

What really let me know this wasn't Father was his mouth. That same mouth that sounded a little like my father was *nothing* like Roscoe Malone's. The man's lips were twice the size of Father's and a big cut with stitches ran from his nose across his top lip into his mouth.

When he looked at me through those swole-up gray-streaked eyes he smiled and I knew I had lost both of my parents, Father to Lake Michigan, and Mother to craziness.

The man had no front teeth at all. My father is very proud

of his teeth and brushes them twice every day. It even looked like the hobo had stitches in his tongue.

Mother said, "Deza, where's Jimmie? Get him up! Run and tell him your daddy is ali—"

Jimmie ran onto the porch.

The poor hobo reached his hand out and mumbled, "My Genuine Gentle, Jumpin' Giant, Jimmie!"

Jimmie's face hardened. "My Fine, Friendly Father Figure?"

Mrs. Henderson walked onto the porch, her hand holding the knitting needles over her mouth.

Mother and the hobo stopped smiling when they saw her.

Mrs. Henderson had lost her mind too. "Roscoe. Please. Where's Steve?"

The man said, "Helen, I'm tho thorry, he didn't make it. He wath with me and—"

Mrs. Henderson's arm jerked and one of the needles left a nasty scratch across her forehead. I snatched the needles away.

She whispered, "Peg, I'm so happy for you," and walked past us toward the street.

Mother said, "Helen, wait!" But Mrs. Henderson kept going.

"Jimmie, walk Mrs. Henderson home. Stay there until I can get someone to look after her."

He gave the hobo a hard look, then ran after Mrs. Henderson.

I followed Mother and the hobo through the front door. She guided him right to Father's chair and helped him crumble down into it. She put Father's blanket over him and ran upstairs to the bathroom.

The man reached a shaking hand to me. He started crying, washing the old gray streaks off his cheeks. He said, "Detha, I've mithed all of you tho much. You're all that kept me alive."

I looked hard into his eyes and saw.

I dropped the knitting needles and slapped my hands over my mouth.

My father was alive!

Chapter Thirteen

The King of Spain Is a Delightful Conversationalist

Father was home, but it still felt like we were trapped in those days that he was missing; everything was the same, but everything was different.

Mother said he was so weak that they didn't want to let him out of the hospital.

She told me, with a very prideful voice, "And girl, once one of these Malone men gets an idea in his hard head it just won't come out. The doctors warned him if he left he might die. Your daddy told those doctors, 'I've gone through all this time without my family, the only thing that's going to kill me now is if I go through one more second without them. Unless you've got a pistol in that coat and are going to shoot me, get out of my way, I'm going home.'"

Mother shook her head. "That's exactly what your daddy said, and he meant it."

She put her hand over her mouth to hide a smile and said, "Well, he didn't say it *exactly* like that, he actually lisped his way through the whole argument!"

We settled into a different kind of day. Every morning Mother would catch the bus to work, Jimmie would go to work for Dr. Bracy and, just like I did for Mother when she had Tic Do La Roo, I would sit next to Father in bed and read. Sometimes out loud to him, and sometimes to myself.

He slept most of the time, which was good because when he was awake it was terrifying. He would wake up screaming from nightmares about Lake Michigan. Mostly he would shout or cry or yell at Mr. Steel Lung. Sometimes he'd apologize to him. Every time he'd yell I'd set my book down and tell him, "It's all right, you're safe at home."

He'd look around, then finally would calm down and go back to sleep.

Every day I did something Mother and Father would do to me and Jimmie whenever we got sick. I kissed Father's fevered forehead three times and said, "Kisses . . . kisses . . . kisses make you stronger."

One day when I kissed him the coolness of his forehead surprised me. His eyes blinked open and he smiled, "Yeth, my Darling Daughter Detha, it worked, your kitheth have made me thtronger."

I plopped down on his chest and hugged him. "Oh, Father! That'th juth what I wanted. Welcome back, my Deareth Delightful Daddy!"

For the first time in a million years my father laughed! It was a rusty old laugh, but it was a laugh, and it felt like chains breaking off of him. It made the hairs on my neck stand up.

"Oh," he said, "how tharper than a therpent'th tooth it ith to have a thankleth, bratty little child. You're actually going to thit there and mock your poor Deareth Delightful Daddy'th new lithp?"

I kissed him again and again and said, "Yeth, yeth, yeth! And it really ith about time you pulled yourthelf together, mithter! But I'm not mocking you."

"No? Well, it thure thoundth like mockery." He put his hand over his chest. "And it thure feelth like mockery to my heart."

I looked to see if he was serious. "No, Father it isn't, it comes from a book I read."

He coughed a couple of times, then said, "I know the book, it'th called *How to Be Dithrethpectful and Abuthive to a Good Man*."

I laughed. "Not that one! I can't remember the book's name but it told about how the people who speak a certain kind of Spanish lisp all the time."

Father said, "I think I know the thtory, but tell me anyway."

"OK." I cleared my throat and waited for a second, settling into the story.

"Once upon a time . . . there was a king of Spain who—"

Father said, "King Ferdinand, right?"

"Father! Who's telling this, me or you?"

"Thorry, go ahead."

"OK." I put my head on the pillow next to Father's. "From the day he was born, this Spanish king was kind and loving and showed great character to everyone. But the whole country felt sad for him because when he talked he had a very strong lisp."

Father said, "A lithp? That'th juth terrible!"

"Father!" I put my hand over his mouth as softly as I could. The stitches in his lip poked at my palm.

"Whenever the king would talk to someone he lisped so badly that people would answer him and lisp too, not to make fun or mock him, but to show him how much they loved . . ."

I kissed Father's cheek.

". . . and respected . . ."

Another kiss.

". . . and honored him."

Another kiss.

"That'th what I'm doing, Father, not mocking you."

Father smiled and said, "Thank you, Detha, that'th beautiful, but I'm afraid it'th a myth."

I said, "What? You're afraid it's a miss?"

Father laughed again. "I thaid it wath a myth. M-Y-T-H, myth, thmart aleck."

"You know what, Father, sometimes myths are a lot better than what really happens, that's why I started that story with 'Once upon a time.'"

His eyes closed. "Hmm, Detha, you're right, thometimeth myth th *are* better than what really happened." Just like that, he was back asleep.

I couldn't wait for Mother and Jimmie to get home so they could see that Father was back to joking and talking and being silly, back to being himthelf!

* * *

Dr. Taylor came by and took Father's stitches out of his mouth and said he was doing much better. Doc said once all the swelling went down Father wouldn't lisp as much. That evening, Mother took Father's supper upstairs, then came back down and sat with me and Jimmie at the dining table.

"OK," Mother said, "we haven't had Chiefs' and Children's Chow Chat for a while. Darling Daughter Deza, what new and exciting things happened to you today?"

I told them everything that me and Father had talked about while they were out working, how he was letting me read to him, and how he was taking himself to the bathroom. He was even practicing putting his tongue up against the bottom of his mouth so he wouldn't lisp as much. Me and Clarice were very impressed.

Mother said, "Now to the Genuine, Gentle Jumpin' Giant, Jimmie. What was your day like?"

Jimmie told about working for Dr. Bracy, about finding coal along the railroad tracks and about how unbelievably fast trains go through Gary.

"They're like rocket ships on wheels! They make your whole body shake!"

Me and Mother held our breaths when he said that. I could see cut-in-half slices of Jimmie flying through the air after he got the speed of a train wrong, but we both kept quiet.

Saying anything would make my brother do something insane to prove he wasn't scared of trains.

Jimmie and me said together, "What about you, our Marvelous Mammalian Matriarch, how was your day?"

Mother told us about what was going on with the Carsdales, how things were so bad in the country that even *he* might lose his job as president of the bank.

"The poor dears might have to cut back to three vacations this year!"

Jimmie said, "Oh, no! They aren't going to have to sell one of their rocket ships, are they?"

Mother started to answer, but before she could we all froze.

Father was standing in the dining room door, looking like a ghost. A skinny ghost with a plate in his hand.

Mother said, "Roscoe Malone! What on earth are you doing? You should've asked. We'd've helped you down."

We all rushed to him and guided him to his seat at the table.

He said, "Thank you, I jutht needed to get back where I belong."

Jimmie said, "Great, Daddy, you had perfect timing! It's your turn to tell about your day."

Me and Mother gave Jimmie a dirty look.

But Father said, "What did I do today? Firth I thlept, then I thlept thome more, then I got up to take my nap, then I ended up the day by thleeping a little more before I finally went to thleep for the night!"

We all laughed.

"I've got to let you know what happened on Lake Myth Again."

"Roscoe, don't you think you should just relax and have your—"

Father said, "All I know ith that I *have* to tell what happened out there."

"Roscoe. Maybe you're—"

"Peg, I really need to talk."

Mother looked at him hard. "Children, go outside until your father and I are done talking."

Father stood up. "No! I need to tell all of you."

Mother stood up and put her hand on his arm. "Roscoe, you're just going to—"

Father snatched his arm away. "Don't worry, Peg, I'm going to tell the truth, I won't lie."

Mother's 1-1-1 lines popped up and she sat very slowly back in her chair.

She picked up her fork and started pushing around the carrots Jimmie'd brought home.

Father said, "No one'th to blame, we had bad luck from the jump. It went wrong right away but we couldn't do anything about it, how can you thay who did what wrong?"

He stared down at his plate.

I looked over at Jimmie. He was just as scared as me.

Mother pointed at us, then the door.

We were happy to leave. Seeing Father like this was worse than seeing him out cold in bed.

I got up, leaned down. "Kisses . . . kisses . . . kisses make you stronger."

He wrapped his arms around me and Jimmie. "Thank you, Detha, Jimmie. Thank all of you for everything. I apologithe, Peg."

We went into the living room and Mother helped Father up. As she passed us on the couch she told Father, "Back to bed for you, buthter. Kids, I'll be right back."

Jimmie reached over and held my hand. "Lockjaw. He's got to fight off lockjaw. . . ."

"No, Jimmie, Father doesn't have tetanus, it's something else."

"Naw, sis, I didn't mean he has lockjaw for real. It's like what Daddy told me. Remember? He said that some of the time you get through whatever hurt you and you think you're all healed up, but there's still something inside that can come back and kill you. Daddy beat Lake Michigan but now there's something inside he's still got to beat. He's not done fighting yet. Almost like he's got lockjaw."

I didn't know whether to be scared about what Jimmie said, or amazed that he was making so much sense.

Chapter Fourteen

The Sad Truth About Jokes

Clarice was early. I was sitting on the couch reading when she tapped on the door.

"You ready?" She had her books in her arms.

We hugged and I said, "Just a second, Clarice."

"Take your time, I want to read this last chapter once more anyway."

I ran up the steps to my room to get the books I had to return to the library.

Me and Jimmie had started taking turns staying with Father.

I'd go to the library with Clarice every other day and Jimmie would go over to Dr. Bracy's and out to the fields to get wild vegetables on the days it wasn't his turn to watch Father.

I started to stick my head into Mother and Father's room to say goodbye.

Jimmie and Father were whispering. Whispers grab hold of your attention like nothing else.

Me and Father never talked about what happened on the lake, so I was surprised to hear him say, "There we were on Lake Myth Again, pulling in fith right and left."

Jimmie said, "Perch?"

"Perch, walleye and bluegillth. We notithed a fog bank further out on the lake and thomeone thought we thould head back, but we thtayed a little longer." He stopped.

I held my breath waiting for what he was about to say, but Jimmie said, "Why's it called a fog *bank*, Pa? It's not like you could get a loan there, or like you could rob it or nothing."

Father said, "Not a bank in that way, Jim, more like a mound, an area higher than what'th around it."

I bet he was staring over Jimmie's shoulder, trying to get deep into his story. I stuck my head into the room. I didn't really want to hear this.

"Goodbye, Father, I'm off to the library."

"No! Detha, you come in and lithen too."

Jimmie said, "Pa's telling what happened out on the lake."

Father said, "We weren't out there for half an hour before the fog rolled in."

Father was talking, but he wasn't talking to us.

"I'd never thought about what a thtrange phrathe 'pea thoup' ith, but when that fog covered our boat I got it. The fog felt like it had weight, that you had to puth it away to even breathe."

There was a long pause and I held my breath, hoping that Jimmie would be quiet too.

"We dethided to get back to thore, but when we pulled on the anchor rope we found the anchor wath gone and we'd been drifting. No one knew for how long.

"Then the thip came. Then everything happened."

His voice changed, sounding like he was fighting to catch his breath, sounding wild and scary. "We'd drifted into the thipping laneth and the wake from a huge freighter hit uth and knocked everyone out of the boat.

"I was in such a thtate of thock that I didn't even realithe I'd been hit in the mouth and all of my front teeth were gone, or how badly I'd been cut. Fear will do that to you, it will make you think about only what'th important, and all that wath important to me wath to get back to my family. That'th all I could think of. Truly."

Most times when Father tells about how his day went he talks like he's painting a picture, but this time there was no picture, just fog. If he was himself, Father would've said something like, "The fog was so thick it should've been spelled with two 'G's!"

But there was something more missing.

Father can't open his mouth without a joke falling out and this story didn't have any.

Maybe it's because the story is so sad. But Father always tells us, "There's a thin, blurry line between humor and tragedy." When he was working regular at the mill he'd told me and Jimmie, "I'll give each of you one whole nickel for every joke you find that isn't cloaked in pain or tragedy."

We'd tried as hard as we could to earn that nickel but couldn't come up with a single joke that didn't have someone getting killed or hurt or made fun of or embarrassed or mocked.

Father told us, "And the more tragic something is, the more jokes you'll find about it."

I couldn't think of anything more tragic than what happened to those poor men out on Lake Michigan, yet Father's story didn't have one smile or laugh in it.

And no alliteration. Something wasn't right.

Father said, "The boat wath upthide down and they all were gone. I tied my writht to the boat with the anchor rope and hung on. That'th the way that thip found me and took me to the hothpital in Thicago. When I came to, they brought me to Gary. That'th the whole truth."

There was another long pause. "That'th everything."

Jimmie leaned his head on Father's chest. "It's OK, Pa, we're all together now."

Father didn't sound like his heart was in it when he said, "You know, Jimmie, when it looked like I wouldn't live, the thing other than my family that I thought about mithing would be theeing Joe Louith knock Max Thmeling back to the fatherland!"

That stupid fight! Father started blabbing about Joe Louis, and Jimmie blabbed right along with him.

I said, "Yuck!" And left them laughing and joking.

Chapter Fifteen

The Brown Bomber Hits Home

Finally Father made the bug about the fight grab hold of my heart. The big day had been postponed to the nineteenth because of rain and that made everything even more exciting.

Since the lake, Father had acted like he was listening when we'd talk about our days during Chow Chat, but we knew his mind wasn't all the way with us. Just two days before the fight, something came alive in him.

We looked at Father to see if he was up to talking. Jimmie saw something that me and Mother didn't. He said, "And what about your day, my Fine Friendly Father Figure?"

Father seemed surprised. "Not much happened." Then he gave us his scary jack-o'-lantern smile. "But I have noticed my

Dar Dawt, the Gorgeous, Gregarious, Glamorous Deza, hasn't found fit to form the flimsiest conversation concerning the coming fisticuffs."

Alliteration! A ton of alliteration! It was like all of the consonants he hadn't used for the past weeks were exploding out of him.

Jimmie laughed. "Wow, Daddy!"

Father said, "So, if none of you mind, I think I'll use my time to explain to the Mighty Miss Malone what's going on that she has so little interest in."

He looked right at me. The first time in a long time he looked any of us in the eye!

"So, Dar Dawt, why aren't you on the bandwagon about Joe Louis?"

"Clarice and me—"

Mother said, "I, Deza."

"I and Clarice—"

"Not funny, Deza," Mother said.

"Clarice and I don't think there's anything about two grown, old, bumpy-muscled men in their underwear trying to kill each other with big, fat, puffy, ridiculous red mittens that's good or important or even worth talking about."

Father put his face in his hand and shook his head.

Jimmie said, "And I thought you were smart, Deza. Even white people are saying they'd vote for the Brown Bomber to be king of the world after he whips Smelling."

Father moved his hand from his face and stared over Mother's shoulder, another real good sign because that meant he was settling into a story or a lesson.

"Deza, this is so much more than just a fight, this is one of those rare occasions where we'll be alive to witness history."

He smiled at me and stuck his left hand out. I put both of mine in it and he covered my hands with his right one. I was surprised at how soft Father's hands felt. They used to be rough like sandpaper or even a hunk of wood, but since the lake they'd got soft as mine.

Father looked real close at our hands and said, "My, my, my. Wasn't it only yesterday that I could close my fingers on yours like this and your whole hand would disappear?"

He was right, my fingers were poking out of the other side of his hands. He brought our hands to his face and kissed my fingertips.

"Dar Dawt, you know you and I are different, right?"

"Of course, Father, you're a man, I'm a girl, you're old and I'm young."

Jimmie said, "Yeah, Pa, plus Deza's got regular teeth and you got them summer teeth. *Some are* in your mouth, *some are* on the bottom of Lake Michigan, *some are* still in the hospital!"

Mother said, "Jimmie!"

Father said, "Ah, I see *both* of my children are reading from that book about disrespecting and abusing a good man. Deza, I meant to say you and I are alike because we're different than most other people."

"Yes, Father, we know the Malones aren't like any other family in the world."

"True, but even *within* the Malone family you and I look at the world in a way that your mother and brother don't."

Jimmie, Mother and me all said, "Thank goodness for that!"

Father laughed. "Good, we're agreed. I hope we can also agree that people tend to leave a trail as to where they've been and from that trail you can tell where they're going, right?"

"Yes, Father."

"All right," Father said. "Another thing we need to get by is faith in one another. Over time we can tell if someone is reliable or not, if we can count on their word or not, right?"

Father *was* starting to come back, this was the way he used to talk, and what he was doing was something he'd taught us to be suspicious of.

He said that people use tricks to get you to think the way they do or to take away something you have that they want. One way they do that is to interrupt your normal way of thinking and take you by the hand and guide you down the path they want you to take.

Father says they make you take a teeny-weeny step in their direction, and then they start to nudge you a little further down the path and before you know it, you're running full speed with them in a direction that you probably wouldn't have gone all alone.

If someone was trying to pull that trick on one of us, Father had come up with a signal. We would take both hands and pretend they were on a steering wheel and move them back and forth like we were driving.

It was called being a passenger in the Manipula-Mobile, and it let all the other Malones know someone was trying to take us for a ride.

I said, "Father . . ." and put my hands on the pretend steering wheel.

He laughed. "Very good, Dar Dawt, I was waiting for you to do that, which is why I prefaced this by telling you that, over time, you know whom you can have faith in, right?"

"Yes, Father."

"Because I want you to consider the source here. Keep in mind that I'm the one trying to educate you on why this fight is so important. There's no Manipula-Mobile on the road here. Are we reading from the same book?"

We were! It was so good to hear Father explaining something to me again!

"And it's a fact, Deza, Jimmie, sometimes getting educated on a subject has a lot in common with being manipulated. The main difference is that you know to trust who's guiding you."

"I understand," I said.

"Great. Here's why this is more than just a fight. Sad to say, the boxing ring is one of the few places in America where your skin color doesn't play a huge role. When you've got two men going against each other wearing a pair of ridiculous puffy mittens, most of the time, it's a reasonably fair fight."

Father looked over Jimmie's shoulder.

"Steel Lung used to say it was the only place where a black man could hit a white man and not get lynched for it."

We all held our breaths to see if talking about Mr. Steel Lung was going to make him stop or take him back out on that lake.

He looked at Mother and said, "Hitler and his boys have said this fight will prove that no black man can ever beat a white man, that we"—Father pointed at each Malone—"and all our neighbors are where we are because we deserve to be here."

Jimmie said, "Yeah, Pops, I can't wait, Joe's gonna show 'em a thing or two!"

Father said, "That's what we're hoping for, James. Joe knows he's *got* to win this fight, he knows how important it is, he'll come through.

"Some of the time life boils down to some pretty ridiculous things, Deza. This is one of them. I agree, it's silly to put so much importance on one fight, but you have to keep in mind that this fight is the one chance we have to show the Nazis, and some of our white brethren here in America as well, that we are people too. It's ironic, but Joe will show we're human by savagely beating the stuffing out of someone."

I would have believed anything my father was saying because it was in his own strong voice. I was going to have faith in Father's word. I was going to try to make a light come on for Clarice, because the more I thought about it the madder I got at myself for not seeing this on my own.

* * *

The man on the radio screamed, "The greatest upset in the history of the world! The greatest upset in the history of the world! The greatest upset in the history of the world!" Mr. Bobbin reached over and turned off his radio.

No one in the barbershop moved or talked or even breathed for what felt like a hour.

No one looked at anyone else.

The most interesting thing in Mr. Bobbin's barbershop was the floor, 'cause as I looked around that was where everybody's eyes were pointing.

The only thing making a sound or moving was the fan as it swept from side to side.

The bell over Mr. Bobbin's door gave that gentle ting-a-ling as people started leaving. Mother grabbed Father's arm, tapped Jimmie and Clarice on the shoulder and nodded at me. The bell tinkled again and we followed Mother and Father outside.

I hope to never see anything else as terrible as that walk home.

Grown men and women were sitting on the curb crying like babies, every light in every store and house we passed was still on, but now they threw jaggedy, sharp shadows onto the street.

Father's lisp was back. "I can't believe it, Peg. It'th like that fog on the lake, I never thought I'd thee or feel anything like it again, but here it ith. Thith ith jutht ath heavy on my heart. Thith ith the thame feeling. Oh, God, Peg, won't I ever get rid of thith? Ith thomething wrong with me?"

Mother wrapped her arm around Father's shoulder.

Clarice was squeezing my left hand and Jimmie was squeezing my right as we walked.

Father said, "What ith going—"

I looked back and Mother shushed Father. "Wait till we get home, it will be OK."

We walked in silence for a couple of blocks and saw a huge bottle that someone had dropped or slammed onto the sidewalk. It had broke into a thousand little puddles of light. The only way you could tell it had been a bottle was because the label was still whole, still hanging on to a few sharp jags of glass.

Jimmie pointed and said, "Look out."

Father scooped me into his arms. "Detha, you know how you are with broken glath."

I almost said, "Father! I'm OK," but then I saw that he was holding me as much to take care of himself as to take care of me.

I let my father carry me like a doll on his hip. I leaned into his neck and Mother grabbed his waist. It was strange, I was squeezing him but it seemed like I couldn't feel him. I was so frightened.

When we got to Clarice's she let Jimmie's hand go and looked up at me in Father's arms. At the same time we put up two fingers, touched our cheeks, then put up one finger and put our hands on our chests.

I didn't notice six or seven of Clarice's brothers sitting on the porch in a little ball crying until the Malones started for home.

Chapter Sixteen

Back in Lake Myth Again

I couldn't sleep that night. I just couldn't ignore the voices coming through the wall from Mother and Father's bedroom.

They'd started out whispering, but their voices were getting louder.

Mother's was the loudest. "That's not true, I heard Mrs. Carsdale say . . ."

Father said, "What choice do I have? It will be better for all of us in the long run."

I shouldn't have been eavesdropping, but the sound of your parents' voices being so frightened is something you can't pull away from. And I'd never heard Mother and Father argue before.

"Margaret, what can I do? What can I say to my babies when there's no work anywhere? Didn't you tell me that they were even making Old Man Carsdale take a pay cut? And if the white president of a bank is having his pay cut, what chance do I have? Look at me! Look at this mouth, I couldn't find work when my face was whole. Who'd hire someone with a busted-up, snaggle-tooth mouth? What chance do I have to find enough work to buy even a loaf of bread?"

"Roscoe, listen, no one's starving here, the welfare food is good enough until—"

Father raised his voice, which was something he usually did only if he was happy.

"Welfare food? How low have we gone that being fed by welfare is normal for us? I heard Jimmie and that Obgurn boy talking the other day and the boy asked Jimmie what kind of cheese was on his sandwich. Jimmie told him, 'Yellow cheese,' and the boy said, 'No, what brand is it?' Do you know what Jimmie said? He told him, 'I don't know, I guess it's 'Not to Be Sold' cheese.' Peg, it's gotten so bad that our son thinks that the label they stamp on all the welfare food is a brand name."

Mother said, "Well, Jimmie is . . . I don't know, Jimmie is Jimmie."

Father said, "Even the welfare food isn't enough for all of us. I feel as though every bite I take is one less for the rest of you. I might as well reach in your mouths and pull it out."

"No, Roscoe, no. . . ."

"And you don't think I see that you eat next to nothing? You don't think I notice that?"

Mother snapped, "*You're* the one who refuses to eat anything. I told you I get plenty at the Carsdales'."

Father's voice got softer. "Peg, haven't you noticed? Haven't you looked in the mirror? Sweetheart, you're the most beautiful woman I've ever seen, but, darling, what is this?"

Their room went quiet.

Father said, "Since when did your cheekbones stick out like this? And why do your clothes hang on you now?"

There was a long pause before Mother laughed. "Me? What about you? If your legs get any skinnier we'll have to use tape to hold your socks up!"

When I heard Father laugh I relaxed a little, but a little too soon.

"Peg, I can't do it. I'll find work back in Flint, I know folks there, there'll be something for me. I can't blame anyone in Gary for not helping, in tough times people tend to look after their own. I'll send money, and once I'm settled, I'll send for you."

Mother said, "Oh, Roscoe, Roscoe Malone. Do you know how many women and children have heard some version of those words and it turns out to be the last thing they hear from their husbands or fathers? Ever."

"Peg, you know me. I give you my word."

"But what if that's not enough? What if this depression goes on for so long that you can't find work even in Flint? What good is your word then? Roscoe, we're at our strongest when we're all together, when we're a family. If you leave, how long do you think it'll be before Jimmie goes? How long before I lose Deza?"

"You're making it sound like this is something I want to do. Peg, do you have any idea how it rips me apart just to come home every day? Every day I go out and there's nothing,

nothing but a city full of other men no one needs, where the next person is desperate enough to work for less than the last person. I just can't do it anymore. There have been evenings when I've stood at the front door for fifteen, twenty minutes, too ashamed to come in, too ashamed to have nothing in my hands but my hat."

Mother said, "Why are you taking this so personal? You have nothing to be ashamed of, Roscoe. No one has work, no one has food."

Father said, "Maybe you're right, maybe it's not shame. Maybe it's fear. Maybe I'm afraid that one day I'll come in here and see the love and concern on all of your faces, see the way you and the kids work so hard to make *me* feel better, and I'll lose my mind. I'll be so hurt, so angry, so desperate that I'll go out in the streets and do something horrible. Something to get food or coal or clothes, something that would allow me to feed my family, something that would allow me to feel like a human being and not some animal in a zoo waiting for a handout.

"What kind of world is it when even when I can find work and even when you work forty hours we still can't afford to have our babies looked after proper?"

"Roscoe, we have to have patience."

"Patience? *Patience?* Do you have any idea how it kills me to come in that door and see my boy and know that he's stopped growing? To know that all we can afford is to take him to Doc Taylor, a man who's so old and stuck in his ways he probably delivered George Washington?"

"Roscoe, listen—"

"No! Do you know what I automatically do every day when

Deza runs up to me to give me a hug and a kiss? Did you know I find myself turning my face or breathing out of my mouth the minute I'm close to her? Do you know why?"

Mother softly said, "Oh, Roscoe, no, don't say that. . . ."

I stopped breathing.

Father said, "It's true, Peg, you don't want to hear it, I don't want to say it, but it's the truth. I've found I can't breathe out of my nose when I'm near Deza because of the smell of her teeth. How sick is that? How pathetic am I that I can't even breathe normally around my own child?"

Their room was quiet for a full minute.

Tears stung my eyes. I tried to stop listening, but . . .

Father said, "And I know you, Peg. I know you're going through the same thing, we both know that that little brown-skinned angel is something beyond special. You know if there's any chance in the future, it's riding on her narrow shoulders. So you tell me, you tell me how can I come home empty-handed knowing that that sassy, smart, beautiful, charming little girl . . . my Mighty Miss Malone . . . is slowly rotting away on the inside and we can't afford to have her teeth looked after, we can't even get them pulled? If I come home and see that the spark that makes Deza so precious is gone, I'll hate myself."

Mother said, "Oh, please, Roscoe, stop. . . ."

Father said, "I don't know which is worse, the smell of her rotting teeth or the smell of the camphor you get from those white people to soak in cotton and stick in her cavities. I'm at my wits' end, I . . . cannot . . . do . . . it . . . one . . . more . . . time! Peg, I'll end up killing someone."

Mother said, "This isn't a good time for you to be deciding

something this big. Don't you see, dear, this is the horrible letdown of Joe losing that fight, this is you still grieving about your friends. You need to heal, you need to give it time. All I ask for is another couple months, we've come this far together and we need to stay together. Give it some time."

I could hear Father jump up. I was surprised that he had his shoes on upstairs this late at night. They thudded over and over as he paced the bedroom.

"Time? What am I supposed to do? Should I tell Jimmie, 'Son, hold on, we just need a little time before we can get you to a doctor who'll tell us why you haven't grown in three years'? And what about Deza? Am I going to tell her, 'Hold on, darling, in another year or two we'll get those teeth taken care of. In the meantime just snap the bad ones off at the roots'?"

His pacing stopped.

"Roscoe, stop and listen to yourself. All we need is a little more time and—"

"We don't have any more time, Peg, we've run out."

Mother's tone changed. "Oh, so since time's run out, your answer is for *you* to run out too?"

There was silence, then, "I'm sorry. I have to go. I'll write soon's I get settled. I love you."

Their bedroom door opened, then shut. I heard nothing from Mother. Father's shoes slowly clomped down the stairs.

I ran to my bedroom door and watched my father sinking down the staircase. He stopped at Jimmie's door, tapped twice, then went in.

I slumped down in my doorway and waited for him to come out.

I was surprised that my second brain was keeping so quiet. It's such a worthless brain. When you don't want to hear from it, it can't stop running its mouth. Times like this, when you could use some noise to drown everything out, or when you'd appreciate a little advice about who you should hurt, that no-good brain chooses to be quiet.

I can't say how long I waited in the doorway.

Jimmie's door came open and Father looked back into the room. "I love you, son. I'll send for you. You'll like Flint. I can't say how long it's going to take, but I promise we'll be back together."

He closed the door and stopped to lean against the railing. I started crawling into my room.

I know Father.

He was coming to see me next.

I wasn't halfway into the room when I heard Jimmie's door come open. Father must have turned around and gone back in to tell Jimmie something else.

I slipped back to look down the steps.

It was Jimmie who had opened the door.

He threw himself at Father and wrapped his arms around Father's waist from behind.

"Daddy, don't go!" Jimmie cried into Father's back. "I don't like school anyway, I can look for work, even when school starts back up, I can help with the bills, just stay!"

Father pulled Jimmie off of his back and the two of them slumped onto the steps.

Jimmie was unconsolable. Father pulled him into his lap.

What broke my heart was that Jimmie, who hated, more

than anything, stuff that made him look small or weak or young, didn't stop Father as he cuddled him like a baby in his arms.

Father kissed Jimmie's forehead and wiped at his tears.

"Son, son, son."

"I can do it, Daddy. I'll have the pie lady paid off in no time. Then I can get a job paying cash. Please, give me a chance. Don't you remember what you call me?"

Father said, "Of course I do, son. You're my Genuine, Gentle Jumpin' Giant, Jimmie."

"That's right, and don't forget about Deza. I bet she'll work too, even with all that reading and studying she does I'll bet you she'll find time to chip in too. With all four of us working we can be good again. Go, ask her, ask her now, she'll do it, Daddy. You know how she is, you know she's a champ!"

Father said, "Yes, she is, Jimmie, but I explained it and you promised me, son. I need all of you to look after things while I'm gone. I'm only asking because I know I can count on you."

Jimmie scooted out of Father's lap and sat beside him. They wrapped their arms around each other.

"I promised, Father." Jimmie sniffed. "And I'm just like you, a man of my word. I'll do everything you asked me to do. We'll look after each other, Pa. I swear we'll be all right, I'll do what I have to. And I won't tell a soul about what really happened out on—"

Father put his hand across Jimmie's mouth and stood up.

"Go try to get some sleep, son. I've got to say goodbye to Deza."

Jimmie ran into his room and slammed the door.

As I creeped back to my bed the second brain finally decided to start. "Oh, God, kiddo, don't let him come say good-bye, just let him leave. If he comes in here I'll hurt him bad!"

I closed my door, then crawled under my blanket. I pulled the pillow over my head but still could hear the slow clomp-clomp-clomp of Father's feet coming up the steps. The sound stopped outside my room and the longest time passed before he tapped lightly on my door.

"Deza?"

I pulled the pillow tighter over my head to stop him from seeing me. And to block the smell of my mouth.

"May I come in?"

I would never answer him.

My door opened and I heard a couple of clomps as Father came to me.

He stood at the foot of my bed.

"Sweetheart, you awake?"

No! Go! Go!

"Deza? I need to tell you something."

I pulled the pillow tighter over my head, held my breath and prayed he'd leave.

Father sighed and said, "I *will* get us back together, Deza. Please take care of each other. I know it's hard, but we'll get this ship righted as soon as we can."

He walked to the side of my bed and I could feel him lean down.

I kept holding my breath and squeezing the pillow tight on my head.

He put his hand on top of the pillow but didn't tug it away.

He said, "Remember, Dar Dawt, that kisses . . . kisses . . . kisses make you stronger."

He pressed his face against my pillow three times and clomped to my door and down the steps.

I squeezed the pillow to my head even harder. I could feel the spot where Father had put his wet face. I threw the pillow at the door as hard as I could.

The second brain yelled, "Quick, kiddo! Push him down the steps! He'll break his leg and then he can't leave!"

I squeezed my jaws together so hard that little fairies of red-hot light shot out of my back teeth and bounced around inside my skull.

Something crunched and crackled inside my mouth and I got woozy. It worked. The bad brain finally shut up.

I knew I could never hurt my father.

I let out a cry and was surprised to see how much blood sprayed onto my pillowcase.

I heard the front door open and close.

And I was glad to see him go.

Chapter Seventeen

The Road to Crime

The people who run the Gary Public Library are very, very smart.

If you're looking for a book you don't have to go through every shelf until you get lucky and find it, all you do is get the book's Dewey decimal number out of a card catalog and you know right where it's going to be.

It's too bad that whoever's in charge of coming up with superstitious sayings doesn't work at the Gary Public Library. They could've saved me a lot of time and frustration in trying to figure out what a saying really means.

The saying "Bad news always comes in threes" is a good example.

I wonder if the bad news is supposed to come three times to each family, or if it's going to come to each *person* in the family three times.

It seems like for the Malones it's three times for each person.

Nearly a month had gone by and the mailman hadn't brought anything from Father.

Mother got home from work at about six o'clock and I met her at the door.

She looked tireder than she usually does.

She kissed me and said, "Hello, Deza, any news?"

I told her what me and Clarice were reading and how Dr. Bracy had started paying Jimmie for the work he did for her, but we both knew that the only *real* news that we all were waiting for hadn't happened.

I could tell by her small smile that she already knew.

"Did you make supper, Deza? I'm so hungry I could eat some bugs."

They weren't ever going to let me forget the heartbreak I'd suffered with the buggy oatmeal.

When we sat to eat Mother said, "Jimmie, Deza, I've been thinking, we haven't heard anything from your father and to be quite frank, I'm starting to get a little worried."

This was very disturbing. If she admitted that she was a little worried, it really meant that she was just about in a panic.

We set our forks down.

"So I've decided we should go to Flint and get some first-hand information. Your grandmother Malone is there and will know something. I haven't been able to get ahold of her but I'm sure we can stay with her until we can get on our feet."

"Get on our feet? Mother, we'll be back in time for the start of school, won't we? Mrs. Needham—"

"Deza, I'm terribly sorry, the Carsdales are moving to Europe. They're starting to close their house down. In two weeks I'll lose my job. Jimmie, you'll be coming with me until then, they'll need help and will pay you."

She looked at me. "I'm sorry, Deza, but you and Jimmie will go to school in Flint and with me and your father working we'll do fine."

I don't know how long I sat there in shock before I heard Jimmie say, "Ma, I can stay here with Deza, you go find Father and—" He slapped his forehead. "Wait! *I* can go find Father, you two stay here and—"

"No! We will stay together. I've asked Mrs. Carsdale to write me a recommendation letter, she's good friends with a lady in Flint whose husband is vice president of a bank there."

She got up and took her plate into the kitchen.

"Well, kiddo," my second brain said, "you didn't really believe any of this good stuff with Mrs. Needham was going to happen, did you?"

I didn't, the only real surprise I had was that my back teeth had gotten so bad that I only had to squeeze them half as much as I usually do to make that stupid second brain shut up.

* * *

I knew how Father felt.

I hadn't had teeth knocked out of my head and hadn't floated around scared to death on a terrible lake, but every morning, after I made breakfast for Mother and Jimmie, I would sneak into my parents' bed and didn't want to move or think or anything. I wouldn't even read a book.

At first I tried to remember that poem Father used to say about how "Hope has wings . . ." but I couldn't.

I just wanted to have my face covered with the pillow that Father used to sleep on.

Three days after we found out we had to go to that miserable place in Michigan, Mother said to me, "Deza, once we leave you are *not* to get back in bed. You are to eat every meal with Jimmie and me, and you will clean your plate. You are to go to the library every day, and you will read and study. Am I clear?"

I shot a look at Jimmie. I was still in bed when he got home every day and he'd ratted me out.

"Yes, Mother."

This was good. I'd learned that sitting in bed all day just made you want to spend all day sitting in bed.

After Mother gave me a kiss and left and Jimmie said, "Sorry, Deza," and went out too, I climbed into Mother and Father's bed just one more time.

And didn't get out until Jimmie got home hours later.

I picked up a book and rushed downstairs but I don't think I fooled him. He hugged me and went in the kitchen.

The next day as soon as they left, I got back in bed again.

There was a loud knock on the front door.

It was Clarice. "Deza! You look terrible." Only somebody you share a heart with could say that and not get you upset.

I gave her the tragic news about how we were going to have to move to Flint.

"Yes, I know. It's my fault that I wasn't here earlier, Jimmie told me yesterday. I would've come but I couldn't stop crying.

I finally ran out of tears this morning, but seeing you like this makes me wonder if I might have some left."

I was so glad she came by. I knew I'd have to give her a good example of being strong.

She said, "The librarians have been asking where you are. You know you *are* such a credit to our race, after all."

I laughed and ran upstairs to get ready. I hadn't read anything in four days and felt like I was starving!

* * *

"Deza! My Darling Daughter Deza!"

Mother was home right on time, and she was singing! I ran downstairs to meet her at the door. She had both of her hands behind her back and a huge smile on her face.

I hugged her, but instead of hugging me back she said, "How was your day?"

"Mother, don't tease! What's behind your back?"

She acted surprised that her hands were hidden and said, "What? This little thing?"

It was a envelope. From Father?

Mother touched my cheek. "No, Deza. It's not that, but it's good nonetheless!"

She said, "*Ta-da!*" I read Mrs. *Ernest Nelson, Flint, Michigan* in very good penmanship.

Mrs. Carsdale had given us the letter for a new job in Flint! This *was* good news!

Not really, but when you're feeling bad you can't be picky about what kind of things can lift you up.

"Oh, Mother, you got it! So now we can move to Flint and find Father?"

Mother said, "Why on earth would a sensible Indiana girl want to move to Flint, Michigan?"

"If Flint's where we'll find Father I'll go. The quicker we find him the quicker we can get back to Gary. Can I read it?"

Mother held the letter over her head.

"Well, I'm not sure, I wouldn't want you to lose it or tear it or—"

I grabbed Mother's arm and we tussled back and forth over the letter. She let me take it.

It was sealed.

I don't know why, but my stomach started folding itself up.

This wasn't good.

"Did you read it, Mother?"

"No. But I told her what I needed and she finally said she'd do it and . . . here it is."

"You trust her?"

I was sorry I'd asked. Mother's good mood was gone.

"Of course I don't trust her, but some of the time you have to have faith, Deza."

"Should we open it?"

Her 1-1-1 lines showed.

"Deza Malone, I'm surprised at you, you know that would be wrong. Besides, if you ripped this expensive envelope open, where in the world would you get another?"

She was right, the envelope felt like it was made out of the same thick, heavy paper as a dollar bill. I knew better than to ask Mother to borrow one from Mrs. Carsdale. She'd see that as nothing but stealing, and me opening the letter would be almost as bad.

"I was just talking." I tried to get her back to feeling good. "Boy, Jimmie's going to be so excited when he hears, can I tell him first?"

Mother smiled but the fun was gone. "Of course, Deza. Now we have to start planning."

She held her hand out. "Let me put this in the filing cabinet so it will be safe."

The Malones aren't like any other family in the world, and one of the reasons is our filing cabinet. It isn't anything like the kind you see at school or in rich people's offices in the movies.

Those filing cabinets have drawers and handles and locks and make a solid echo-y kra-bang sound when they're closed.

Ours is a lot quieter. It's as soft and comfortable and quiet as a couch. That's because it *is* our couch. Mother lifted the middle cushion and stuck Mrs. Carsdale's letter on top of some other papers.

She patted the cushion back in place. "Now, what's that delicious smell, Deza?"

"Just supper." I smiled and headed to the kitchen, but my mind was under the couch cushion with that letter.

* * *

After we ate and Mother went over to see Mrs. Henderson, I went in the filing cabinet, got the letter and took it to Jimmie.

"Great. We can go find Father now."

"Not great, Jimmie, we can't trust that woman."

"What you mean, sis?"

"We've got to open this letter."

"No problem. Put the kettle on."

I knew he'd be able to get into the envelope without anyone knowing, he'd opened every sealed report card and letter from teachers he'd ever gotten before he gave them to Mother and Father.

After the kettle boiled, Jimmie took it off the stove.

"The most important thing is don't get it too wet. Most folks mess up by soaking the glue too much, that way the envelope gets bumpy and people know it's been opened before."

Jimmie is always very generous, even with his lessons on how to be a criminal. He held the envelope over the kettle's neck and slowly pulled at the flap. "You have to take your time. With everything, not just steaming open letters. Be patient and take your time. Remember what Pa says, 'All things come to the person who waits.'"

I didn't correct Jimmie because in every movie I'd ever seen and every book I'd ever read if one criminal criticizes what their partners do or say it always ends up with someone in prison.

What Father *really* says is "All things come to the person who waits . . . if that person works like mad while they're waiting."

Jimmie got the last part of the flap from the envelope and it was absolutely flat!

"Wow, Jimmie, that's great!"

"Hold on, we ain't all the way done yet. This is just as important."

He blew along the envelope's flap. "This stops the glue from clumping up. All set."

I pulled the letter out. It was on three pages of fancy writing paper. My stomach was folding, not because I knew this was wrong, but because I was afraid of what the letter might say.

While Jimmie put the kettle away I quickly read through what the woman had written. I got happy and mad at the same time.

Happy that my gut feeling was right, and mad at what that horrid woman had written.

"All right, Deza, what's it say?"

I read parts of the letter to Jimmie.

Dear Marilyn,

I'm certain you've heard about the tragic situation here in Gary. Charles has been ordered to take an unheard-of twenty-five-percent cut in his salary. He's a man of integrity and refuses to accept this.

We have made the heartbreaking decision to close Grace Hall and to travel the Continent for the next three years or until such time as this country gets back to normal.

As you can imagine, this has placed a tremendous stress and burden on me as I arrange for lodgings with kind and generous friends in six countries.

I'm left to wonder at God's mercy. Thus far I have been able to keep a strong and cheerful face for the sake of Charles and the children. Speaking of which, how are Ernest and your young ones? Please forgive me for waiting so long into this correspondence to inquire after their well-being. I'm certain you can understand the unimaginable stress under which I operate daily.

Has this horrible depression devastated your family as much as it has devastated ours? Remember, Charles says it shan't be long before this great country comes to its senses, throws off that filthy communist Roosevelt and is returned to its rightful owners.

I shall write from Burton-on-Trent, where we will be staying with Lady Chigwell for the next six months. Who could have dreamed that it would come to this?

Sincerely,
Milly
(Mrs. Charles Carsdale)

Postscript

The colored gal bearing this letter has been in our employ for the past twelve years. She missed an entire year for some cause or other. She is a competent worker so I relented and rehired her. I've always believed 'tis better to stay with the devil you know.

I skipped reading the next lines to Jimmie.

In that time she has also missed four or five days to tend to a sickly boy who has not grown properly. I'm sure it's nothing more than the terrible food those people enjoy so much.

I read aloud.

I've never been able to catch her stealing. If your experience has been anything like mine, you know them as well as I. I've found that one is a carbon copy of the next. Hire her at your own peril.

My hands were trembling. Jimmie was looking down and shaking his head.

"Man, Ma's gonna be mad."

"No, she won't, we can't let her see this. I wish I could get some of this woman's writing paper, I know I can copy this penmanship in a flash."

"You know I'm going to the Carsdales' with Ma for the rest of this week, I'm getting a dime a day to help them close their house up."

"Jimmie, I don't know—"

"You hit the nail on the head, sis, you don't know, and you don't want to know. Let Jesse rob this train. Give me some skin and leave the rest up to me."

I slapped Jimmie's palm and had never felt like such a big crook in all my life. And doggone it all, the second brain was taking over, because I *really* liked the feeling!

* * *

Mother and Jimmie came home together the next day and as soon as he saw me Jimmie made his eyebrows go up and down over and over.

I followed him into his room.

He smiled. "*Ta-da!*" He opened a paper sack and pulled out ten sheets of the beautiful paper and two envelopes.

It wasn't until that second that I saw that Jimmie'd stole this stuff for nothing. We didn't have any ink or a good pen so I could copy the woman's writing.

Jimmie read my mind. "*Ta-da!*"

He reached into the bag and this time he was holding a

gorgeous pen and a inkwell. "What'd I say? You got to let Jesse rob this train. I knew you were gonna need the ink too. I'll take anything you don't use back tomorrow. Now it's your turn."

* * *

After I practiced on some of my foolscap, I only messed up one sheet of the pretty paper when I wrote the new letter. I kept in mind what Mrs. Needham said about good writing being short and to the point.

Mrs. Carsdale was far too verbose.

I was kind of upset that I was making this woman look good by improving her writing.

I got my thesaurus and dictionary and after about a hour I came up with:

Dear Marilyn,

The woman bearing this letter has asked for a recommending letter and my heart is filled with joy to give her one. She is kind and loving and helpful in every way. She has worked for us for the past twelve years and we wish she would stay forever but she is moving to Flint to be with her husband who is also kind and loving. She is trying to keep her delightful family together.

If you give her a job she will work as hard for you as she did for us. She never lies or steals, because that is against everything she's taught her children. One of them is a charming, kind and loving boy. He sings like a angel. The other one is a girl who is very humble.

Don't answer this missive, I shall write from Burton-on-Trent which is geologically located in England where we will be the guests of Lady Chigwell for a very long time.

Sincerely,
Milly
(Mrs. Charles Carsdale)

Postscript

God bless President Roosevelt, America and all the world.

"Jimmie?"

He came upstairs into my room.

I read the letter.

He gave me a thumbs-up sign and said, "Put it back in the filing cabinet, Deza, and let's get ready to say goodbye to Gary."

Jimmie's words brought all the sadness back out in me. It was true, I was going to have to leave my home, just when it seemed my luck was turning. I'd have to say goodbye to Mrs. Needham, and worst of all, I'd have to say goodbye to Clarice.

But the chance of finding Father and bringing him back home was worth even this.

Chapter Eighteen

Deza Steers on the Last Days in Gary

If I ever found that Dewey decimal system for superstitious sayings and looked up "Bad news comes in threes," I would've seen that for the Malones, it meant three times every hour.

At supper Jimmie asked what kind of truck we were going to use to move.

Mother said, "Children, give me your hands."

A not-so-good sign.

"Jimmie, Deza, there isn't going to be a moving truck, we won't need one."

My heart flew! "Oh, Mother! I knew it! We aren't moving!"

"Yes, Deza, we are. We just won't need a truck to do it.

Most of this furniture . . ." She looked around. "Who am I kidding? *None* of this furniture is ours."

"*What?*" I wouldn't have been more surprised if Mother had told me that after twelve years of being on the end of my leg, my left foot belonged to someone else!

"No, dear, we rent this place furnished. Pretty much all of this belongs to the landlord."

I was shocked and mortifried! The first thing that came to my mind was the wardrobe. That *had* to be ours, we'd been writing on it for years and Mother and Father wouldn't tolerate us writing on someone else's furniture.

"Mother, what about the wardrobe?"

"What about it, Deza?"

"We wrote all over it. It's always been part of our family history."

Well, it had been part of the Malone history for a while. Ever since I was two and Jimmie was almost five, on each of our birthdays, we would stand next to the opened wardrobe door. We'd stretch our necks as long as they'd go without letting our feet come off the ground.

Then Mother and Father would put a ruler on top of our heads and take a pencil and make a mark to show how tall we were. That way we could keep track of how much we'd grown.

All that stopped around the time Jimmie turned twelve. I was nine when, after measuring me, Father put the ruler on Jimmie's head.

It was right at the same mark it had been last time.

Father looked at Mother, then made a mark that was half a inch taller than Jimmie really was.

I almost said, "Hey! That's not fair!" But Mother shot me a look and I kept quiet.

Jimmie was so happy that he had grown even that much. But after while, when my dress had to be let out, Jimmie was wearing the same clothes month after month. We stopped going to the wardrobe on our birthdays.

"Yes, Deza, we wrote on it because we thought, a million years ago, that we were going to buy the furniture from the landlord, but just like with so many other things, life got in the way."

Which is just a unpoetic way of saying, "gang aft a-gley."

Mother was so sad that I said, "I guess that means we've got a lot less to worry about, right?"

She smiled. "When aren't you right, my Mighty Miss Malone?"

"It's only because I've got the blood of the Malones in my veins!"

"You also have the blood of my family, the Sutphens, in there too. Let's not forget that."

We looked around at what we'd need to pack. There wasn't going to be much.

Mother said, "OK, Deza, Mr. Rhymes is going to give us a ride as far as Detroit. I've got three dollars for gas for him, then another two dollars for bus fare to Flint.

"Jimmie, we'll be leaving in three days, you've got to say goodbye to your friends. I'd much prefer you write, rather than visit in person, those who are currently in jail."

Mother could still make jokes.

She told me, "Sweetheart, you have permission to walk

over to Mrs. Needham's and Clarice's to say goodbye. Jimmie, walk with your sister, please. Give them my love, Deza."

This was going to be terrible.

* * *

I was relieved when no one answered Mrs. Needham's door. She was counting on me so much that I knew it would break her heart that I was leaving. But I stayed strong.

It wasn't until we were walking to Clarice's that I could feel tears swelling up in my eyes.

How can you say goodbye to the best friend you've ever had?

I reached over and took Jimmie's hand. I knew he wouldn't try to pull away.

"Come on, sis, don't cry. We gotta get this over with. It's just like when you pulled that tape off of my eyebrow. Do it quick, that way it don't hurt as much."

Jimmie knocked and Mrs. Johnson answered.

"Why, Jimmie, Deza, come on in. Child, what's wrong with you?" She pinched my cheek.

Jimmie said, "Bad news, Mrs. Johnson. We gotta move to Michigan and Deza's come to say goodbye to Clarice."

"Oh, dear."

She wiped at my tears and said, "I'm so sorry, Deza, did you forget? Clarice and Mr. Johnson and the big boys found some work with Uncle Boo in Nashville. They left an hour ago."

I'd forgotten all about Clarice telling me this.

"I'm not expecting 'em back till next Thursday. Can you come then?"

Jimmie told her, "No, ma'am, we're leaving on Wednesday."

Secretly this wasn't such bad news. I knew if I saw how Clarice would take me leaving, it would scar and bruise my soul in a way that wouldn't heal for centuries.

Jimmie said, "Do you want to write her a note or something, Deza?"

I tried to talk but only sobs came out. I nodded my head.

Mrs. Johnson said, "Hold on one minute, darling, I'll get you a pencil and some paper."

Jimmie hugged me hard.

She came back. "I swear, these children must eat pencils. All I could find was these crayons, Deza." She handed me a old Prince Albert cigar box full of broken, speckled crayons. She also gave me a piece of blue-lined paper.

Mrs. Johnson pulled out a chair at the gigantic table where her family ate. I sat down, took the stub of a black crayon and wrote, *My dearest sister Clarice . . .* My hands started shaking too much and my eyes started getting too cloudy to write.

For me to write a letter telling Clarice a proper goodbye would take years. This letter had to be the best memory Clarice would have. I needed it to be so special that she'd keep it folded up in her pocketbook for centuries and would show it to her great-great-great-grandchildren and tell them, "*Once upon a time . . . in a city named Gary, Indiana . . . there lived two great and loving friends.*"

My head plopped down on the table.

Jimmie put his arms around my shoulders. He took the crayon out of my hand. "You want me to write it for you, sis?"

I looked up and shook my head.

Jimmie said, "Well, someone's gotta write something. What should I say?"

I just blubbered.

He looked over at Mrs. Johnson. I could see where my dear Clarice got her kind and loving nature, her mother was close to blubbering too.

Jimmie said, "OK, sis, how 'bout if I just draw something for Clarice?"

Oh, no! Not one of Jimmie's drawings! Could Fate be any crueler? Not only was I losing my best friend, but Jimmie wanted one of his horrid drawings to be the last thing Clarice heard from me.

I had to pull myself together and stop Jimmie from drawing anything, but the heaviness in my heart had swole up into my head too, and it plopped back down into my arms.

Jimmie tugged at the piece of paper I was crying on. "Raise up some, sis, just give me a minute." He started drawing. "There."

He gave the paper to Mrs. Johnson. She looked like she wanted to say something kind about it but couldn't find the words.

I was going to have to translate. I wiped my eyes and blinked at the piece of paper.

It was another very bad drawing.

Under where I had written, My *dearest sister Clarice* . . . Jimmie had used the black crayon to draw two frowning girls standing with their arms spread all the way out to their sides.

There was a capitol "D" over the left-hand one. That was supposed to be me. There was a capitol "C" over the girl on the right-hand side.

My left arm and Clarice's right were as long as giraffe necks and reached to the center of the page. Each of us held one side of a red, dripping blob.

Both of us had huge, fat drops of water squirting out of our eyes and spraying all over the page. Right in the middle of both my and Clarice's stomachs there were two big, red, colored-in circles.

Jimmie'd printed "DEZA STEERS" by the girl who was supposed to be me.

There was one arrow coming from those words that pointed at the water Jimmie had drawn coming out of my eyes and another arrow that pointed at a half circle near the bottom of the page.

Inside the half circle was a spot where the blue lines of the paper had got blurry and looked like a beautiful turquoise puffy cloud floating at the bottom of the page. It was where my real tears had blurred the paper's blue lines.

I could see that "DEZA STEERS" should have been spelled "Deza's tears."

I pointed at the two big red circles on our stomachs.

Jimmie said, "It's that corny hand signal you and Clarice give each other about having one heart. And those are two holes where it use to be before it got broke in two."

What could I do? I hugged my big brother and choked out, "Thank you so much. Jimmie, this is perfect."

He smiled, "Yeah, I thought so too. Come on Deza, we gotta make sure Ma's OK."

Which is exactly what you'd expect from the best big brother in the world.

Chapter Nineteen

The Malones Meet Marvelous Marvin

Three days before Mr. Rhymes was supposed to give us a ride to Detroit and it started like so many other days lately: gang aft a-gley.

It was far too early in the morning for him to be awake, but Jimmie hollered up the stairs, "Ma! Ma! It's the landlord!"

Mother jerked up in our bed and yelled, "Tell him I'll be down in a minute, Jimmie."

I did my morning wash-up as fast as I could. I heard Mother's raised voice as soon as I got to the stairs.

"You simply cannot do that! We're paid until the end of the month, that's three more days!"

"Mrs. Malone, what can I say? You've been good tenants,

this is just as hard on me as it is on you. But I got kids that like eating too, and I got three families who're gonna pay me four times as much to live here as you do. Two of 'em were ready to move in yesterday, I can't afford to lose 'em to someone else. My hands are tied. It's nothing personal. You gotta go. Now."

"No!" Mother said. "We have rights."

The landlord said, "Fine. Go hire a lawyer or call the police, but until I hear something from a shyster or a cop, you're out of here. Fellas, start moving their junk out. The furniture stays."

Jimmie yelled, "If you touch one thing I'll gut you like a chicken!"

"*Jimmie!*" Mother screamed.

I got to the porch just as Mother pulled a straight razor from Jimmie's hand. "Where did you get this?" She looked so shocked, I think she'd forgotten all about the landlord and his workers.

Jimmie said, "A man's gotta look after things, Ma."

Mother said, "Since when does carrying a razor make anyone a man? You get inside and get dressed."

Jimmie scowled at the landlord and the three other white men, but he went inside.

Mother said to the landlord, "Give me until noon. I have to walk over to a friend's house and see if he can come pick our things up. You know we weren't supposed to leave for three days."

The landlord said, "Noon. Only because you've been such good tenants." He got in a truck with the other men and drove away.

Mother went into the house and came back with her pocketbook and Jimmie.

"Deza, I don't trust that man, if he comes back early don't interfere, just make sure they don't steal anything. Go in and pack up the rest of your clothes, strip all the beds and bring everything downstairs. Jimmie, you're coming with me."

Jimmie said, "What? You're leaving Deza to look after the house, to do my job?"

"I don't have time to walk over to Mr. Rhymes's house, get him and come back and get you out of the hospital or out of jail for attacking somebody. Besides, I need an escort, you know how that side of town is."

Jimmie put his hands up like he was driving the Manipula-Mobile.

"You have a choice, walk beside me like a gentleman or . . ."

Jimmie scowled.

"If Mr. Rhymes is home we shouldn't be long." She gave me a kiss and I went back inside.

I stripped the beds and put everything in boxes. We had packed most everything else, and our clothes. All that was left was my Sunday school dress, my books and essays and tests and Mrs. Needham's niece's dress and shoes.

I folded my Sunday school dress and wondered if I could run it over to Clarice's. Maybe if Mr. Rhymes had time he could drive by that way and I could leave it for her.

I left it on my mattress, just in case.

I took the few boxes from Mother's room and all but the last one from mine downstairs.

I started looking through my essays to see if there was

anything to throw away. Before I knew what happened I was sitting on the bed reading them. It was a pleasant way to forget about a unhappy job.

I read through one essay and decided I'd make two piles, one for essays and tests that would come with me and one for those I could leave. I read some others and they all went in the go-with-me pile.

Nothing wrong with that.

The next time I looked up, the go-with-me pile was huge and the other pile was still empty.

The screen door slammed.

Oh, no! Mother and Jimmie! Had I been reading that long?

I put all of the papers, the dictionary and thesaurus, the clothes and the shoes in the box and slid it under my bed.

I ran downstairs and my heart near exploded into my throat!

A huge, strange white man was in the middle of our living room with a box in his arms!

I screamed as loud as I could.

The man dropped the box, screamed too, then flew out of the front door.

I ran behind him and slammed and locked the front door.

Someone said from behind me, "What in Sam Hill . . ."

The landlord came out of the kitchen with a mop in his hand.

"Time's up, girly, unlock that door, I gotta get this cleaned out now."

I screamed again. It had scared that first white man, maybe it would scare this one too.

He set the box down and waited patiently for me to breathe.

"Are you done?" he said. "Neither one of us wants the cops, but I'll call 'em if I have to. Unlock that door and get out of my way! Your mother asked for until noon and it's past that."

What could I do? I unlocked the door and went outside.

The men had already moved most of our stuff out onto the sidewalk. I'd have to sit and watch to make sure no one walking by would steal anything.

Not that there was much to steal.

After while the landlord put the broom, a mop and two buckets on the sidewalk and said, "That's everything. Tell your mother I do feel bad, but business is business. I don't have to do this, but here's something for leaving early."

He handed me four one-dollar bills. I stuffed them in my pocket.

"I got mouths to feed too."

After he left, a old car stopped in front of the house. A Mexican woman called out of the window, "Excuse me, miss, is this 509 Wilbur Place?"

"Yes, ma'am."

She said something to the others in the car and they cheered. A big family got out of the car.

"It's beautiful! Are you going to be sharing the house with us? Do you need help carrying these in?"

She pointed at our boxes.

"No, ma'am, we're moving out."

"Oh! I hope your next home is as beautiful as this one."

"Thank you, ma'am, I hope so too," I said. "Ma'am, do you

mind if I sit on the step until my mother comes back? She's getting a car so we can load our boxes."

"Please," she said, holding my screen door open, "you can come in to wait if you want."

This family seemed like they were of good character but I couldn't stand to see them living in my home. "Thank you, ma'am, but I have to watch our things."

She said, "Rosario can keep you company. Maybe you can tell her about the neighborhood and school and any nice little girls she can be friends with."

A girl a little younger than me said, "Hello."

"Hi."

We sat next to each other but neither one of us felt like talking.

Her family was inside screaming and yelling as they went from room to room. You'd have thought they were finding gold nuggets.

Every time they yelped the girl would look toward the front door, then back at me. She had the most beautiful, sorrow-fulled black eyes, and eyelashes that were as thick and black as the teeth of a comb.

I told her, "You can go in if you want, I'm fine out here."

She said, "Really?"

"Sure."

"Thank you." She jumped up to the front door.

I said, "Be careful, if you let it go, the screen bangs loud and disturbs people."

"OK."

She seemed like a sweet person so I said, "If you look under the welcome mat there's a little knothole in the porch that my brother and his friends used to shoot marbles into. If you can figure a way to get underneath the porch there must be a million of them down there. Jimmie and his friends think the marbles fell all the way to China, which is geologically exactly on the other side of the Earth from Gary, but that's nonsense, they're still under the porch."

She laughed and said, "*Dios mio*, all brothers are *idiotas*. *Muchas gracias*."

Another whole family walked up and moved into our house and still no Mother and Jimmie.

I looked in one of the boxes and found the kitchen clock. Two twenty-eight.

I knew it would make time stand still, but I set the clock next to me.

At three-thirty Mother trudged up the sidewalk, looking like she'd walked a hundred miles.

"Mother! Where have you been?"

"I'm so sorry, Deza. Let me sit for a second."

"What took so long?

She sat next to me on the step. "We waited at the Rhymeses' house for hours. When they came back we found out Mr. Rhymes has lost his car. The bank took it back."

"Where's Jimmie?"

"I sent him to the post office to have any mail we get forwarded to general delivery in Flint."

"To what?"

"General delivery. Since we're not sure what our address in

Flint is, any mail we get in Gary will go to Flint. We'll have to go to the post office there and pick it up."

That made this whole moving-to-Flint-story seem a lot realer. And a lot sadder.

Mother picked up the clock.

"Goodness, it's that late? Jimmie said he might not come straight home, that he knew someone who could help us. I was too tired to fight him."

"There are people living in our house."

She looked at the front door. "I'm so sorry, Deza, don't worry, we'll—"

A long, shiny black car stopped in front of the house. My smiling brother and a man jumped out. "Ma! Deza! This is Marvin, he can carry our stuff to his girlfriend's house and for five bucks we can stay there for a week!"

Mother and me looked at Marvin. His skinny, skinny mustache matched the rest of him. He was dressed in a fancy suit that had such sharp creases on the trousers that if you brushed against them, they'd cut you like a razor. His shoes and hat were the exact same color as the suit and so clean that he looked like a movie star. A hunk of gold on his finger sparkled like the sun.

When he took off his hat and tipped it at us his hair was jet-black, slicked back and wavy.

He said, "Marvelous, absolutely marvelous to make your acquaintance, young ladies."

Mother looked at him for the longest time before she said, "Hello. Jimmie, can I talk to you for a minute, please?"

"Sure, Ma. Gimme a minute, Marv."

"Cool."

Mother and Jimmie and me walked to the side of the house. Mother said, "James Edward Malone, isn't that the man they call Marvelous Marvin Ware?"

"Yeah, isn't it great he's going to help?"

Mother snapped, "Isn't he the numbers man?"

"Yes, Ma."

She slapped the back of Jimmie's head. "How on earth do you know him?"

"Ow! Ma! He's heard me singing in the park, he's always liked my voice."

"The numbers man?"

"Yes, Ma, he ain't so—"

"You're riding in a car with the numbers man?"

I said, "Mother, what's the numbers man?"

"Jimmie knows exactly who he is. He steals poor people's pennies with a gambling scheme."

Jimmie said, "And he's the best, always pays off. He's the honestest numbers man in Gary."

Mother looked at the pile of boxes on the sidewalk, sighed and reached in her pocketbook.

She counted out five one-dollar bills and gave them to Jimmie.

"Any port in a storm."

* * *

Me and Mother sat in the back of the car.

Jimmie and Marvelous Marvin loaded all of our things

in what Jimmie called the trunk. It wasn't like any trunk I'd ever seen, it was really only a door that raised up at the back of the car.

The trunk door slammed shut and both me and Mother jumped.

I had never been inside a automobile except for Mr. Steel Lung's truck. But this car, this car was amazing!

The seats were made of a brown cloth more beautiful and softer than anything I'd ever seen. There was a brown carpet on the floor and more of the brown material on the ceiling of the car. This automobile was the kind of place that you felt like you should wipe your feet two or three times or even take your shoes off before you got into it.

There was even a radio!

The middle of the steering wheel spelled out B-U-I-C-K. I'd have to ask Jimmie how to pronounce that later.

I looked at Mother to see if she was as excited and amazed as me, but she'd crossed her arms and was staring sadly out of the window at our old house. I did the same.

Jimmie and the numbers man got in the car and Marvelous Marvin said to Mother, "I know you must be very proud of little Jimmie here, Miss Malone. . . ."

Mother never looked away from the window. "It's *Mrs.* Malone."

"Sorry, ma'am. But I ain't never heard no one, kid, grown or otherwise, who can sing like him. Yeah, the little man's marvelous, absolutely marvelous."

Jimmie stretched and looked over the back of the front seat at us, his eyebrows jumping up and down. He could see that

Mother wasn't very impressed and I was giving him my angriest look. He turned around.

Marvelous Marvin said, "Y'all mind if I fire up a square?"

Jimmie translated, "Is it OK if he smokes, Ma?"

Me and Mother said, "No!"

"Cool."

"Yeah," Jimmie said, "that's cool."

We stayed quiet for most of the ride. But my goodness, what a ride! Mr. Steel Lung's truck was nothing but bump after bump, this car was like a magic carpet! We floated all the way through Gary heading west. We drove further and further.

Jimmie laughed. "Did you see that, Deza?"

I looked at Mother but she was staring out of the window, lost.

"What?"

"Those signs on the side of the road. There are five of them in a row and they got poems on 'em."

"Poems?"

Jimmie said, "Yeah, poems. Nothing like the ones Pa makes up, but at least these rhyme. Look! There's more of 'em coming up."

Marvelous Marvin said, "Oh, yeah, them's Burma-Shave signs, that's what I use to keep my skin soft as a baby's behind."

He rubbed his hand over his chin, it looked like he was wearing nail polish!

I told him, "I don't think I'd like to be compared to anybody's behind."

Mother slapped my hand. "Deza, hush."

Jimmie said, "Here comes one!"

It was a skinny red sign on a post at the side of the road.

Jimmie read,

"When driving the roads . . ."

The next sign was a bit further along.

"Keep your hand in the car . . ."

Then,

"Or it may end up . . ."

Next,

"In some doctor's jar!"

Me and Jimmie and Marvelous Marvin shouted the last sign out,

"Burma-Shave!"

We burst out laughing. Except for Mother.

Jimmie read the next signs,

"He chose not to shave . . .
With our famous brand . . .
That's why he's known as . . .
The loneliest man!"

Everyone but Mother shouted, "*Burma-Shave!*"

Before long Jimmie said, "Dang, Marv, where's this house at?"

Marvin said, "Chi-town, baby."

Mother said, "*Chicago?*"

"Yes, ma'am. We got another ten, fifteen minutes. This

gal's from Gary, but she wanted to stay near her momma in Chi-town. She shares a place with her sister, who's out of town for a while, so I convinced her to put y'all up till then."

Mother shook her head and looked back out of the window.

We stopped in front of a house that was just as nice as the automobile.

The numbers man said, "Home again, home again, jiggity-jig."

On the front porch, Mr. Marvelous knocked. The door opened and a soft, sweet smell whooshed out.

Chapter Twenty

The Girl in the Mirror

The woman who answered the door was strikingly beautiful and long-limbed and dressed in a flowing robe that looked like a orange cloud had left the skies and was floating around her legs.

She smiled and hugged Jimmie. "Little Jimmie! I know you from the park! I love your voice, poppa!"

Mother was so mortifried that I thought she was going to swoon.

The woman told the numbers man, "I'm only doing this because it's Little Jimmie's family. You already dumped that Carter woman and her brat in the basement and that's that. This ain't no hotel or no orphanage neither."

Marvelous Marvin said, "Woman, please."

She pointed at me. "I'd best not catch you snooping round my sister's room neither."

My second brain said, "Kiddo, one punch and she's down for the count."

Mother said, "We won't be a bother, ma'am. We'll be out of here as quick as we can. Thank you for having us."

The woman snorted and pointed at a closed door. "That's where y'all's staying. Cynthia's only gonna be gone for a week so don't get too comfy. Little Jimmie can sleep on the couch."

"Thank you very much." Mother pushed me toward the room. Inside she leaned against the door and put her hand over her eyes.

It was the most beautiful room I'd ever been in! It was like it came out of a magazine! The bed had fancy blankets and fancy pillows and the lampshades were pink and frilly and everything matched, even the curtains! There was a small low desk with a little chair in front of it. A long tall mirror was in the middle of the desk. Sitting on the desk was a bunch of exquisite different-color little bottles with gold tops and rubber bulbs held to their sides by a little skinny piece of hose, looking like gigantic diamonds or rubies! There was also a picture of a beautiful woman and a little boy in a gold frame.

"Oh, Mother!"

She wasn't as impressed as me.

"Be careful, Deza, all of this nonsense is very expensive."

"What are those bottles?"

"They're called atomizers, you squeeze the rubber bulb and it shoots out a mist of perfume."

Mother went to the desk and picked up one of the bottles. She sniffed the top.

"I can't believe it, they're living just as well as the Carsdales. On second thought, I do believe it, both they and the Carsdales live off of poor people's nickels and dimes."

"Can I smell one?"

"Of course, dear."

I walked over to the desk and reached for the darkest blue bottle.

I closed my eyes and brought it to my nose.

Yuck! It was too strong, like kerosene and flowers mixed together.

Something caught my eye.

I said, "Oh!"

A little girl was staring at me.

I put the beautiful blue bottle in my left hand and brought my right hand to my face.

The girl's cheeks were hollow and her face was thin. She was doing the same thing I was.

Her dress was clean but raggedy-looking.

Her hair was neatly braided and greased.

Her left hand was touching her cheek.

Her mouth was open a little bit like she was saying, "Oh!"

She had a beautiful blue perfume bottle in her right hand.

Her eyes were tired and sad and she stared right back at me.

Over the girl's shoulder Mother was sitting on the bed with her face in both of her hands.

I looked back into the girl's sad brown eyes.

"Well, kiddo, what do you think?"

I bit down on my back teeth and the girl's face twisted in pain.

I couldn't look away.

There was a knock and Mother looked at me and whispered, "Deza! Quick! Put that back."

She called, "Come in." I put the atomizer back and turned around as the door opened.

Jimmie closed the door behind him and his eyebrows were jumping all over his forehead. He was smiling like a Cheshire cat. "Well," he whispered, "Pretty cool, huh?"

Mother reached out and slapped Jimmie's cheek hard! "How dare you? How *dare* you?"

"What?" Jimmie said.

Mother reared her hand up again but stopped. "How dare you associate with this criminal? What do you do when you're supposed to be at school? Do you think your father and I raised you to be in the company of people like this?"

"Mother!" I said.

Jimmie said, "What? I didn't do nothing wrong. Nothing!"

"How do you know that man well enough to have him put us up?"

"I told you, when I sing in the park lots of people listen to me."

"So this is the kind of life you want to live? All fancy and big-shot like this? Driving around in a brand-new Buick? Wearing trashy clothes? If Roscoe Malone saw this he'd strangle both you and that man!"

Jimmie busted out in full tears. "I ain't done nothing wrong, he just likes my singing."

Mother grabbed his shoulders. "Don't you see this is how it starts? Don't you see one minute you're carrying a straight razor and the next it's a gun? Or do you already have one?"

"Ma, I swear, I don't do nothing wrong. I only went to him 'cause we didn't have nowhere else to go and he always said I should look him up if I needed something."

"Jimmie, this is how young men get trapped. You think he's doing you any *favors*? You'll owe him. I guarantee he'll have you doing little things for him in no time. I guarantee. . . ."

Jimmie wiped at his eyes. "Ma, how come you always think I'm gonna do wrong? I know what's right, he's been trying for the longest to get me to run numbers for him, I always said no, I ain't stupid. I was only keeping my word to Pa, I was only trying to look out for you and Deza."

He pulled away from Mother. "You don't give me credit for nothing. Nothing!"

He turned, walked out of the door and closed it softly.

Mother sagged onto the bed and I sat beside her. We hugged each other.

I got up and put my hand on the doorknob. "Mother?"

"Go ahead, Deza, bring him back, I don't want either of you leaving this room."

* * *

I heard squeals and giggles coming from the backyard. A girl about six or seven years old was getting pushed in a swing by a woman. Jimmie was sitting on another swing.

The girl dragged her feet so the swing stopped. "Are you Jimmie's sister?"

"Yes, my name's Deza."

Her nose twisted. "That's a funny name. My name's Eppie, but my real name is Epiphany."

I said, "That's a beautiful name, it means you're like a light coming on all of a sudden."

The little girl had a very fresh mouth. "You've got a weird name and don't know nothing, I'm named after a song, not no light."

Jimmie said, "'Sarah's Epiphany'?"

The woman said, "How'd you know that song?"

I said, "He's a singer, ma'am, he knows just about every song in the world."

"Y'all from Chicago?"

"No, ma'am, we're from Gary."

"You must be kin to Marvin or that sad excuse for a woman."

"No, ma'am, we're just staying here for a few days before we get a ride to Flint."

"In Michigan?"

"Yes, ma'am."

"That's north of here, right?"

"Yes, ma'am."

"Ooh, girl, how old you think I am? You gotta quit calling me ma'am. I'm Miss Carter."

"Sorry, Miss Carter."

"Flint anywhere near Detroit?"

"It's geologically located sixty miles northwest of Detroit."

"So y'all are going through Detroit to get to Flint."

"I think so."

"Who's carrying you to Michigan?"

Jimmie said, "I might ask Marvin how much he'd charge to take us in that big Buke."

She started pushing Eppie again. "Don't do it. The sooner you get away from that character the better. But if you hear of someone else going that way let me know. There's suppose to be lots of work in Detroit."

"You're leaving too?"

"Child, as soon as I can. The friendlier Marvelous Marvin gets the meaner that woman does."

I asked, "What will you do if you can't find anyone to take you?"

"If nothing else comes up in a day or two me and Eppie won't have no choice but to ride the rails. We did it before. I'd rather get drove, but you gotta do what you gotta do."

Jimmie said, "Ride the rails! You really hopped a train before?"

"It's not like we jumped on no moving train. This is Chicago, son, there's a million boxcars sitting at the yard and someone always knows where they're going."

Jimmie's eyes met mine.

What choice did we have but to try to get Mother to go along?

* * *

After Miss Carter and Eppie went back to their basement, Jimmie and me sat on the swings and talked about how we could get Mother to hop a train with us.

Jimmie said, "What do you always tell me, Deza? The truth

is the best way. We just gotta ask her what other choice we have if we're gonna get to Flint and Pa."

"You're right." But it wouldn't be that easy.

When we went back into the room Mother hugged Jimmie and apologized.

Jimmie said, "It's OK, Ma, I know you're just worried. But, Ma, we gotta get outta here."

"Yes, son, we do."

I explained about Miss Carter and the train. We were both stunned when Mother said, "Let's talk to her and see what we have to do."

* * *

Miss Carter stood in our room and looked at our boxes. "The main thing is, you have to travel light."

Mother said, "We only have these seven boxes."

Miss Carter said, "You each can carry one blanket full of only the most important things."

Mother sighed. "Well, let's see what we can leave."

Uh-oh. Even though a dictionary and thesaurus were the most important things to me, they wouldn't be for most people. And how many essays could I take?

We set our boxes on the bed and Mother took three blankets and spread them out. We emptied the boxes and started putting things in a blanket or back in a box to stay in Chicago.

A few pots and pans went in Jimmie's blanket along with the kitchen clock and some knives, spoons and forks wrapped in towels.

Miss Carter said that anything made out of glass, like the plates, the drinking glasses and the bowls, would have to stay, they'd just end up breaking. We took three tin cups.

Miss Carter said, "Most camps have cans you can use for plates, but it's best if you find some tin plates and hold on to them."

Mother said, "We don't really intend to spend any time in a camp."

Miss Carter smiled. "Believe me, no one ever does. But, sweetheart, better safe than sorry."

The last box on the bed was opened and Jimmie pulled Father's old work boots and some of his trousers and shirts and winter coat out.

Miss Carter said, "Whose are these?"

Jimmie picked up one of Father's boots. "They're Pa's."

"Is he waiting for you in Flint?"

Mother said, "We're not exactly sure where he is, but . . ."

Miss Carter said, "You gotta leave 'em, only take what y'all need."

Jimmie wouldn't let go of the boot. Mother took it from him and said, "I'm sure your father has plenty of things in Flint, Jimmie. We'll have to leave these."

She set Father's boots on the floor.

She said, "Well, that's it."

"Wait! There's one more box. My essays and dresses and shoes."

We looked around. There was nothing.

I slapped both of my hands over my mouth and felt like the ceiling was crashing down on me.

"Oh, Mother! I left my box under the bed in Gary! We've got to go back and get it."

Even before Mother could tell me what we all knew, I heard, "Well, kiddo, the best-laid schemes of mice and men . . ." The pain that ripped through my heart and soul shut the bad brain right up.

Chapter Twenty-One

Riding the Rails

If you could forget about the way the boxcar smelled like a toilet and ignore the heat and the darkness and the hard floor and the flies you could say it was pretty comfortable. You could say that, but you'd be telling one of the biggest lies ever.

We sat with our backs against the front of the boxcar on old pieces of cardboard. There were two other families sitting at the other end. Jimmie and Eppie left me alone with Mother and Miss Carter. They wanted to sit closer to the huge, half-open door to watch Illinois, then Indiana, then Michigan zoom by.

Miss Carter said, "Breathe out your mouth till the train moves and air starts circulating."

Mr. Steel Lung's truck was bouncy and bumpy, but compared to this train it was like riding in a brand-new Buke.

It would take eight hours to get to Detroit. Miss Carter said then it would be easy to find a freight to Flint. If we felt up to it we could even walk there in a day and a half.

As the train got moving air swirled through. The flies stopped buzzing, and once we were in the country, breathing got a lot easier. We rolled through green fields, past farm after farm, and every time we went by a road we could see cars waiting for us to pass. Bells warned people that our train was barreling east.

I was glad Epiphany wasn't sitting with us. Not only did she have a very fresh mouth, she was also very verbose. And not in the good way.

She was leaning a little too far out of the door when my second brain said, "Ooh, kiddo, one quick kick and 'Bye-bye, Eppie!'" That was the first time the bad brain ever made me smile.

Mother said to Mrs. Carter, "Julia, isn't this terribly unsafe?"

"Shoot, girl! Yeah, it's *all* unsafe. You gonna have to be *extra* careful when you get to camp, that's unsafe too, if you don't know what you're doing."

"What do you mean?"

"It's just like anything else, there's just enough bad folks in camp to make it so you got to keep your guard up at all times. It's especially hard on women, and even worst for little girls."

She looked at me and a shiver went through my heart. "You just gotta keep your wits about you and don't let no one in on your business. Keep it to yourself why you're on the road alone."

Mother's 1-1-1 lines jumped out.

"Always let folks think your husband or your brother is with you, always tell 'em that he's gonna be back later tonight. There's strength in numbers so let folks think there's a lot of y'all. You're a good-looking woman, you gonna have to be careful not to draw a lot of attention you don't want."

Mother's jaws tightened.

"And don't let no one get too familiar either, man or woman. Don't let 'em know where y'all are really from. They'll start prying and before you know it they're looking to help you out in some way that ain't no kind of help at all. Just keep your head low. Don't look weak or scared."

The train stopped in a city called Battle Creek and two white women climbed in with us. The next time it stopped, what felt like four days later, someone walked by and said into the boxcar, "Detroit. All clear. Detroit. All clear."

Miss Carter said, "Come on, Peg, we need to find a hobo and see what's going to Flint."

Jimmie whispered in my ear, "A hobo's someone who rides the rails all over the country."

I already knew that but I said, "Thanks, Jimmie."

Once we got our bundles and stepped off the train we walked up to a rough-and-tumble-looking old white man. He told us which cars were going toward Flint.

Epiphany said, "Ick, he smells bad."

The old man heard her. "If I was you I'd quit worryin' 'bout how folks smell. You got bigger fish to fry. You need to start worrying 'bout that man with three eyes and a hunting knife that was asking round 'bout where you gonna be sleeping tonight, girly!" The hobo walked away. "Sweet dreams!"

Mother frowned, looked at the boxcar we were supposed to get in and said, "Julia, why don't you come to Flint? You said there's strength in numbers."

Miss Carter hugged Mother. "Peg, you'll be fine. Flint's too small and country for my tastes. You're welcome to come with *me* if you want."

Mother said, "Thank you, but we have to find Roscoe."

"Get right into the shantytown. You'll need somewhere to rest at least one night."

"Thank you, Julia."

"You're good people, I wish y'all the best, travel safe and look after each other."

* * *

Time has a way of misbehaving when you're anxious or nervous. When Father was lost on the lake, time lollygagged and every second took a hour to pass. When we were on the train to Flint, time hitched a ride on Jimmie's rocket ship and the trip took two seconds. I spent half my time wondering what we'd do if we found Father. I spent the other half wondering what we'd do if we didn't.

The train stopped and someone banged on the side of the boxcar. "Flint. All clear. Flint. All clear." He was a raggedy man with a beautiful curly black-and-white beard.

Mother said, "Excuse me, sir, do you know how we get to Flint?"

"Flint's down that way and the camp's up there."

Mother said, "How far is Flint, sir?"

"Downtown's about half a hour's walk. Y'all look fresh, shouldn't have no troubles there."

Jimmie said, "How far's the camp, sir?"

He pointed at some woods. "See that glow? Supper's just 'bout ready."

Mother said, "Thank you. Do you know who we see to get somewhere to sleep?"

"A train just left going west, should be plenty of huts opened up. Ask for Stew."

"Is there a charge?"

He laughed. "If there was, ma'am, this place would be empty. You just give what you can, food, work, anything. Folks find a way."

"Thank you very much."

"Don't suppose none of y'all smoke or chaw tobaccy?"

"No, sir, we don't."

"Well then, may peace like a river come to you." He tipped his rough hat and walked on.

Mother said, "It won't be bad, we'll only be here for a night. I'll go to your grandmother's tomorrow and we'll be able to leave."

Jimmie said, "Don't worry, Ma, whatever happens don't forget what Pa said about us being a family taking a trip to somewhere named Wonderful. We're gonna get there sooner or later. Right, Deza?"

"You know it, Jimmie."

He pointed at the orange glow and bowed. "Now, lay-deees and ladies, next stop, a place called Wonderful!"

Part Two

Gone from Gary
Late Summer 1936/Late Spring 1937
Flint, Michigan

Chapter Twenty-Two

Learning How to Settle in Flint

You'd need a really exploding imagination to call this camp anything like Wonderful. But it was OK.

We asked the first person we saw how we should get a place to stay. He said, "Look for Stew, white lady with a long gray braid. She's at the crick."

Stew was leaning on a stick by the water. She saw us and limped over. She stuck her hand out. "My name's Donna Stewart, everyone calls me Stew. You're new here, you need a place to stay?"

We introduced ourselves and Mother said, "My mother-in-law lives in Flint and since we got here so late we thought we'd better stay."

The woman said, "There's plenty of room, and you're welcome to stay as long as you need."

Jimmie said, "It's not going to be long—"

Mother tugged at her earlobe, the Malone signal for "Stop talking . . . start listening." She said, "My husband is going to be here in a bit."

Jimmie was confused but had sense enough to keep quiet.

Stew said, "Fine, let's find you a place."

We followed Stew along one of the trails that led back to the fire. She and Mother walked slowly ahead of me and Jimmie.

"I twisted my ankle on a root a couple of weeks ago, you gotta watch where you're going. This your first time staying in a camp?"

Mother said, "Is it that obvious?"

Stew laughed. "Painfully."

Jimmie whispered, "Dang, see what being seen with two soft little cream puffs like you and Ma has done to my reputation?"

I slapped his arm.

Stew said, "Where're you from, if you don't mind me asking?"

Mother stuttered around a bit before she said, "Uh, Lancaster, Pennsylvania."

She was very bad at lying. Which is a good thing. I guess.

Jimmie nudged me. "*What?*"

I whispered, "I'll tell you later."

In camp people said hello to us, then came up to Stew to

say things like, ". . . And you know we've asked them three or four times to stop, and nothing's been done. My husband is about to take matters into his own hands and no one wants that. . . ."

Or, "Sorry to disturb you, Stew, but have you heard anything on that job . . . ?"

Or, "Thank you so much, Stew, we owe you big. . . ."

Or, "Anyone going in to the post office tomorrow . . . ?"

She was patient and kind with each person.

Jimmie said, "Wow, Stew! It's like you're the mayor or something!"

She laughed. "Well, let me know when the next election is so I can be sure not to run again!"

She walked us toward the fire. "Now, you don't want to choose a spot so close to the fire that you get smoked if the wind's wrong, but it's nice to be close enough that you can hear the fire burning down. How do you feel about music?"

Jimmie said, "We love it."

"Good, that's another advantage to being close to the fire, some nights folks sing and play instruments there. I warn you, though, the quality varies, it depends who's in camp."

Jimmie looked at me and made his eyebrows do that crazy up-and-down dance.

Stew asked me, "You're about twelve, thirteen?"

"Yes, ma'am."

We stopped in front of a tent that sat between two cardboard, wood and cloth huts. There were boxes set like porch chairs outside the tent.

She said, "This is the Smalls' place. They've got a girl named Loretta that must be around your age. The places on both sides are open. Take your pick."

Mother said, "It is for just one night, so . . ."

The opening of the hut that caught my eye was closest to the fire. There was a cloth pulled to one side that you could drop down to cover where the front door was supposed to be. Even in the dark I could tell the cloth was gingham. It was too dark to be sure if it was blue.

I walked over to touch the material. It was a little dirty and a lot stiffer than Mrs. Needham's dress, but it was still beautiful. And it *was* blue.

Mother smiled. "Deza, which one?"

I said, "It's got to be some kind of a sign!"

Stew said, "Good choice. All we ask is that you not leave anything outside your place, that you respect your neighbors' privacy, any garbage goes to the dump, which is that way, and finally we ask that *you*"—she looked square at Jimmie—"not water any of the trees or plants, there are latrines near the dump."

Jimmie said, "I don't—"

Stew interrupted. "I'm not singling you out, young man, it's a general rule."

We said goodbye to Stew and set our bundles in the hut.

Mother said, "We'll just open the one with blankets."

I can't believe how something as easy as sitting in a couple of boxcars can get you so tired. We opened the bundle that had the bedding in it and even before it settled to the ground I was surprised to see Mother standing over me saying, "Sleep well, my lamb. Tomorrow we'll be with your grandmother."

I heard Jimmie say, "Sweet dreams, sis," and I wanted to answer him, but before I could open my mouth, I was out so quick that I didn't have time to think about the first night in my life that I wasn't sleeping in a real bed.

* * *

The blue gingham curtain was the first thing I saw and I wondered why Mrs. Needham's niece's dress was hanging that way. I yawned, stretched my legs, and the hard ground reminded me I wasn't in Gary.

It was morning and I could hear the very pleasant singing of birds and voices outside. It sounded like Jimmie, a couple of girls and a pack of robins.

I stretched my arms and looked to where Mother had slept. She was gone.

I smoothed my hair back, pulled my dress over my slip, dipped my washcloth in baking soda and ran it over my teeth, then put my shoes and socks on.

I pushed the curtain aside and walked into the bright morning sunlight. Along with the birds' singing there was the soft smell of firewood in the air. I blinked to get my eyes used to the light.

"Hey, sis! Come and meet our neighbors."

Jimmie was sitting in front of the tent next to our place.

He said, "Loretta and Kathleen Small, I'd like to present to you the Mighty Miss Malone!"

"My name is Deza."

The oldest one said, "Hey, Deza, nice to meet you. Jimmie says you're twelve?"

"Uh-huh."

"Are you going into seventh grade?"

"Yes."

"Good, we'll be in school together."

I looked at Jimmie. Why hadn't he told them we weren't going to be in the camp that long?

Kathleen said, "You don't have no idea how great it is to see you! I thought since Katherine Williams moved off I was gonna be the only colored girl in seventh grade."

"There are only white kids in seventh grade?"

"There's only eight of *us* in the whole school."

That was going to be different.

"What's that like?"

"Most of 'em treat you OK, you find out real quick who's the prejudice ones, especially the teachers. But you don't have to worry, I'll look out for you, Deza."

She was talking to me but looking at Jimmie.

"Thank you. Jimmie, where's Mother?"

"She's gone to Flint to find Grandma."

Loretta said, "She's with my momma. Ma might get her some work cleaning offices or working at the Durant. She's gonna have to show she can work good for a while, then she'll get paid. I get to help sometimes too, maybe we can get you some work, Deza."

"That would be great, but I don't think—"

Jimmie said, "I was waiting till you got up, sis, I'm gonna

head into Flint and see what I can get percolating. Y'all two girls take good care of my baby sis."

They both had dreamy eyes when they said, "We will, Jimmie."

Yuck.

He handed me a knife, a apple, a hard piece of corn bread and a tin cup full of water. I didn't know how hungry I was. I cut the apple into small pieces and dipped the corn bread in the water to soften it up a little so my teeth wouldn't hurt when I chewed. It went together with the apple real nice. But when you're hungry *any* two things together are real nice.

Jimmie rooster-strutted away.

Kathleen said, "Your brother sure do look good!"

I changed the subject. "What do you do all day here?"

Loretta lost interest in me and left the second Jimmie was gone. Kathleen said, "Most of the grown-ups go into Flint every morning to try to find work. Us kids got lots of chores to keep everything tidy and safe and neat out here. These folks here are crazy 'bout keeping neat, don't dare drop nothing or leave nothing outside your place or they act like you robbed a bank."

Kathleen looked up and said, "Morning, Miss Stew."

I stood up like Mother and Father say you're supposed to whenever a adult comes up to you. She was leaning on her walking stick and smiling.

"Morning, girls, I see you've made a new friend. Young lady, I've forgotten your name."

"I'm Deza Malone. Remember? From Lancaster, Pennsylvania?"

"Sit, sit, Miss Malone. Have you been explaining to Deza how we do things here?"

Kathleen said, "I was just fixing to, ma'am."

"I'm making my rounds. Come with me, Deza. You can learn a little about the camp."

I went, even though we weren't going to be here long enough for me to need to learn anything.

We started walking along one of the trails.

"You ever seen a camp before, Deza?"

"There was one in Gary, but only three or four families lived there. This place is huge."

"It is, and that causes problems. Everyone who's been on the road for a while comments on how clean this camp is, and it's not by accident. We work hard at keeping it that way. We may be poor but that isn't any excuse to live poorly. Cleanliness costs next to nothing."

"Yes, ma'am."

We walked past hut after hut and tent after tent. Some of the places looked like Father or some other real carpenter had put them together, some of them looked like they'd just tumbled down off a tornado. Miss Stew showed me where she lived with her little boy, it was just like all the other places, neat and tired.

The strangest-looking place was made out of stacked old automobile tires.

Stew said, "The Goodyear Mansion. Smells terrible inside once the weather gets hot."

Another place we passed was called the Ford Mansion. It

wasn't anything but a old panel truck with the wheels gone from it.

She showed me where the outdoor toilets were and where we'd go to do dishes.

There were more little kids than any other kind of people in the camp. It seemed like they'd been glued to each other, leaning heads on each other or hooking arms or holding hands. They had eyes like really old people, and they all looked tired and beat and hungry.

"Ma'am, how do people eat here?"

"Not very well, I'm afraid. You're on your own for breakfast and lunch. There's the mission in Flint, but it's not the most welcoming place. We throw together a community pot when we can, Sundays, Wednesdays and Fridays for sure, maybe a couple other times a week depending on what folks can catch. We've been doing good lately and having supper nearly every night."

Every once in a while Stew would stop at a place and ask, "Anyone home?"

If a child answered she'd ask them to tell their mother about some piece of trash or something left near their hut. If no one was there she'd write something in a notebook she carried.

"So your mother's going to look for your grandmother?"

"Yes, ma'am."

I remembered what Epiphany's mother said about not letting anybody know our business. Miss Stew seemed kind and of a good character but it's better to be safe than sorry.

"Ma'am? Does Flint have a library and what's the limit of books I can check out?"

"Of course! It's 'bout a twenty-five-minute walk from here. But you won't be able to check out any books unless you've got a Flint address to put down. You a big reader?"

"I live for books! One day I may even be a writer."

"You don't say? I've got plenty of *Reader's Digests* you can read. I like 'em because they don't let all the extra words writers want to cram in a story get in the way."

I bit my tongue.

After a hour of walking and listening to a million different complaints from a thousand different people we had circled back to our blue gingham front door.

"Deza, I hope you're able to get with your grandmother, but if you do need to stay here for a while it will be a pleasure to get to know you better. Stop by my place later and I'll have a couple *Digests* ready for you."

"Thank you, ma'am."

Mother was inside the hut lying on her side, asleep like a baby. I pulled the blanket over her and her eyes came open. "Deza! My goodness, I can't believe how tired I am, I'm not used to walking so much."

I kissed her cheek.

She said, "So, Miss Malone, do you want the good news first or the bad news?"

"You know the news I want."

"Sorry, Deza, no news there. No news about your grandmother either. Her house has been turned into apartments and none of the neighbors know anything. Flint's as bad off as Gary."

I didn't expect to hear anything but bad news, but my spirits sank anyway. I shoved my hands into my dress pockets.

"I do have a bit of good news, though."

"You went to the bank lady with Mrs. Carsdale's letter and got a job?" Mother's lines went to 1-1-1. She looked at me for a uncomfortable long time before she said, "I went to the woman but she didn't need anyone. I didn't give her that very interesting letter, though. We'll talk about that later on."

Uh-oh! I wonder if Jimmie ratted me out on that too?

"The good news is that I'm getting a chance to work with Mrs. Small at night cleaning offices. I won't get paid for the first week, it's like a tryout. If they like the way I work they'll hire me."

My fingers folded around the four dollar bills from the landlord in my pocket.

I pulled them out and Mother whispered, "Deza! Where did that come from?"

"I forgot! The landlord! He gave us this because we had to leave early. It seems it was so long ago but it wasn't even a week!"

"Thank goodness! I'll be able to get a few things in Flint."

"Since Grandma's gone does this mean we'll go back to Gary?"

Mother's lips moved. I'm sure she said something in English, but all I heard was "gang aft a-gley."

* * *

Mother is a fantastic worker and very proud of everything she does so after trying out for a week she got hired working three nights a week cleaning offices. She even found another job picking up both day and night shifts at the Durant Hotel.

* * *

Before long Jimmie didn't have trouble finding odd jobs and fruits and greens for us to give to the community pot. We even started saving a few pennies. The camp got easier to live in every day, but Mother said we needed to get a room in Flint as soon as we could.

Miss Stew and me got along just fine and she asked me to go on rounds with her every morning. We'd walk, she'd scold people and we'd discuss those horrible chopped-up stories from *Reader's Digest*. We were together so much that people started calling me Little Stew.

Time played its tricks on me. One day we got up and Mother said, "There was a nip in the air last night, Deza, I know Flint winters can't be anywhere near as bad as Gary's, but I really don't want to be out here once it starts getting cold. And there is school to consider."

"School?" It sounds foolish but I always thought I'd be back in Gary by then.

"Mrs. Small said you've got to go register next week."

I'd been having such a good time being Little Stew and trying to fill in all the missing words from the *Reader's Digest* that time had completely run off and forgot all about me!

"But, Mother, Miss Stew needs me to—"

"You aren't suggesting you stay here and help Stew instead of going to school, are you?" When she said it like that, it did seem silly.

* * *

On the outside, schools in Flint seemed a lot like schools in Gary, but they weren't. Instead of having one teacher all day, in Flint we went from classroom to classroom and teacher to teacher for each subject. The teachers were different too. First, all of them were white, and second, they weren't anywhere as nice as the teachers in Gary. But one of Mrs. Needham's lessons stuck: I was learning how to toughen up.

I got my usual As on the tests in mathematics, geography, civics and history.

After my first mathematics test, when class was dismissed, Mrs. Scott called me to her desk.

"Deza, have you always done so well in math? You're the only student who got a perfect score."

I sounded very humble, but the truth's the truth. "Yes, ma'am. Mathematics is one of my favorite subjects."

It was great to be back in school!

"Could I ask you a favor?"

Maybe she wanted me to help some of my classmates. Even though they were white, some of them were the spittin' image of Dolly Peaches and Benny Cobb.

She slid a paper toward me. It had five unsolved story problems on it.

"Could you sit right there, right now, and solve these for me?"

Maybe Mrs. Scott was seeing if I was ready for harder work. I finished in no time.

She looked them over. "Hmm, perfect again, but next time you *must* make sure to show all your work. You're dismissed."

I was surprised that was all she said.

In English class I *really* showed how much I'd toughened up.

Flint teachers don't have the imagination that Gary teachers do, so instead of giving grades back so everyone knows what you got, they just walk around the class and hand your test or your paper back to you. Upside down.

Mr. Smith was passing out our first essay. I'd followed all of Mrs. Needham's advice. I'd written it at the Flint Public Library and was very careful not to use the dictionary or the thesaurus too much. And I didn't digress at all.

I made sure my posture was good, crossed my ankles and folded my hands on the desk when he got close to me.

He handed me my paper and smiled. "Very good job."

My heart flew! "Thank you, sir."

I turned my paper over.

He'd written, "Good for you!" and put a giant C+ with three exclamation points.

I turned the paper back over. Maybe I saw it wrong.

I looked again but it was the same.

One sign that I had toughened up was that instead of crying I thought of a little joke that Jimmie said he did whenever he didn't like his grade.

"I turn the paper over, then, the same way people bang on a machine if it ain't acting right, I smack my hand on the paper. Maybe if I bang it hard enough my grade will jump up a mark!"

It was nonsense, but I slapped my hand on Mr. Smith's essay.

I turned the paper back over and smiled.

I'd have to tell Jimmie that it still wasn't working.

Mrs. Needham would've been proud. Instead of bawling I looked at Mr. Smith's back and said to myself, "OK, buster, I'm going to make sure my next essay is the best thing I've ever written. You won't have any choice but to give me my A plus."

When me and Loretta were walking back to camp I asked, "What grade did you get on your essay?"

"I don't know, the same old D. What'd you get?"

"C plus."

She stopped walking. "Uh-uh, no, you didn't!"

I showed her my grade.

"Ooh, girl, you must be *real* smart."

"For getting a C plus?"

"All these teachers up here at Whittier's prejudice. Katherine Williams was the smartest colored girl in the school and all she use to get was a C. You must be a genius to get a C plus!"

She laughed. "I'm gonna see if I can sit next to you when we take our next exam!"

* * *

Early every morning, Mother and I would leave the camp and walk for half a hour to downtown Flint. Jimmie would go his own way.

After school I'd go to the library and read until Mother picked me up. We didn't have a official address so I couldn't check out any books, but I still got to read.

It wasn't long before we stopped looking fresh and had seniority in camp. Stew said I had a bubbly personality so she had me help the new children get used to living here. Some of them didn't have any idea what to do, mostly the boys.

I pretended they were my students and was very patient.

Two little boys from Flint came in one day all by themselves. One of them reminded me of myself. He seemed scareder than his friend so I took him under my wing.

He was very nervous and shy, but you could see how sweet he was too.

His first evening in the camp, I didn't want him and his friend to think they were going to get a free ride so I had them help me with the dishes. I took the little boy and showed him the creek where we clean the camp's pots and dishes. We sat on a big rock and I washed and had him dry.

He said, "Are you leaving on the train tomorrow?"

"Uh-uh." I'd been lying so much about how we weren't alone that without thinking, I said, "My father's going out on it, he might leave for a day or two for work."

"Where do you go to school?"

"Well, Mother says I might have to keep going here in Flint at Whittier."

The sad-eye little boy said, "I'm hopping the freight to go west, me and Bugs are gonna pick fruit."

"I wish you two well."

I'd hand him the dish after I'd washed it and when my hand touched his he'd start blinking a lot and would get twitchity and fumble the cloth when he tried to dry the dish.

After while I started touching his hand just to make him squirm. And squirm he did!

He counted softly, "One, two, three . . . ," then blurted out, "I'MNOTAFRAIDOFGIRLS!"

I laughed. "You aren't?"

"Uh-uh. I even kissed some in the home."

"Really?"

"Yup, I got three kisses."

He held up four fingers.

I looked up at the moon. It was huge and yellow and yolky. "Isn't the moon lovely?"

I looked back. The little boy had closed his eyes, puckered his lips and leaned in toward me!

I started to slug him, just a arm punch. But looking at how sad he was made my heart melt.

He was all alone except for a person named Bugs.

What else could I do?

I kissed his forehead three times and said, "Kisses . . . kisses . . . kisses make you stronger."

He blinked six or seven times and when his eyes came open he looked lost and befumbled.

I put his hand in mine.

The harmonica man started playing "Shenandoah."

"Do you know that song?"

His head was wobbling back and forth and I wasn't sure if he was saying no or getting ready to swoon.

I said, "It's about a Indian princess who hasn't seen her husband for seven years."

I sang a little.

He said, "You sing beautiful."

Wow! He *was* befumbled!

"You should hear my brother, now that's a real singer."

I helped him up and we carried the dishes back to the camp.

As bad as things were for me, they were much worse for

him. I still had my family, and like Mother always says, without a family you're nothing but dust on the wind.

I hoped he'd find kindness somewhere, but even with my exploding imagination, I couldn't figure out where that would be.

Chapter Twenty-Three

Jimmie Blasts Off on His Rocket Ship

Later that night a few people were still sitting around the big fire, talking and laughing softly.

Pieces of wood crackled and hissed. I started counting the seconds between each snap.

Mother had left for her night job and I looked to see if Jimmie had fallen off yet. There hadn't been any of the twitching or soft whining he does most nights, but that didn't really mean too much, especially since I knew he'd found work earlier. If the job had been a tough one he'd climb under his blanket and sleep without fighting against it too hard. But not tonight, he was looking right back at me.

"Something wrong, sis? Can't sleep?"

"No, Jimmie, I'm doing fine, I was just about gone. You?"

"I'm fine. I was hoping that mouth organ man was gonna play, but it looks like he's through."

I said, "He played 'Shenandoah' earlier, your song. Could you sing it for me, just once?"

"Sure, sis."

Jimmie sat up. He says singing is like eating and serious thinking, things that shouldn't ever be done whilst lying down.

He took three deep breaths, held the last one, then sang, "*Oh, Shenandoah, I long to see thee . . . ,*" and you would have put your life on the line believing him.

"Way-eh-hey, you rolling river . . ."

He waited, shook his head and sang more. I closed my eyes. I imagined him getting taller and taller.

"Oh, Shenandoah, I'm bound to leave thee . . ."

Jimmie's slowness when he's singing is all part of settling into the song. It was the same thing Father did when he told us stories back home in Gary. I'm not saying anything bad about her, but Father's way is *so* different from the way Mother tells stories.

With her it's like we're in a race, like she's scooped us up and is flying with us to "*. . . they all lived happily everafter.*"

When Father would tell the same story things were easier, slower. It didn't take much to see yourself dropping bread crumbs right along a trail, or hear yourself scheming right along with High John the Conqueror, or feel yourself riding a golden horse behind Sir Lancelot with your arms wrapped around his waist and your cheek surprised at how cool the armor on his back was.

Hearing a story from Mother is like you're looking at the story from inside that boxcar. Things are swooshing by so fast that it wouldn't pay to get too interested or curious about any of them. With Father it was like you were strolling along a road, holding his hand and stopping whenever something caught your fancy.

"Way-eh-hey, we're bound away . . .
'Cross the wide Missouri."

After a long sigh, Jimmie was through. I opened my eyes. He had shrunk back to his normal size and dropped down his shoulders and was hanging his head.

He said, "Sweet dreams, sis."

A gentle tap-tap-tap came from the wooden frame of the door.

Jimmie jumped up. With his right hand he swiped the gingham curtain aside. He dropped his left hand behind him and my breath caught. He was holding another long, open straight razor!

He deepened his voice. "What do you want?"

A man said, "Hello, sonny, we wanted to have a word with your sister."

"You can have a word with me first. What do you want to talk to her about?"

"It's her voice, we—"

Jimmie butted in. "Why? We ain't being loud, y'all couldn't have barely heard us."

Four or five people laughed, and they were kind laughs but Jimmie's body tightened. I came up behind him and pulled the razor away. I closed it and held it against my leg.

It was the harmonica man who'd knocked. He said, "No, sonny, no complaints, far from it." He looked at me. "Evening, missy, how are you?"

There were six or seven men and women. Three of them were white. They all smiled at me.

I stepped in front of Jimmie. "I'm fine, thank you, how are you?"

The man pulled his hat off and said, "I'd have swore *I* was doing just fine up to a few minutes ago, then I fount out I was doing something terrible wrong."

He opened his hand and showed me his harmonica. "I thought I owned 'Shenandoah.' Thought I played it like it was me what wrote it. But tonight you took that song right 'way from me and made it so's I seen how it's supposed to be done. As of tonight I'm signing it over to you! You are spectacalar!"

People called out, "Amen!" and, "Hear, hear!"

A woman said, "Child, do you have any idea what kind of gift you have?"

"That's right!"

"A pure gift."

"But it wasn't me singing, it was my brother, my big brother!" I don't think a prouder sentence has ever crossed my lips. I stepped aside so they could see Jimmie. "We tell him all the time that there isn't anyone else in the world with a voice so beautiful."

The harmonica man said to him, "I played all over this country and I ain't never heard nothing like that in my life. Now, *I* ain't trying to boast, but I used to travel with Bessie Smith, and—I don't mean to disrespect her none, but she ain't half the singer you is. Not half. Not on her best day."

He reached his right hand toward Jimmie. "My name's Zeke Greene, folks call me Saw-Bone Zee, and it's a true honor to make the acquaintance of a brother musician like you, sir."

Sir!

It's horrible what one tiny word can do to you. You can talk yourself into believing that you're tough, then one tiny three-letter word gets said and smashes everything apart.

Sir!

I'd learned not to cry or even get angry when all sorts of calamity befell us. I'd learned not to take it personal when people barked at Mother and Jimmie and me about walking across their property, I knew how to swallow the sadness that would wash over me when Father used to come home and we could tell by the way he worried the brim of his hat when he asked how we were doing that there'd been no work. I thought I could control it all.

And then this man called Jimmie "sir" and all my hardness melted away.

It was wonderful that these people liked Jimmie's singing, but horrible too because I was still at the mercy of someone else's words. And Mother had told us so many times that that's something neither me nor Jimmie can afford to let happen, that we should take everything someone says, good or bad, with a grain of salt.

Jimmie took the man's hand. "My name's Jimmie Malone, sir."

"Pleased to meet you, I take it you're a natural, you ain't had no training?"

Jimmie looked surprised. "They can train someone to sing?"

"Not like what you done. That cain't be taught, that's from inside."

"Yes, sir, it is."

"You mind I ask how old you is?"

"I'm seventeen years old, sir."

With Jimmie, lying was just like singing, they both came natural to him.

"I knowed you was older than you look, ain't no kid gonna sing like that. From your singing I see you's a full-growned man."

Jimmie had hardened his heart twice as much as I had mine, but from the look that came over him I could see that when it came to those words *he* was totally lost.

Jimmie said, "You used to travel around with Bessie Smith? Really? You got paid to play with her? Cash money?"

"I ain't gonna say it always worked out that way, but that was the idea."

"And you really think I sing good as her?"

"I didn't say that, I said you's *better'n* her, raw, but better. With a little work y'all wouldn't even be playing in the same ballpark. Son, if things was the way they use to be you could make you some money traveling, might've even got someone to make one 'n'em Victrola recordings of you singing."

"Naw!"

"I said if things was the way they *use* to be. Ain't a whole lot of cash out here now for nothing. But if anybody was gonna rake in the little bit there is it'd be you. You got a true gift, son."

One of the women said, "Young man, can you and Zee sing a couple of songs? It's late, but tomorrow's Sunday so won't be no work nowhere."

I said, "Go on, Jimmie! Mr. Zee, do you know 'Motherless Child'?"

"You ain't gonna be able to name no spiritual I don't know. Young man, you up to giving these folks a little happiness?"

Jimmie slipped his feet into his brogans.

He said, "I ain't never sung with no one playing a instrument, don't we have to practice some first? How'm I gonna know when I'm suppose to come in and when I'm suppose to be quiet?"

"Don't worry none 'bout that. It's my job to know when to blow and when to shut up."

I pulled on my shoes. Me and Jimmie were smiling like a couple of Cheshire cats on Christmas Day in Gary.

I said, "We've enjoyed your playing ever since you came, sir. I told Jimmie and Mother that right along with Miss Toland, our Sunday school piano player back in Gar— back in Lancaster, you were the best musician I'd ever heard."

I slapped Jimmie's head. "We told you you were great! And you just didn't believe it!"

As we walked toward the fire Mr. Zee put his hand on Jimmie's shoulder. "When you working with other musicians you got to know your part. If it all come together right it's like that stew they made for supper. Everything blended just right.

Waren't too much of any one thing. When you and me play together, I'm suppose to make sure ain't too much mouth organ and too little you. You the meat in the stew, I ain't nothing but the salt."

There were about seven people still at the fire. Some were leaned up against each other close to sleep.

Mr. Zee sat on a stump. "What key you sing in?"

Jimmie said, "Key?"

The man smiled. "Hum the first bit of 'Shenandoah' again."

Jimmie did.

Mr. Zee blew some notes that blended in real nice with Jimmie.

He said, "It's on you, young man, 'Motherless Child.'"

Jimmie was staring into the fire, waiting until he was good and ready.

Some people started giving each other sideways looks, thinking he'd chickened out.

After the longest while Jimmie took a deep breath.

"Someti-i-i-imes I fe-e-el . . ."

The gooseflesh jumped through my palms as Jimmie sang:

". . . like a . . . motherless chi-ild.
Sometimes I feel like a motherless
chi-i-i-ild . . ."

A woman yelled, "Yes, Lord!"

Mr. Zee brought the harmonica in, and it was a perfect match for Jimmie's whispery voice.

A man said, "Testify, brother!"

Mr. Zee's playing danced around Jimmie's words and reminded me of something. In Gary on Friday nights, after dinner, a lot of the Mexican people and the black people would go to the church hall for storytelling.

I was shy when I first met the people from Mexico. They didn't look like us and they didn't look like white people. They had skin like ours and hair like white people's, only lots stronger and darker. They spoke a different language too.

Father was the best American storyteller, and a woman named Senior Rita Morales was the best one from Mexico. Miss Morales was a small-boned woman but when she spoke she was like Jimmie, she seemed to grow. She'd use her hands, and if she was talking about a star she'd reach up and gently pluck it. Then she'd look in her hand, like the star was resting there. If you followed her glance you could see it too, you could even see a shadow on the ground underneath.

Some superstitious Americans stopped coming because they said Senior Rita Morales was hypnotizing everybody, and who knew what she'd have folks doing once she got their minds?

Mother pooh-poohed them and said Senior Rita Morales was someone who could have words do magical things.

Miss Morales told the stories in her own language and in English both, and you could still understand everything! Even if you didn't know the word, something about the way she'd unfold her hands, or the way she'd smile, or the way she'd look at you when she talked let you know what she meant. If you waited it would come.

Jimmie and Mr. Zee were doing the same thing with their

music. They finished the song and Mr. Zee said, "Uh, uh, uh!" Jimmie grinned.

A white woman said in a dreamy voice, "My Gawd! Danny, go get your daddy's gee-tar!"

The white man Danny was sitting with put his hands on the boy's shoulder. "Rest easy, son. Thank you, Connie, but we're gonna let that gee-tar be tonight. I ain't got no intentions of being the alley cat at a gathering of lions."

In the middle of the third song I jumped when a hand lighted on my shoulder.

"Boo!"

"Oh, Mother!" I pulled her to sit next to me. "Do you see how they're watching Jimmie?"

Mother hugged her knees.

Jimmie would say a song and Mr. Zee would nod and play.

I poked her. "He isn't being even a little bit shy!"

"Singing belongs to him as much as writing does to you, Deza. Plus talking, we can't forget how comfortable you are with that." Mother loved teasing me for my verboseness.

People clapped as Jimmie walked over to us. "Can I stay awhile and talk to Mr. Saw-Bone? Tomorrow's Sunday."

I answered for Mother. I know her well enough that talking to me is like talking to her. Least I thought so up to this time. "Oh, yes! Stay as long as you'd like."

That wasn't how Mother would've answered. Her eyes widened just the littlest bit. But she said, "Yes, Jimmie, have a good time."

"Wow, sis, hasn't this been the best night ever?"

I laughed. "Indeed it has, indeed it has!"

Mother said, "Let's go down to the creek, Deza, the sound of the water is so soothing." She wasn't mad, but there was a sadness in her as we turned away from the dying fire.

* * *

"Mother, was I wrong?"

"No, Deza. It's fine that he stays. He works like a grown man so it's only right that he starts living like one too. Much as I may want to, I can't hold him forever."

I did what all good conversationalists do when they don't like the direction a talk is going, I changed the subject. "Tell me what it was like when you and Father met." That always made Mother light up.

She held my arm tighter and smiled. "Oh, Deza! We had that kind of happiness that can't help but draw attention to itself. We weren't trying to show off or anything, but there wasn't a bushel basket big enough or thick enough for us to keep our happiness hidden under."

I loved the times when Mother talked about Father courting her. The man she talked about who was serious and shy seemed different than the happy, jokey man I knew.

I dropped my head onto her shoulder and squeezed my arm around her waist. I knew all the answers but I asked anyway. "Were you two excited when me and Jimmie were born?"

"Your father told me, 'If I ruled the world, Peg, I'd give every brown-skinned baby a note as soon as they were born. It would read, *Hold tight, because the only thing guaranteed is, one way or the other, you're going to have a very interesting, very busy life.*'

"I said to him, 'Roscoe, that could be said about any baby.' He smiled and said, 'Maybe, but not to the same extent.' "

Mother and I laughed and teased all the way down the trail.

At the creek I squatted down to toss a twig into the water. I watched the twig bob along. It spun twice like it was trying to decide which way it should go, then bobbed off downstream.

I could hear the smile in Mother's voice. "You know one of the things I love most about my baby girl? You know one of the things I'm so thankful for?" I looked over my shoulder at her.

"I love the fact that you're so much smarter than I am. Took him a while to catch on, but you're smarter than your father too."

I studied her face. How could I be smarter than the smartest two people I knew?

"Really. No use pretending, Deza. I'll never forget the first time we realized how special you are. You never talked until you were almost three years old. Other than a lot of laughing and some crazy noises that your father called squinking, you hadn't said a peep.

"We told each other we weren't worried, though, because you were such a watcher. We could see you were understanding and taking things in. So we had strong hope that you were fine."

Mother smiled. "I admit I was a *little* worried, but your daddy said, 'Uh-uh, I got the feeling this one will talk when she's good and ready, and once she does, watch out!' "

"So what was my first word?"

" 'Why?' "

"Because I'm curious, Mother."

She slapped my arm. "No, silly, I wasn't asking 'why?' 'Why?' was your first word. Your grandmother Malone was visiting from Flint and she was moaning about the fact that we only had milk for her coffee and not cream. It went on forever. You were sitting in my lap and she said, 'What's a woman got to do to get some cream for her coffee around here? I've told Roscoe again and again that nonsense like this is why I stay in Flint.'" Mother laughed. "You piped up clear as day, 'Why don't you go to the store and buy some?' We wouldn't have been more shocked if the salt shaker told us it wanted to go for a walk."

"That was the first thing I said?"

"No, not 'that.' It was 'why?'"

I splashed her. I hadn't seen her acting silly for the longest. "*Mother!*"

"Your grandmother was not amused. She wanted to skin you alive. You always frightened her. She said she never liked the way you watched everything like you were a spy and that if she was raising you she'd get that smart-mouthedness out of you in two shakes of a lamb's tail.

"Imagine that, instead of being amazed and thrilled that you were saying full, grammatically correct sentences, she was mad because you hadn't called her ma'am! And your father was right, you talked nonstop the rest of the day. I couldn't wait for him to get home to hear!

"When he got off work and came in the front door I told you not to say anything to him till he talked to you first so we could surprise him.

"He picked you up, said something ridiculous like, 'How's

Daddy's Darling Daughter Deza doing on this delightful dusky day?' and child, he nearly dropped you like you were on fire when you said, 'Fine, thank you, but Gram is mad at me, Daddy. She wants cream for her coffee, not milk.'

"He bawled like a baby, and you wiped his tears and told him, 'Don't cry, Daddy, she's mad at Mommy and me, not you.' He'd been scared to death that there was something wrong. That was when we first knew what a special child we had."

Mother leaned down and splashed some of the creek water on her face. Seeing Mother like this was beautiful.

Jimmie was right, this had been the best night ever.

Chapter Twenty-Four

Losing Jimmie

I couldn't tell what had been said but I went from deep asleep to wide awake. It was still dark outside. Mother was sitting up, looking at the closed gingham curtain with her mouth half open. Jimmie's blanket was empty.

"Mother?"

She shook her head. "I don't know. Someone shouted."

We asked each other, "Where's Jimmie?"

The shantytown was coming alive, not like it did most mornings, with gentle sounds, tonight it was feet hitting hard on the ground and quick broke-off conversations.

I jumped to the door and looked outside. The fire had burned itself into a dull orange glow.

People were snatching their things and tossing them into blankets and sacks. Mostly men.

One ran by our door.

I asked him, "What's wrong?"

"Those dirty dogs are trying to sneak the train out early!"

I looked back. Mother had spread her blanket and was tossing everything we owned onto it.

"It's not the police, Mother! They're taking the train out early."

More and more men and boys ran past our door. The little boy I'd done dishes with stumbled past, looking more lost than he had before, squeezing a ratty old suitcase to his chest.

I said, "Hey!"

But he didn't hear me.

I stepped back into the shack. Mother reached out her hand. She was holding a folded page from my notebook.

"Not another drawing."

"Worse."

I took the paper and walked out of the shack where there was more light.

Dear Mother and Deza,

mr. Z thinks we can fine werk in chicargo or new yerk I no youd want to stop me but a mans got to do what a mans got to do I have to try plees understand I will rite and sen all I urn to genurel delivry in flint I promise I sware rite to me genurel delifery in chicargo or may be new yerk sis keep up the job in skool you make us all prowd and Ill make you prowd to I sware please don't wory I love both of you Jimmie Malone.

Mother said, "I knew he wouldn't stay much longer."

"We have to stop him! Jimmie can't be on his own, we don't even know who Mr. Sawbuck Zee is." I pulled my shoes on. Mother hadn't moved.

"Deza, once one of these Malones decides it's time to go nothing can stop him."

I stood in the door. "Can't I try? What harm would that do?"

"Go ahead, sweetheart, but be careful."

"When I'm done with that Jimmie Malone he'll be wishing he never thought of leaving us!" I stepped outside our shack. I couldn't believe how many people were living in this shantytown. I'd never seen everyone at the same time.

I started in the direction the men were running. I began going faster and faster, it felt like something was coming off of the running men, pushing and pulling at me to keep up. Someone would bump into me, say, "'Scuse me," then hurry on. Once I was running all-out the crowd got thicker and thicker and just before we crossed out of the woods a explosion of sparks and smoke came from the right. We all stopped and looked at the reddish fireball that danced over the tops of the trees.

A man yelled, "They're firing it up!"

The stream of people began moving forward.

When I broke out of the trees it was like I'd walked into a battle from King Arthur's times.

The freight train stretched out like a gigantic dragon. What looked like a black-and-orange smoky genie squatted down over the top of the engine's smokestack.

People stood waiting, but it wasn't a patient wait, it was more like the spring on a clock that was being wound tighter and tighter. Then I saw why.

About ten policemen stood with billy clubs all along the sides of the train cars.

The crouching genie exploded up and out of the smokestack, as tall and dangerous as a volcano erupting, dancing over the stack with a roar that made the hair on my neck tingle.

Everyone looked at the dark cloud and river of sparks that belched out of the smokestack, then turned their eyes back on the police. At that second the spring had been wound as tight as it could go and snapped.

A policeman threw down his club and stepped aside. Then two more did. Then the rest.

I hung on to a big tree as the men ran past me toward the train.

The train's wheels groaned and the cars banged and clanked ahead. Those sounds made the men move faster. There was no way in the world I'd be able to find Jimmy amongst all of these people.

I promised myself to remember everything about the last time we'd talked and how happy he'd been. I grabbed hold of the last thing Jimmie had said to me. "Wow, sis! Hasn't this been the best night ever?"

Whatever else happens, this is what I'll always remember about Jimmie. Not the twitches and jerks he does when he's trying to sleep, not the way his expression never changes when Mother shakes her head to let us know there's been no word from Father, not the sadness in his eyes ever since we figured out he was going to stay the size of a twelve-year-old-boy his whole life.

No. I'm going to remember the way he looked so proud and

lit-up and carefree a few hours ago when he ran back to talk to Mr. Sawbuck Zee. It was like he was driving his rocket ship.

When the train disappeared and I couldn't hear the chugging of the engine, sounds came from the direction of the shantytown that had me running toward our shack faster than I'd run away.

I yelled, "Mother!" and had to dodge three children who were coming from the shantytown like they'd seen a ghost. A woman screamed over and over as gunshots bounced around in the woods.

"Mother!"

Chapter Twenty-Five

Back on the Road

I ran toward the orange glow right in front of our shack. The fire had grown much larger. Something flew through the air and landed in the middle of the flames. The fire whooshed and sparks flew up like a swarm of fireflies and flickered in the dark sky. A big-boned white man was throwing the sides of people's homes into the fire. Something that looked like a wildly flapping pack of pigeons flew straight into the sky, then landed in the fire. It was Miss Stew's *Reader's Digests*.

I looked over toward our place. The blue gingham curtain was still hanging down.

I started toward the shack to see if Mother was inside, then stopped as gunshots banged out twice more. I ducked. A white man on the other side of the fire was pointing down with a gun and shooting. He reached his gun down into the big stew kettle and fired. He was ruining it so no one could use it.

I pushed the curtain aside. For the second time Mother was putting everything back into the blanket. She'd already bundled and tied the one that I'd carry.

"Thank goodness you're back! Move quickly, I might be able to get us back into Flint."

"Might? Can't we just take the road there?"

"The police said no one's to go into Flint. They'll block all the ways into the city."

Mother tied the four corners of her blanket together and the bundle clanged as she threw it over her shoulder. She gave me a tired smile. "OK, Miss Malone, once more into the breach."

I picked up my bundle and slung it over my shoulder. Mother had made mine half as heavy as hers. "We'll take turns with the big one," I said.

We hugged. "Sweetheart, I'm so glad you're here for me to lean on."

I held the gingham curtain aside, and once Mother was out, I looked back into the place that had been our home for the past months. Now that we didn't know where we were going next, this raggedy hut seemed pretty wonderful. I held the curtain up. "Will they throw something this beautiful into the fire?"

"Deza, let's go! I promise, one day I'll get yards of store-bought gingham and make you a dress."

Outside, a big white man with a tired voice was saying over

and over, "Keep up that road there, and if you don't want no trouble don't come back."

We followed the crowd away from the fire. We'd only been walking for a few minutes when Mother steered me to the side of the road. "Deza! I left my wedding ring in the shack!"

Since we'd left Gary, Mother's wedding band had gotten so big that it was slipping off her finger at work. She put it on a string and wore it around her neck.

I pointed. "No, the string is right around your neck."

Her hand flew to her throat. "Oh! No, no. I took the ring off the string last week."

Mother was acting odder all the time. I put my bundle down. "I'll be right back."

"No, I'll get it! I know exactly where it is. Don't leave this spot no matter what."

I watched as she ran toward one of the policemen. My stomach knotted when he raised his club and jabbed his hand toward the road.

Oh, please, please . . .

Mother pointed back at me and kept talking.

Stay back, Mother, don't get too close . . .

He kept his club raised and with his other hand jabbed at the road again.

Please, please . . .

Mother kept talking and finally the cop brought the club down to his side. Mother headed into the woods to where the shantytown was slowly being turned to ashes.

I sat on the side of the road and watched our neighbors walk away.

They were mostly women with children tied to their backs or hanging on to their clothes or trailing behind like tired duck-lings. A few old men hobbled along with the group. Anyone who was strong enough to work was on that train with Jimmie.

No one complained. This was just the way it was.

If somebody came along and saw us walking they'd mistake us for a very quiet parade instead of what we really were, a river of people who didn't know what city we'd be in tomorrow, or what we'd be eating, or even where somebody would let us stop and rest.

The only way someone might suspect something was wrong was because of the fresh ones. I hadn't understood what the hobo with the beautiful beard had meant when he said we were fresh, but now I got it.

There weren't a lot of them, but all of the fresh ones, young and old, had a certain look, a expression that anyone who's been on the road for a while has had scrubbed off their faces.

It wasn't like they were worried or feeling sorry for them-selves, they had a look of surprise, like they couldn't believe what had happened. You can't know that feeling unless you've had it.

One day you're living in your own home, and then it seems like with no warning, the next day you're carrying everything you own in a blanket or a sack or a ratty suitcase while being shooed from one place to another like a fly.

"Little Stew, you all right? Can we help you carry some-thing?" A white man and his son had come over to me.

"No, thank you. My mother had to run back, she'll be along in a minute."

The man said, "You sure? Camden here is strong as a ox."

The boy, who looked about six years old, made a muscle with his right arm. "Wanna see?"

I laughed. "Thank you, Camden, but we're OK."

He kept his fist balled. "You *sure* you don't wanna see?" He looked like he'd explode if I didn't feel his muscle. I squeezed his skinny arm.

"Wow! With muscles like that you could probably lift a whole automobile over your head!"

He smiled. "Well, maybe I could get the front wheels off the ground."

"Thanks, Camden."

They headed back down the road. In the next couple of minutes five other people stopped and asked the same thing.

Mother finally came back.

I said, "Did you get it?"

She looked like she had no idea what I was talking about.

"Your ring."

She touched her throat. "Yes. That was close."

I was starting to worry about her.

We fell in line with the other people. We'd walked for a half hour when the road split in two directions. People started dividing into two groups. There were hugs, pats on backs and even tears as they said goodbye.

Most of the white people started down the road leading south. Most of the black people walked north.

Someone told Mother there might be work in Saginaw, Michigan, which is geologically located about twenty miles north of Flint.

But Mother steered us south.

"We've got to get back into Flint. I have to work, and you have to go to school."

"But how will we get past the—"

"I don't know, Deza, but where there's a will there's a way."

* * *

"A way" meant we did a whole night of walking to circle the city.

It was very late when we knocked on the door of one of the women Mother worked with.

Even though we woke her up, Mrs. Brand said we could sleep on the floor of one of the two rooms she shared with her family.

When I woke up the next morning, Mother had already gone to her first job.

I was surprised I was so tired the night before that I hadn't seen how many people were in the room, and I felt terrible that we'd taken over the little bit of space that was left. I stepped over three of them and headed toward the tiny kitchen.

"Good morning, Mrs. Brand."

"Morning, Deza. You've got another hour before you need to get up for school."

"Yes, ma'am, but I thought I could help you."

"Thank you, dear. You can go out back and get some wood if you don't mind."

"How much do we need?"

"Just enough for the stove, we got some grits and greens I'll hotten up for breakfast."

The house started waking up and more and more people walked by the kitchen on the way to the outhouse. All but two of them were kids.

I missed Jimmie already. But I couldn't let myself worry about him. Or Father. That made two of them I wouldn't think about.

When it was time to go to school Mrs. Brand said, "Your mother told me you're to come here after school, she won't come back between jobs, she's going to look for a room to rent. She knows you two are welcome here as long as you need."

"Thank you, ma'am." Me and one of the big girls, Analise, walked the youngest kids to Clark Elementary School. Then we went on to Whittier Junior High.

Mother and Mrs. Brand were sitting on the front porch when I got home.

Mother was smiling!

She dangled two keys. "Deza, we've got a place! It's just one room, but it's right between Whittier and downtown. No more half-hour walks for us, my dear!"

"What about the post office?"

"It's not far at all. You can check every day!"

Chapter Twenty-Six

Settled

We shared the kitchen and indoor bathroom with two other families and a teacher from Clark Elementary School. Our room was almost perfect. We had everything we needed, a table, two chairs, a wardrobe and a bed that had a big dip in the center.

Me and Mother would get up and fix breakfast. She'd go to her first job, check the post office on the way home in the afternoon, then take a nap. She'd be up when I got home from school, we'd chat, make supper and she'd go to her evening job at the hotel.

Since we had a address now, I wrote to Jimmie at general delivery in New York and Chicago. Maybe he'd answer. I could also check out books from the library! After school I'd choose two, and since I wasn't doing very much studying, I could go home and read. On Fridays I'd take out six books for the weekend. I'd also check for word from Jimmie or Father at the post office.

I got to be friends with the postmistress, Mrs. James, a kind old white woman. She knew we were waiting for news and promised to keep a extra-sharp eye open for me.

One day I went by and said, "Hello, Mrs. James."

"Deza, how are you, I haven't seen your mother for over a month, is she OK?"

I knew it! I knew Mother had stopped checking!

I said, "She's working two jobs."

"I see. How's school going?"

"Fine, thank you. But Flint schools are a lot easier than Gary's. The things they're teaching here I learned two years ago in Indiana. I don't even have to study." So that wouldn't sound like bragging I said, "But I can't believe how much I've forgotten."

She smiled, "Sorry, no mail today, Deza. I'll keep hoping for you."

"Thank you, Mrs. James."

Hoping is such hard work. It tires you out and you never seem to get any kind of reward. Hoping feels like you're a balloon that has a pinhole that slowly leaks air.

If Mother wasn't even checking the mail, that meant she'd stopped hoping. But who could blame her? I was pretty close to being through myself.

* * *

And school was making things worse.

Mrs. Scott never asked me to help other students and

never gave me any tougher work. Mrs. Dales in geography, Mrs. Foley in civics, Mr. Alton in history and Mr. Smith in English never called on me when I raised my hand. So I stopped raising it.

The Deza Malone in Gary would have been crushed. Her heart would have withered like grapes left on a vine at the North Pole in the middle of winter.

The Flint Deza didn't care.

I toughened up so much that I stopped even caring about literature in English class. The less I cared at school, the more I read.

And it wasn't long before that wasn't the same either.

When I was in Gary and would read novels I used to put myself right in the middle of the story. I knew it was a great book when it felt like the author was writing about me. Some of the time I'd get snapped out of the book when I read things that I couldn't pretend were about me, even if I had the imagination of Mr. William Shakespeare.

Words like "her pale, luminescent skin" or "her flowing mane of golden hair" or "her lovely, cornflower-blue eyes" or "the maiden fair." I would stop and think, No, Deza, none of these books are about you.

I'd decided in Gary that when it came to reading those kinds of words, I had four choices: one, I could pretend I had blond hair and blue eyes. But that didn't feel right. Two, I could start reading the novels like they were history books, just a bunch of facts put together. But that wasn't what the authors wanted, they wanted me to enjoy the story the way they wrote it. Three, I could change a word or two here or there and keep enjoying them by pretending they *were* about me, or four, I could stop reading novels altogether.

Jimmie was right when he said I couldn't stop reading if I wanted to, and a whole lot of the enjoying comes from imagining it's you charging at windmills or asking for more gruel or trying to wash invisible blood off of your hands.

I'd decided a long time ago that I'd ignore those interrupting words and keep reading.

I look at my novels the same way Mother looks at buggy oatmeal: there might be a few bad things in them, but if you plugged your nose or sifted them out, there was still something pretty good left.

But some of the books Mr. Smith assigned were just too terrible to pretend that they were anything but stinkers. And the biggest stinkers of all were some of his favorite books, stories about a rich, bratty little white boy named Penrod.

One thing being a student at Whittier did was make me understand, for the first time, how other kids didn't think waking up to go to school was the most wonderful thing in the world.

I got it now.

* * *

October turned into November, then December. Even though we heard nothing from Jimmie I kept sending letters to general delivery.

1937 came and January changed to February. I came home on the twelfth and Mother and the people we share the house with—Mr. Alums, the Wilsons, and the Eppses—gave me a huge surprise!

I walked up to the porch and thought it was strange that no children were playing there. I walked down the hall to our room. It was funny that there wasn't any noise or talking anywhere in the house. I unlocked our door and eleven people yelled, "Happy birthday!"

I'd forgotten! I was a teenager now!

The Wilsons gave me a pair of their oldest daughter's shoes! They fit like a glove. The Eppses gave me their son's coveralls that he'd outgrown, they were practically new!

But the two best gifts came from Mr. Alums and Mother.

He's the only black teacher in Flint, he teaches at Clark Elementary and has all of the kids terrified of him. But he's always friendly to us.

He said, "Miss Malone, I've noticed the books you've been reading, and I think you are quite capable of handling these."

He handed me *The Quest of the Silver Fleece*, by W. E. B. DuBois, and *Quicksand*, by Nella Larsen.

"Thank you, Mr. Alums!"

Mother said to Ronald Epps, "Go get it, please."

He came back holding two one-gallon tubs of ice cream! One chocolate and one vanilla!

We ate like pigs and laughed for the longest time. After everyone left and me and Mother cleaned up she smiled. "I've got one more gift for you, Deza."

"Really?"

She reached under the bed and handed me a neatly wrapped package. It was soft, like it had clothes in it.

I sat on the bed. "What style?"

"Whichever."

I chose Flint style and shredded the wrapping.

It was the kind of blouse worn by the white women at the front desk in the hotel where Mother cleans. It had HOTEL DURANT written in fancy letters on a pocket on the chest. It was nicely pressed and starched and crisp.

Mother said, "I bought it from one of the girls who works up front."

"I love it!" We hugged and she reached under the bed and pulled out another package.

I opened it and was shocked!

Mother had given me the best gift I ever could get.

It was a jumper made from blue gingham!

"Mother! How could we afford this?"

"It was free!"

"*Free?*"

"Free. Remember when we left the camp?"

"Of course."

"Remember how I went back to get my ring?"

"Yes."

Mother slapped my arm. "I can't believe you fell for that! Did you honestly think I'd leave my wedding band anywhere?"

"Well . . ."

"Deza! You even saw the string around my neck and *still* didn't catch on!"

"Catch on to what?"

"The curtain, Deza, I went back for the blue gingham curtain!"

"This . . ."

"Yes, my sweet, naïve darling, yes!"

I felt like such a idiot!

Mother said, "After I'd cut away the worn parts there was only enough material to make a jumper, that's why I bought the blouse. No one will ever see 'Hotel Durant' written on it when you wear the jumper. Try them on."

They were even more beautiful together.

We laughed and twirled for the longest time.

For two more hours I thought the jumper was the best gift I'd ever get, until . . .

* * *

I was too excited to sleep. Mother fell off and I quietly got out of bed.

I picked up the two books Mr. Alums had given me. They both had nice covers. I'd read about Jason and the golden fleece so I started reading about the silver one.

It started in a swamp. It said something about a boy's brown cheek and I read it again to make sure. Yes, his brown cheek.

I got a sinking feeling, so many times stories that have people with brown skin turn out terrible, but I read on.

The book grabbed me and shook me like a soon-to-die rat in a terrier's jaws! It was about black people and they had real problems and thoughts and did real things, not like the black people in so many other books. Nothing like in *Penrod.*

I started to read it a second time.

I was so startled that I screamed at the top of my lungs when the alarm clock rang.

Mother screamed too.

In a heartbeat Mr. Alums banged on the door. "What's wrong? Are you all right?"

Mother went to the door. "Sorry, Mr. Alums, we startled each other, we're fine."

I yelled, "Mr. Alums! I read *The Silver Fleece*. This book . . . what a tragedy . . . a true tragedy it had to end. This is a work of true genius! The people in it are so real and so much like people. This is the best book I have ever read!"

Mr. Alums was my new hero!

Chapter Twenty-Seven

The Letter!

Mother had warned me time and time again. But I couldn't help it.

One day at school Mr. Smith got tired of teaching and gave us assigned reading time halfway through class. I had another horrible Penrod book on my desk, but I was really reading what was in my lap, *The Quest of the Silver Fleece*, for the fifth time.

You can tell you're reading a really good book when you forget all about everything else and know you'll die if you don't get to at least the end of the chapter. That was what Mother had warned me not to do anywhere but home, but Mr. Alums was giving me more and more books that I loved and couldn't put down.

And that can be dangerous.

I didn't hear the bell dismissing class.

Mr. Smith said, "Well, Deeza, I suppose Mr. Tarkington and I should be flattered you're enjoying *Penrod* so much that you don't want to leave, but I've got to lock up."

"I'm sorry, Mr. Smith, I was just—"

"No problem, you're a real credit to your race. See you tomorrow."

As I walked from school I still had about ten pages till the end of the chapter. I did what Mother had warned me not to and walked and read at the same time.

When I looked up I'd walked three blocks past the post office!

Maybe I'd just keep walking home, it wouldn't be a big deal if I came next Friday.

But I turned around.

I didn't stop reading, though, I knew when I finished the book my hands would shake, my eyes would rim with tears and I'd say, "A masterpiece, a work of true genius! What a tragedy, a true tragedy that it had to end!"

I pushed the post office door open and everything froze.

Mrs. James was holding a envelope over her head and screaming, "Deza! I've been waiting! I think this is it!"

My book crashed to the floor. I was dumbstruck.

She came around the little gate waving the letter.

"It was postmarked in Cleveland and it's to you and your mother!"

I stared at it. This was what I wanted more than anything else in the world and now I couldn't even move.

She put her hand on my shoulder. "Deza, dear, do you want me to open it?" She picked up my book and led me to a chair.

I took the envelope. It was written by a typewriter.

Mrs. Margaret Malone and Mistress Deza Malone
Care of General Delivery
Flint, Michigan

"Deza? Are you all right?"

"Oh. Yes. I . . . I . . . I . . . it's not from my father, it's from my brother."

"How can you tell?"

"If it was from Father he would have put all three of our names on it."

I turned it over and over.

"Is it against the law for me to open the letter or should both me and Mother do it?"

"Your name is on it so you can open it." She smiled and patted my hand. "Besides, Miss Malone, I bet it's an absolute impossibility for you to walk all the way home and get there with that envelope still sealed."

Father would have been proud of the Flint-style way I ripped the envelope open.

Mrs. James picked up the pieces and said, "Dear me, Deza, I know you're excited, but this is the U.S. Mail, sweetheart, you have to be respectful!"

I unfolded the page inside. I expected one of Jimmie's

terrible drawings, but the letter was typed. He must've got someone to do it for him.

Dear Peg and Darling Daughter Deza,

I looked at the first words over and over, it didn't make sense, why would Jimmie . . . then it hit me, this *wasn't* from Jimmie, it had to be from Father!

I stopped breathing and had to read each sentence twice before I could understand it.

It was from Father!

I have missed you two so much, every day has been a heartache for me. Don't worry, I am fine, I have asked a friend to type this since I hurt my right hand in an accident. It is not very serious, I am able to work but I still can't hold a pen properly. The doctor told me it will take maybe a year before I am completely healed.

Now for the great news. I have found work as a traveling carpenter! I make good money and travel all over the country. I will send money every two weeks. We will be able to rent a house in Gary before much longer.

I hope this finds you well and in great spirits.

Love,
Father

I read it again.

And again.

The fourth time through I had to stop, tears were clouding my eyes so much I couldn't see.

Mrs. James said, "Oh, please tell me it's good news, Deza."

"Oh, Mrs. James, Father's OK! He got a job! He's working as a carpenter."

We fell into each other's arms.

"Child, I am so happy for you."

She handed me something that had fallen out of the envelope when I ripped it apart. It was a piece of paper that had been folded and taped shut.

Out fluttered two of the greenest, brightest, cleanest-looking dollar bills I had ever seen! I picked up the money. They weren't dollar bills. They were *five*-dollar bills!

I had never seen this much money in my life!

"Oh, my, Deza. In the future you must treat the mail with more care. Look at this!"

"Are these real?"

She took the bills. "I went into the wrong profession, I should have become a carpenter!"

I hugged her again, put Father's letter in my book and flew home. I couldn't wait to see how flabbergasted Mother was going to be!

* * *

As soon as I got home I started arguing with myself about how to give Mother the good news.

It isn't the way of the Malones to come right out and tell anybody anything, so I had to think up a way to surprise her.

Should I pretend I was so sad about something that she'd pull me into her lap and say, "Kisses . . . kisses . . . kisses make you stronger"? And then give her the letter?

Should I put the letter under her pillow so the next morning she'd find it like the tooth fairy had visited? The more I thought about it the more confused I felt.

I put on my Hotel Durant blouse and blue gingham jumper. When I climbed on the bed and read the letter for the fifth time, I started crying, I don't know why.

I remembered how my tears messed up Clarice's goodbye note, so to be safe, I got up and put the letter in our new file cabinet under the mattress.

I curled back up on the bed. I wished Mother would hurry home.

I didn't want to, but I bawled and bawled and bawled.

And that's how Mother found me a hour later. I pulled the letter out and handed it to her.

She didn't act near as excited as I thought she would. She kept looking from the letter to the two five-dollar bills. She flashed her 1-1-1 lines before she said, "Oh, Deza, isn't this wonderful?"

Her heart wasn't in those words. Maybe it was just relief, maybe you can hold on to something bad for so long that when you put it down you don't trust the feeling.

That had to be why both of us weren't bouncing around the room.

"I'm still going to check at the post office every day," I said.

"Deza, it says he'll write again in two weeks, why don't you start checking closer to then?"

"I'd just die if Father's next letter sat at the post office one day longer than it had to."

She smiled. "Fine, but leave the library fifteen minutes early and come right home afterwards."

That night, I thought I'd have trouble sleeping, but when Mother kissed me and said, "Good night, my darling," the last thing I remember thinking was, Two weeks. Two long, slow weeks, then I *know* something good is going to happen.

* * *

I had just left the library when a man called out, "Miss Jones?"

I kept walking.

He yelled again, "Miss Jones!"

There was no one around but me. I could hear him coming nearer. I closed my book and started walking faster.

The man started running at me!

I looked for help, but I was on a block of vacant lots and empty homes.

"Wait! Miss Jones, hold on for a minute."

I turned around and did what Mother and Father always told me to do if something like this happens, I yelled at the top of my lungs, "*My name is not Jones! Leave me alone! Someone help me! This man is bothering me!*" I took in a breath to keep yelling but the man stopped and put both of his hands up.

"Whoa! Whoa! It's me, Saw-Bone Zee! Don't you remember? From the camp, the harmonica man? I'm sorry, missy, I mistook you for Jimmie's sister."

"Mr. Zee! You scared me to death!"

He laughed. "I *thought* that was you. How are you and your ma?"

"Do you know where Jimmie is? Is he here with you?"

"Y'all ain't heard?"

"Oh, please, Mr. Zee, if it's bad news just tell me."

"Bad news? Your brother is doing real good. I thought for sure he was writing to y'all. Must've got lost in the mail."

"Please, Mr. Zee, what happened to Jimmie?"

"He's doing just grand, he's singing in nightclubs."

"*What?*"

"It's like I told y'all, if there was anybody who could squeeze a penny or two outta folks in these hard times it would be him and that voice."

"You aren't traveling with him, he's all alone?"

"Well now, that's sort of a sore subject with me. Jimmie's fell in with a shady manager calls hisself Maxwell. I got cut loose."

"Do you know where he is?"

"He travels a lot on the chitlin' circuit, but I'm pretty sure that right now he's singing mostly outta Maxwell's nightclub in Dee-troit, joint called the New Turned Leaf."

"What's a nightclub?"

"That's just a fancy name for a blind pig or a speakeasy."

I'd heard lots of horrible things about speakeasies, they were where people went to drink alcohol and fight with each other. "Mr. Zee, can you wait so I can write this down? I'm so excited I know I'll forget." I got my pencil and opened my notebook. "Sir, Jimmie and my last name is Malone, not Jones."

He snapped his fingers. "I forgot! That Maxwell clown had Jimmie change his name to Jones."

"What? Why?"

"Who knows, but ask near anyone in Dee-troit 'bout Little Jimmie Jones and they'll know who you mean."

Mr. Sawbuck Zee gave me the address of the nightclub in Detroit. Then he said, "When you see him tell him I ain't mad, he done what he had to. I been in this business long enough to know what's what."

"Thank you again, sir, and I'll tell him." I started running home to give Mother the news!

Three things stopped me.

First, my heart was pounding so hard and fast and my legs were so wobbly and weak that it felt like I'd already run a mile. I bent over to catch my breath.

The second thing was I could almost hear Mother say, "Deza, that's just a rumor, if Jimmie was making money you know he'd write to us," or, "If Jimmie was as near as Detroit he would've come to see us."

But he hadn't.

And the third thing was when I heard my second brain, "OK, kiddo, you know doggone well Mother isn't going to run to Detroit to try to find Jimmie. In a speakeasy?"

My second brain laughed at me, then added, "And you know you don't have half the nerve it would take to even *ask* her if you could go by yourself!"

I squeezed down on my back teeth.

That second brain was right, I'd never be brave enough to do it on my own.

Unless . . .

Chapter Twenty-Eight

The New Turned Leaf

Mother's favorite saying is "Where there's a will, there's a way," and my will was strong enough to find a way to write her a note, borrow money out of the filing cabinet, buy a Greyhound bus ticket and come to Detroit. All by myself.

It was ten o'clock at night and for the first time in my life I wasn't in bed asleep. Instead I was squeezing my pocketbook to my chest, standing behind a tree in Detroit, Michigan. Across the street was the address that Mr. Zee said was the New Turned Leaf, a speakeasy! A nightclub!

I kept peeking at the house trying to figure it out. I know you can't read what someone's like by the way they look. The person who seems to be kind and understanding may be using that look to hide something horrible, while the person who at first sight scares you might turn out to be the gentlest soul you'll ever meet. And things like houses hide their secrets even better than people do. Things don't even have to try.

My heart sank. Nothing seemed to match up with the horrible rumors I've always heard about speakeasies.

The minute I decided I was going to come to Detroit by myself I'd been scared to death about what I'd see once I got to the New Turned Leaf. I thought there'd be all sorts of loose grown-ups half-undressed shouting and fighting. I thought there'd be drunken men laying in the mud next to a pile of people who'd been stabbed or shot or had drunk themselves to death that night.

I imagined having to cover my ears to block out the gut-wretching wails of children who were crying to their mothers or fathers not to spend all the grocery money on whisky and beer or dice.

But if those things were going on in this place you could have fooled me. This New Turned Leaf was about the most unexciting thing I could think of. It looked the same as any other very nice house that rich people lived in.

The curtains on both floors were drawn and were so thick that if there *were* lamps on inside you'd never know. The front yard was tidy, with a strip of geraniums growing along the sidewalk. There wasn't even a sign that let you know what this was, only the number 3121 lit up under a porch light.

The only thing that made me think this was more than just a regular rich person's home was that in the few minutes I stood behind the tree, four couples and three or four men by themselves walked through the gate and followed the sidewalk to disappear around the back of the house.

The men were all wearing very fancy suits and hats and ties. Mr. Marvelous Marvin would have fit right in here. The women were in some of the most beautiful dresses and shoes I'd ever seen! A lot of Sunday-going-to-church hats had escaped from their boxes a couple of days early!

I was so glad I was wearing my blue gingham jumper. I'd stick out like a roach floating in buttermilk in my other dress.

One or two of the men were walking in that rooster-strutting way that Jimmie and his hoodlum friends did back home in Gary. Everybody nodded or shook hands with the short, thick man half hidden in shadows leaning against the side of the house.

I got the feeling he wasn't about to let just any-old-body go past him without some kind of trouble, even a scared-looking girl dressed in very nice blue gingham.

The curtains in one of the windows came apart and a triangle of light shone through the darkness. A tiny head, it looked like a five- or six-year-old girl's, was at the base of the triangle of light and a pair of eyes locked right on me. She must've been watching me as long as I'd been watching the house. She raised her hand to wave, then jerked her head around to look back into the room. The curtains fell and smothered the light.

I started walking to the corner so I could circle around the house but hadn't gone five steps before my second brain started filling my head with its usual nonsense.

"Well, kiddo, what if that child is a prisoner in this speakeasy? What if the little girl was getting ready to signal you to call the police when one of the murderers or drinkers or thieves or gamblers who were holding her prisoner came back into the room to make sure she hadn't escaped? What then?"

"Concentrate, Deza!" I kept walking toward the corner.

My heart started pounding once I turned down the alley. Maybe Jimmie wasn't here after all, maybe he was traveling, and maybe I should give up and go back to Flint.

I kept walking past the speakeasy, cutting my eyes at it so if someone was watching they'd think I was just a girl walking through a alley, not someone looking to find their brother or rescue a little girl who'd been kidnapped by gamblers.

Then something made the doubts go away. A door on the side of the house that didn't have any kind of knob on it opened and a man came out.

He only took a few steps, then dropped to his hands and knees. Two times his back bucked up like one of those rodeo horses in the movies. He started throwing up more junk than you'd think a human being could ever have swallowed! And the best thing was, when he finally got up and started running on his tiptoes toward the front of the house, I saw that the door hadn't closed all the way behind him!

Doors without knobs? People coming out to throw up? Guards hiding in the shadows? Little girls held prisoner upstairs? When you added everything up, this was a for-sure speakeasy!

I watched the man on tiptoes until he turned the corner. Once he disappeared I held my breath and slowly walked to the door.

I put my ear near the crack. No screaming or loud noises.

I put my fingers in the door and pulled it open so I could peek in. My head started spinning and I don't know if it was from relief or disappointment. There was nothing but a narrow hallway. A bright lightbulb hung from a wire and there was another closed door at the other end. This one had a knob on it.

I stepped into the New Turned Leaf and shut the door behind me.

I walked to the second door, and without thinking what might be on the other side, I grabbed the knob, turned and pushed at the door.

It didn't budge.

I leaned my shoulder into it and pushed really hard. It came open a crack. I put all my weight into the next push and the heavy door moved far enough for me to stick my head through.

For the second time that night my head started spinning.

But this time it had good reason!

Chapter Twenty-Nine

The Man in the Beautiful Two-Tone Shoes

It was like I'd rubbed the magic lamp of the Forty Thieves! A strong smoky smell slipped through the crack of the door. Hard adult laughs laced themselves up in the smoke and rolled out with it. I had to blink and wipe at my eyes as the cigarette smoke stung them. I saw three round tables in a large dark room. Each table had six chairs set around it. There was a candle in a glass jar in the middle of the tables.

A woman turned to look in my direction.

The light from the hall was drawing attention so I stepped inside, closed the door, pressed my back against the wall and slid to the left. The woman stopped looking and I kept sliding until I came to a stack of chairs. I squeezed behind them so that I was hidden.

My heart was slapping at my ribs and I was having a hard time catching my breath. If my head felt any lighter I was going to end up swooning behind this pile of chairs.

I remembered what Jimmie had said once about being scared, that if you pretended you were watching what was going on through a telescope you got a lot calmer.

"And take three of the deepest breaths that you can, three's a magic number and if you breathe deep three times you ain't got no choice but relaxing."

By the third breath I had to smile. Even though I'd pulled three giant puffs of stinking, smoky air into me it worked and I was a lot calmer.

Now that my eyes were used to the dark I peeked from behind the chairs to get a look around the inside of the New Turned Leaf. It was more like a cave instead of a room! There must have been ten other round tables full of people spread out across one half of the place.

The other half of the room was empty for a bit, then there was a piano, a set of drums, a giant fiddle, a beautiful, shining gold saxophone and a microphone. Seeing the microphone gave me hope, maybe, just maybe, Jimmie *was* singing here.

I began noticing other things in the room. On one side was a swinging door with a round window and each time the door swung open kitchen sounds joined with the voices in the speakeasy. Women were going in and out. Mother would say their clothes were scandalous, their skirts didn't seem to be much more than a couple of handkerchiefs sewn together. The skirts flapped and sparkled in the light.

There was just as little to their blouses. Their shoulders and arms were bare like movie stars in Hollywood magazines.

I nearly jumped out of my shoes when a loud boom came from the stage.

Lights came on and four men were sitting on the stage with instruments in their hands.

My heart sank. No Jimmie.

People started clapping and a little cheer went up.

The musicians started playing and I was shocked!

I'd heard music on the radio and in moving picture theaters before, but this was different. It was beautiful and warm and went right into my body!

The man at the piano said into a microphone, "Good evening, ladies and gentlemen, thank you for joining us this evening in beautiful Dee-troit, Michigan!"

I guess all Michigan people are like Father, they seem to be very proud of where they're from, the loudest cheer came when the man said "Detroit."

People bounced their heads up and down and snapped their fingers and smiled like a whole herd of Cheshire cats.

When the first song was done the crowd whistled and clapped.

The man said, "Thank you so much. And now, what you've all been waiting for, our featured vocalist . . ."

The people stood up and cheered and screamed and banged their hands on the table and stomped their feet and made the house shake.

He said, "Originally from Lancaster, Pennsylvania . . ."

Lancaster! I screamed like the people did when they heard "Detroit"!

A curtain split in the middle and a man in a beautiful blue suit with a pair of two-tone blue shoes and a matching blue hat stood with his head bowed. His face was completely covered by the brim of the blue hat. He was holding on to a microphone.

I froze. Maybe this man was going to introduce Jimmie.

The drum banged. The people cheered louder. The drum banged one more time and the music stopped.

The man kept his head down and raised the microphone to his mouth. He waited and waited.

I stopped breathing.

Then a clear, strong voice sang, "*More or less resigned to crying over Angela* . . ." The band jumped in, the crowd screamed louder and I found out for a fact that I am not a swooner, because if there was anything in the world that could make you swoon, it was the air of the New Turned Leaf, the music of this band and the voice of the Genuine, Gentle Jumpin' Giant, Jimmie Malone!

He looked up from under the blue hat and sang,

> ***"I watched my heart leave the station***
> ***The day she said we were no more. . . ."***

It *was* Jimmie! In a suit!

Jimmie sang two songs and the crowd never calmed down. I raised my hand, hoping he'd see me but knowing it was impossible. I came out from behind the chairs. People were too busy staring at Jimmie to notice me, maybe if I got to the front of the room . . .

I was this close to Jimmie when the man who had been standing outside by the door stepped in front of me like a wall. "How'd you get in here? Let's go."

He left his gut wide open.

I know it was wrong, but I twisted my hips and swung as hard as I could. My fist crumpled against him and pain shot through my arm like a epiphany.

He looked at me like I was a mosquito. He reached at me and I screamed as loud as I could.

People around us jumped back like we were on fire. The band and Jimmie stopped and moved off the stage through the curtain.

Three other big, square men were just-like-that standing around me.

The only sound was people's shoes as they shuffled to the door I'd snuck in through.

I yelled, "Jimmie!"

The first man lifted me like I was as light as a pillow.

"*Jimmie!*"

Through the microphone I heard, "Sis?"

The curtain opened and Jimmie stood there without his hat.

"Fellas, hold on, that's my sister."

He said, "Folks, please, please have a seat, we'll start the show in a minute. Please don't go."

The man I'd slugged put me down as Jimmie jumped off the stage and grabbed me.

We cried and cried. "Aw, sis, it's so good to see you!"

I said, "Jimmie, I missed you so much."

He walked me onto the stage and through the curtain to a stool. "Let me take care of my business, Deza, sit here till I'm done."

The band started up and it looked like they weren't ever going to stop. Four times, after they finished playing and stood up, people yelled and stomped until Jimmie did another song. When someone finally came and moved the drums and instruments off the stage, a white man smoking a cigar took Jimmie's hat and walked around the crowd.

People started tossing in coins and even some folding money!

Jimmie grabbed me. "Come on, sis, I live just around the way, we've got a lot to catch up on. I see you're still the Mighty Miss Malone, I can't believe you slugged Tito like that!"

Jimmie and me and the band went out the back door and got into a car just as marvelous as Marvin's. It wasn't a Buke, but it *was* great!

Chapter Thirty

Father's Feet of Clay

It was so strange, but as me and Jimmie stood in his little room I didn't really know what to say.

I didn't want to start in scolding him, but I couldn't help it. "Why are you calling yourself Jones, what's wrong with being a Malone?"

"It don't mean nothing, sis. Mr. Maxwell thought Jimmie Malone sounded like a white Irish guy's name, he thought it might confuse people, thought more folks would come if they knew what I really am."

"You gave up our name?"

"It don't mean nothing. Us musicians change our names all the time."

"And James Edward Malone, you knew we were in Flint, you were only sixty miles away! You couldn't write to us or come see us to let us know you were OK? Do you have any idea how we've worried about you for all this time? Why wouldn't you at least send a letter?"

"Aw, sis, you see where I'm living and working, what would Ma say about me making money in speakeasies? It was better that she didn't hear nothing from me until I got things right."

"You were going to throw us away that easy?"

"Aww, Deza, you know that's not true, I was gonna write before much longer."

He cleared his throat and said, "Deza, I gotta tell you something I've been carrying around with me and after I done lots of thinking it's only fair you know."

Oh, no.

He said, "I promised Pa I'd never tell anyone about this, Deza, especially you and Ma. But I think it's the right thing to break my word." He looked so sad and serious I could tell this was something I didn't want to hear. But I had to. I sat down.

"Go ahead, Jimmie."

"It's about Pa, and it's going to be a surprise."

I smiled. "OK, you tell me what you know about him first, then it's my turn. We'll see who's most surprised."

"Sis, this is serious."

Jimmie looked so sad that I wondered if he really did know something terrible about Father. I grabbed the arms of the one chair in the room and sat in it. "Well, kiddo, here it is." I bit the second brain quiet.

"You remember Pa's story about being trapped out on Lake Michigan?"

I nodded.

Jimmie looked at me hard. "Swear you'll never tell Ma this."

I nodded again.

"Pa told me what really happened on the lake. It was the last thing he told me when he came to my room that night he left. He lied to us, Deza."

I got out of the chair so quick that it fell over. I turned my back on him and walked to the door. He blocked my way.

We stood that way for what seemed like forever. I looked down into my brother's eyes. I could smell cigarettes and something else foul on his breath. Just like Dolly Peaches and the guy named Tito, he left his belly wide open. I clenched my left fist and was getting ready to sink it into his stomach when he touched my arm and said, "Please, Deza, I'm sorry I said it like that, but I have to tell you."

I opened my fist the second time he said, "Please?"

I turned and set the chair back up. But I didn't sit. "Father lied?"

"Everything about them going out in the boat was true. The lies started right after the fog came in."

I sat down.

"Pa said everything went good until they'd been on the lake for a couple of hours. That's when someone noticed a huge fog bank further out on the lake. Pa and Mr. Henderson thought they should go back in, but they were catching so many fish that the other guys wanted to wait awhile longer.

"Mr. Henderson finally had had enough and started to pull up the anchor. But somehow the anchor had come off the rope and they'd been drifting. No one knew for how long. When they looked toward shore they couldn't see it. Then the fog bank rolled over them."

Jimmie sniffled. I stayed quiet, wanting to hear and not wanting to hear at the same time.

"Pa didn't know how long they were in the fog bank, but a lot later they heard a ship. They could even see the light from it. They cheered and screamed, thinking they were gonna get rescued. But the ship came right at them and they had to row like mad to get out of its way."

I covered my mouth with my hand.

"The ship missed them, but it sent out a wave that rocked the boat so hard that it just about tipped them over. They were all soaked except for Mr. Williams. At first they laughed because it was such a close call, but they noticed that the oars were gone and soon Pa and the guys who got wet started getting cold and shivering. Pa said being cold and scared did something to them and . . ."

Jimmie sniffled again.

"After they drifted for hours and hours Mr. Coulter's eyes got really big and were shooting from side to side in his head. He started talking nonsense and wondering why Mr. Williams was the only one who wasn't wet. He said Mr. Williams must've planned this to get all of them killed."

Jimmie stopped. I didn't want to talk or do anything to stop him from telling me what really happened.

"Pa said that's when Mr. Coulter jumped up and grabbed Mr. Williams around the throat and they both fell overboard, tipping the boat over. Pa said he thinks it was the cold, it had to be the cold. He said they lost their minds, that being scared and cold made them kind of crazy. That's why when the boat tipped and Pa went underwater he thought about how easy it would be just to stay there and die. But he thought about us, Deza, he thought about our family and knew he had to fight to the end. He scratched and clawed and finally got back to the upside-down boat.

"First thing he saw was Mr. Steel Lung. Father grabbed him and they hung on to the boat. Father tied the yellow anchor rope around their wrists so they wouldn't fall asleep and fall off.

"He said that every once in a while he'd wake up and remember he was still hungry, cold and scared. He started hearing voices and seeing things. He thought Ma was whispering to him and saying over and over, 'My job? My job? You think you gonna take my job?'

"Then Ma takes the anchor rope and wraps it around Pa's neck. Pa fights back and sees that it isn't Ma at all, his senses clear and he sees it's been Steel Lung hollering at him. He's untied the rope from around his wrist and is choking Pa with it.

"Steel Lung screams, 'Taking food out my babies' mouths? You think I'ma lay down and let that happen? We'll see who dies out here!'"

Each time my heart beat it felt like it was getting smaller and smaller.

Jimmie said, "Pa got the rope off but Mr. Steel Lung wasn't through, he got one of the oarlocks and started swinging it at Pa.

"Pa said he begged him to stop, he told him, 'No one's going to take your job, brother. It's me, Roscoe.'

"But Mr. Steel Lung screamed, 'Get off my boat!' and kept

swinging. He was so weak that he couldn't get a good hit in, so Pa just covered his head hoping he'd tire himself out. He finally stopped.

"Pa moved his arms off his head and looked up, but that was what Mr. Steel Lung was waiting for, he swung one more time and caught Pa right in the mouth. He knew his teeth had been broken out."

I couldn't move, it was horrible hearing the truth.

Jimmie said, "Steel Lung got his hands around Pa's throat. . . ."

Jimmie covered his face and cried through his fingers. "What choice did Pa have? He wasn't trying to hurt him, he hit him with the oarlock. Not hard. Just once. Once."

I told Jimmie, "Father didn't do anything wrong, Mr. Steel Lung was trying to kill him."

"Next thing Pa remembered was waking up on that ship heading to Chicago."

Jimmie's eyes were red and swollen. "That's it, sis, that's what happened on Lake Michigan. That's why Pa left, he wasn't looking for no job, he was running away, he was looking for somewhere to run off and finish. Finish dying."

"No!"

"I'm sorry, Deza."

"You're wrong. Maybe he felt bad for a while, but he got work! That's why I've been looking for you. We can get back together, Father's sent us money! Father's OK! Look!"

I took Father's letter out of my pocketbook. Jimmie took it and said, "That's great, sis." There wasn't any excitement or happiness in his voice. "Does Ma know you're down here?"

"I left her a note."

Then to hurt him I said, "Just like you did. Saw-Bone said you might be here and I had to come tell you we heard from Father! We can go back home and be a family again."

"That's great, but I'ma have to stay here for a while, working, then I'm back to traveling. We can talk about it later. You gotta go back to Flint. Maybe I can get someone to give you a ride, that's a pretty long trip."

I was too tired to fight anymore. I couldn't believe he wasn't as excited about Father as I had been, or as I was now about finding him.

"Come on, Deza, we've got a lot to talk about and catch up on. But now it's sleepy-bye time for you."

Chapter Thirty-One

Jimmie's World

The next morning I was dreaming about Father. He was in a beautiful suit and tie and was standing in my doorway back in Gary. I'd never seen Father in a suit.

"Deza?" he said. "Are you going to let a gorgeous day like today get away from you?"

"Oh, Father, you're not going to believe it! I found Jim—"

I jerked awake and looked at the door. It was Jimmie.

He did look a lot like Father, just smaller. "Get dressed, we're going out, I got a surprise for you, but you gotta hurry."

I rubbed my eyes. "Jimmie, where are we going? I'll look all raggedy next to you."

"You look fine, but if you want, I'll go put on some walkin'-round clothes."

I remember what he said when I wore my blue gingham dress. "Nah, Jimmie, you are one sure-enough sharp scrap of calico in that suit!"

"*Deza!* That's something you only say to girls! But thanks anyway."

I got dressed and cleaned up and we started down the stairs.

The white man who took all the money that people put in Jimmie's hat was sitting on a couch.

"Jim-Jim! Great show. Outstanding!"

"Thank you, Mr. Maxwell."

"And who's the beautiful young lady?"

"This is my sister, Deza."

"Delighted, delighted. Does she sing too?"

"Deza don't need to sing, she's gonna go to college!"

"Good for you, girly."

I was happy Jimmie pulled me by the elbow out of the front door.

"Who is he, Jimmie?"

"That's my manager, he's like my boss. He's the one that give me a contract."

"A contract?"

"It means he has to give me money for singing."

"You're kidding! That money people put in your hat last night was for you?"

"Naw, that's the tip money, he takes it and divides it up with me and him and the band. I'm suppose to get fifteen dollars plus room and board on top of that."

"*Fifteen dollars?* Every month?"

Jimmie had us turn at the corner. "Naw, Deza, every *week*!"

We walked out on a huge busy street called Woodward Avenue.

So many people in Detroit knew Jimmie! Near every person we passed stopped to speak!

One old man said, "When y'all going back to Chicago, Jim?"

"'Bout two weeks, I expect, Mr. Pierce."

"I need you to take a message to my brother, if you don't mind."

"No problem, write it down, though, you know I ain't got the best memory."

"See you in a bit, Jim."

Three very tall, breathtaking women wearing gorgeous hats stopped us. One of them said, "What's this, poppa? You know how jealous I get, who is she and what is she to you?"

She was smiling but I knew I'd be able to knock her out with one punch.

"This is my baby sis, down from Flint. Deza, this is Saundra and Shayla and Kendra."

The women said, "Nice to meet you."

After they passed I sang, *"Jimmie's got a girlfriend, Jimmie's got a girlfriend!"*

"Naw, sis, if I had one she'd be a whole lot younger than them. Kendra's old, gotta be about twenty."

Even people in cars honked their horns and waved out their windows at us as we walked!

"Jimmie, you're famous!"

"These are just folks that come to the club. When I really

do get famous people all over the world will know me, not just in Detroit!"

I put my arm in Jimmie's. "Well, you're the most famous person *I've* ever met!"

We stopped in front of a very, very tall building and went in through some glass doors that spun round and round! Before I could ask, Jimmie said, "They're called revolver doors, Deza."

Next we stopped in front of three separate metal doors that were divided in half. They didn't have one doorknob or hinge or lock anywhere on them. Jimmie pushed a button on the wall and I heard a whirring, clankity sound.

A bell rang and one of the doors split right in half!

Behind it was a lit-up closet. A man sat on a stool in a red suit covered with two rows of gold buttons, and a little red cap. He was behind something like a cage. He smiled out at me. "Going up!" He pulled aside the metal cage and Jimmie walked right into the closet so I followed. "What's shaking, Jim?"

"Not a thing, Clarence."

"Who's the lady?"

"My sister, Deza."

The man tipped his cap at me. "Welcome, missy. Doc's office, Jim?" He pulled the cage back in front of the door. He slid a handle to the side and the metal doors closed.

I had to grab Jimmie's hand when the little room started shaking. One at a time, buttons on a board that ran from L to 26 started lighting up.

The room banged and jerked one more time and the man said, "Twenty-fifth floor. Attorneys Greene, Rubinstein and

Kramer to the left, Doctors Fortuna, Lyon and Mitwally to the right."

The metal doors came open, the man slid the cage aside. We were in a whole different place!

"Later, Jim."

"Later, Clarence." The doors closed behind us. "It's called a evalator, Deza. It's kind of scary at first, we'll use the steps down if you want."

"Are you kidding? That was a great surprise, let's do it again!"

I started to push the button pointing down but Jimmie grabbed my hand. "The evalator isn't the surprise, Deza, the surprise is Doc. Look."

He opened his mouth wide so I could see his teeth. I couldn't believe it! There was something in all the cavities.

"What happened to your teeth?"

"Isn't it great, sis? Doc Mitwally filled my cavities up, I don't get no more headaches and don't wake up in the middle of the night neither. I'm gonna get him to fix your teeth up too."

"Aw, Jimmie, thanks, but my teeth don't . . . That's OK, I'm used to it."

"Sis, that's what it is, you just got use to it. I know how much they hurt. Doc says bad teeth let bad blood get in your system. He says he gets kids young as eight years old whose mouths are so rotten he has to pull all their teeth. He says some of 'em waited too long and even die."

"They die? From *cavities?*"

Jimmie nodded. "If I'm lying, I'm flying. You won't believe how much better you're gonna feel. I promise you. Food's gonna taste better, you'll start smelling stuff a lot clearer, and your mouth is gonna be sweet as a baby's breath."

"It really doesn't hurt?"

"Naw, he gives you some gas and a shot while he's doing it and some pills for after. You'll just get dizzy and sleep a lot."

"I don't know, Jimmie, I've got to get back to Mother, I wrote I'd only be gone two days."

"Deza, we'll send her a telegram soon's we leave Doc's. We'll let her know you're safe with me and see how long it's gonna take Doc to fix you up, then I'll put you on a bus back to Flint. Ma'll be all right. Besides, I don't see you for all this time, then you come here and expect to leave me after only two days? My Mighty Miss Malone would never be so unconsiderate."

I moved my hands back and forth like they were on the steering wheel of a car.

Jimmie laughed. "Yeah, yeah, yeah. It's the Manipula-Mobile, but I'm not letting you go."

He opened a door and walked in. I looked inside but didn't move.

"Trust me on this." He reached out to me. I took his hand and let him pull me inside. I only did it because something was telling me that Jimmie and the dentist weren't joshing. Anything that hurt this bad really could kill you.

I only did it because of that. And because I *can* trust my brother.

Chapter Thirty-Two

Going Back to Gary

I know I said you can't read what a person or a house is like by the way they look, and that's mostly true. But some people have kindness and gentleness wrapped around them like a blanket and there's no doubting who they are. Jimmie's Dr. Mitwally was that way.

That's the only reason I didn't run when he told me to sit in a strange, horrible chair with a big light over it. The chair was like something that Jimmie would sit in when he drove his rocket ship to the moon.

Jimmie took my hand. "Hey, Doc, I wanna save a little money on this, so instead of using that numbing stuff, do you have a washrag she can bite down on whilst you fix her up?"

Dr. Mitwally said, "I can knock a little more off the bill if

I use a pair of pliers and hammer instead of any of this fancy dental equipment."

I was so nervous that I couldn't laugh at their jokes.

But once I sat all the way back in the chair it was a miracle! My teeth stopped hurting!

Before I could let them know, Dr. Mitwally said, "Open wide, Deza."

Dr. Mitwally didn't say anything then but Jimmie's face twisted.

The doctor poked around in my mouth, shooting red lights of hurt into my scalp.

He said over and over, "Sorry, sorry, sorry . . ." Each time he did, more lights flashed.

The doctor said, "We need to get these X-rayed. Come in the next room with me, please."

Jimmie took my hand and we followed the doctor.

We finished taking the X-rays. Then me and Jimmie went back to the rocket chair. I sat and he held my hand.

After a while the doctor came back in and said, "I've seen worse, you're going to lose a few, I'll be able to give you some relief immediately, but there are some things that are going to take more time."

Jimmie said, "You know I'm good for anything, Doc, just fix her up, please."

"We're talking about months of work, James."

"She's gotta go to school in Flint, but we'll get her here, Doc."

Dr. Mitwally said, "I can recommend a good dentist in

Flint." He smiled at me. "You are one tough cookie, my dear, I can't believe how you're able to think, much less excel in school. By the way, don't let him know, but everybody's sick and tired of hearing Jimmie brag about how smart his baby sister is. You'll feel a hundred times better when you leave here, and once you get everything taken care of you'll be as good as new. Now wipe those tears and let's get to work. You're going to feel a little pinch." The needle he'd been hiding behind his back came at my mouth, and then he put a little triangle-shaped mask over my nose and mouth.

Jimmie said, "Sweet dreams, sis," and that was it. The next thing I knew I was floating out of the office, getting into a taxicab with Jimmie and trying to talk.

"Deza, your mouth's all swole up. Just try to sleep."

"Bud Musser? Wud abows musser?"

"I sent Ma a telegram, she's gonna pick you up from the bus tomorrow. Doc said you were a real soldier. I told him he wasn't telling me anything I didn't know."

For some reason that was very funny and I started saluting.

Jimmie saluted back. "Time to fall out, General."

* * *

I woke up crying. It felt like a million little metal mice were chewing on my gums.

Jimmie came into the room with a glass of water and a little brown bottle. "Doc said you might feel pretty bad once the numbing wore off. He said take these."

I swallowed the two little pills and drank the water. It was like I was swallowing fire.

Jimmie held my hand. "It hurts for a while, Deza, shoot, even I cried like a baby."

I wanted to say, "Not *you*, Jimmie!" But sleeping seemed like a much easier thing to do.

* * *

The bus from Detroit got to Flint in no time, not that I was noticing much. The pills Jimmie gave me made everything foggy and far-off seeming.

I got off the bus and Mother kissed me. "Deza, what did they do to your face?"

I hugged her and we both cried. "Jimmie got my teeth fixed up, I'll feel better in a few days."

"Oh, sweetheart, I can't wait for you to feel better because the minute you do I'm pulling those teeth out one by one with a pair of pliers. Do you have any idea how much I've worried?"

"Yes, but I knew I'd find Jimmie. I'd do it all over again."

As we walked home Mother asked me a million questions about Jimmie, had he grown, was he eating, did he look healthy, did he seem happy? My head was spinning so much and my answers were so short that she finally said, "We'll talk tomorrow."

I said, "That's fine, Mother, but you can write to him at the New Turned Leaf. He wrote the address down for me." I don't remember anything after that.

* * *

Once all the swelling went down I felt so different!

I started chewing all of my food instead of biting it a couple of times with my front teeth before swallowing it, and everything tasted as good as one of Dr. Bracy's pies! Dr. Mitwally gave me the name of a dentist in Flint that I was going to have to go to, but once I saw how good this made me feel I couldn't wait!

It looked like the Malones had finally used up all of their three pieces of bad news. The only thing that wasn't perfect was school. And Father. And Jimmie not being here.

I had to hide my first terrible Flint report card from Mother. I didn't care, though, Flint teachers were so unfair. I'd gotten As on every test I'd taken but when the report card came it was all C pluses and a C in English. The teachers all wrote the same thing, I was a good student but didn't participate in class. Mother never asked to see the card, but I'd always showed her my exams so she didn't know anything was wrong.

The letters from Father came like clockwork.

Every two weeks he'd send ten or twenty dollars and a note telling about how his hand was getting better. He was still working as a traveling carpenter, mostly in cities geologically located in the South. The letters came from Jacksonville, Florida; New York City; Washington, D.C.; Baltimore, Maryland; and Atlanta, Georgia.

It all ended one Friday in May when I went into the post office and Mrs. James said, "Sorry, Deza, there's no letter today."

I wasn't going to let it bother me too much, Father's letters had been late a couple of times.

But Mrs. James laughed and said, "But there is a package!"

She waved a box at me.

It was from Father!

I said, "Mrs. James, you like teasing so much you could be one of the Malones."

She said, "Why, thank you, Miss Malone, it would be an honor to be in your family."

I hadn't meant it as a compliment.

The package was addressed to Mother only. It was postmarked from Jacksonville, Florida. I'm really growing up, I was able to walk all the way home without opening it. I set it on the kitchen table and waited.

* * *

Mother did the same thing I did when I first touched the package, she shook it, held it to her ear, then turned it over and over before shaking it again.

"Something's rattling in there, Deza, what do you think it is?"

"Gold?"

Mother laughed. "Well, if it is we shouldn't waste another second."

I screamed, "Mother!" as my Indiana mother tore at the package Flint style.

She laughed and finally got the paper off.

She said, "Here goes . . ." and opened the lid of a blue cardboard box.

Inside was a envelope, a letter and two keys held together by a piece of wire.

I took the keys and Mother read,

"Dear Peg and Deza,

I told you. When one of the Malones gives you their word, we keep it. These keys are for 541 Jackson Street in a beautiful city in

Indiana called Gary. I have paid the rent for six months and you can move in at the beginning of June. My hand is still injured and I am still traveling and working. I have sent some extra for your move. I will still send money. Take care of each other.

Love,
Father"

"Oh, Mother, he did it! Father did it! When do we leave?"

I opened the cash envelope. There were three tens and a five inside!

Mother looked befumbled. "As soon as school is over, Deza. I do miss Gary."

Part Three

A Little Closer . . .
Early Summer 1937
Gary, Indiana

Chapter Thirty-Three

The Quest for Jonah Blackbeard

We got a taxicab at the Gary bus station and told the driver the address. He stopped in front of a beautiful little house with a porch and a green door. I have never been so excited in my life!

We were dumbstruck.

"Deza, are you sure this is the right address?"

"Yes, Mother, this is it!"

"Let's see if that key fits."

We left our bundles on the sidewalk and went up the walkway like a couple of thieves waiting for someone to shout, "Hey! Get off that porch!" But no one did.

My hands were shaking too much to get the key into the

lock. Mother took it from me, stuck it in, held her breath and turned it to the left.

Nothing.

She turned it to the right.

The lock clicked and Mother pulled the door open.

We walked in and I yelled, "Hello?"

The word echoed around the empty rooms.

Mother said, "Deza, we're home!"

We hugged each other before I started running through the house. I knew how the little girl Rosario and her family felt when they first looked through our old house, every room was so beautiful that it might as well have been filled with gold nuggets!

We didn't have any furniture but we were used to sleeping on the ground so spreading sheets and blankets on the bedroom floor didn't feel all that bad. With the money Father was going to send it wouldn't be long before we'd have beds and tables and chairs and maybe even a new wardrobe of our own.

I pulled my blanket up to my chin and said, "Mother, isn't it wonderful? We're back in Gary, Father kept his word!"

Mother sighed. "Darling Daughter Deza, it's been a long day and tomorrow's going to be another. I've got to find work. I'll look up Mrs. Henderson and the Rhymeses, and I know you've got some searches of your own to do. As much as I'd love to chat with you right now, button that lip and let's get some sleep."

She smiled and leaned over to kiss my forehead.

"Kisses . . . kisses . . . kisses make you stronger."

* * *

Jimmie was right, if you're getting a bandage ripped off it's best to do it in one quick snatch. Same way with getting bad news, find out and get it over with. Or as Father would say, "Deza, my Darling Daughter, don't dillydally!"

On our first full day in our new house I decided to get two pieces of very bad news out of the way; Mrs. Needham's house was empty, and as I walked to Clarice's house my stomach started folding itself up a couple of blocks off. I was pretty sure they wouldn't be there, but I had to try.

I stood in front of her house and knew right away. When a house has twelve boys and one girl living in it it's different than an empty house, even if they've all gone to the park or for a walk. Clarice's house looked the same, but I knew right away something was wrong. It reminded me of the spot in my gums where Doc had pulled my tooth. Even though you couldn't tell it from the outside, something big and important was gone. For everafter.

Maybe that's what I felt, or maybe it was me knowing I'd have to go through the rest of my life with half a heart, but this second piece of bad news made me want to leave without even asking her neighbors if they knew anything.

I'd wait until the next day to see if Dr. Bracy being gone was the third piece of bad news. Instead I went to the library to find out if I could still use my card.

Mrs. Ashton remembered me and was very pleased things had turned out so good for us. Even though I didn't have a card with my new address yet, she let me check out four books!

I was reading and walking and got right up to our new front porch before I noticed there was a taxicab sitting in front of our home. Jimmie? Father!

I fumbled for my key and ran onto the porch. Mother called from inside the taxicab, "Deza!" She sounded very nervous.

I froze. "Well, kiddo, here's part three of your bad news."

I ran to the taxicab. "Mother, what's wrong?"

"Get in."

I climbed in next to her. "What? What happened?"

"I got a letter from a place in Lansing, Michigan. There's a man who's been in a poorhouse there for the last year. We have to check, Deza."

"Check what?"

"There's a chance the man may be your father."

"*What!*"

"Lower your voice, Deza."

"Mother, what are you talking about? A man in a poorhouse? How could it be Father? Father's been traveling all around the country and sending us—"

A million more questions bounced around my skull but Mother said, "Deza, think it through. If those letters were from your father, why didn't they ever mention Jimmie?"

"I'd thought about that. . . ."

"And how does a carpenter make a living with a hand so badly injured he can't hold a pen?"

"But—"

"And besides, Miss Malone, who on earth has ever heard of something called a traveling carpenter?"

"Well—"

"There wasn't one bit of your father in those letters. It's just like that letter to Mrs. Carsdale's friend in Flint, why do you think I never used it?"

"You didn't?"

Mother said, "Jimmie opened it for me, and once I read it I saw that letter was pure Deza Malone, not Mrs. Carsdale."

Mother is so smart!

"You and I know Roscoe Malone, we *know* him. We both know that wasn't his writing in those letters."

"No, it had to—"

She gently squeezed my cheek. "You knew, Deza, you wanted so desperately for them to be from your father that you just couldn't admit they weren't. But you knew."

"But why didn't he write to us? Father would never have let us worry so long. And who wrote—"

"Something must have happened, Deza. Something terrible."

She looked out the window. "I thought about bringing Mrs. Kenworthy. I couldn't do this alone. But you've grown so much lately, and there's no one else who understands this like you, Deza. No one."

Mother was right, I felt so proud that I could really do something to help.

Mother asked the taxicab driver, "Ten dollars flat, right? Round trip."

We started driving back to Michigan.

* * *

If hospitals took that horrible smell they have, bottled it up and mailed it away, this poorhouse in Lansing, Michigan, must have been where the postman had been delivering the bottles.

Mother is much more used to bad odors than I am, and as we stepped onto the porch even *she* took a surprised quick breath. My hand flew up and pinched my nose shut.

She said, "Breathe out of your mouth, Deza, we can't be rude."

She took a letter out of her purse and knocked on the front door. After her second knock a man in a white uniform answered. "Yes?"

"Hello. I've been writing to a Mr. Jackson, he said there's a possibility my husband is here."

"I'm Mr. Jackson."

"Fine, I'd like to get some information on the man you call Jonah Blackbeard."

"Oh, yes, you're the lady who wrote looking for her husband. But, ma'am, I told you I don't think Jonah is him. You said your husband was a carpenter. We don't know much about old Jonah, but we're pretty sure he was a sailor or in the merchant marine."

"Mr. Jackson, I have absolutely no clues where my husband is. I'd like to see this Jonah Blackbeard, the things you wrote about him made me wonder."

"Come to the office, let me get his file. I'm sorry, but I think this is wasting your time."

Mother grabbed my wrist and we walked into the house.

Breathing out of your mouth was worthless once you got inside. The smell was like a living animal, it clawed at your nostrils and rubbed against your legs like a overfriendly cat. Rotten meat and leaking toilets and perspiration were bad enough, but what made it worse was it seemed like someone had sloshed a bucketful of strong cleaning fluid all over everything to fight the bad odor.

My eyes watered but I kept breathing out of my mouth.

In his office, Mr. Jackson opened a drawer that was choked with files. After thumbing through them, he took one out. There was one piece of paper in it.

"It says some hobo brought him into the colored hospital in Lansing. He was barely conscious, trouble breathing, high fever, they thought he was going to pass but he just kept hanging on." He read, "'Name: Unknown. Age: Unknown. Occupation: Thought to be a sailor. No known next of kin, no identification.' After while the hospital figured he'd had some kind of attack. Maybe asthma. Whatever it was might have triggered a small stroke too. He was confused, but he's shown real improvement over the months."

As he talked Mother twisted the strap of her purse.

"He talks so little about himself that we thought he was on the run from the law, but once you spend time with him you see that's not likely. He's a smart man but he doesn't talk much. Won't tell anyone his name. There's five or six others here with stories like his, we don't try to push them to talk about the past. If they want to talk they do. If not, who am I to say they should? There's lots of folks who want to forget or be forgotten.

"He was brought here on July seventeenth of last year." He sighed. "'Bout a month after Joe got beat."

Mother said, "Where is he?"

"Everyone's in the backyard getting some air."

All three of us stood up.

Mother said, "Deza, you wait here."

"But—"

"Deza!"

I sat back down . . . and waited long enough for Mother to follow the man out of the room. I was right behind them. Mother went with him through a long dark hallway toward the back of the house. She said, "If this man won't say his name, why are you calling him Jonah Blackbeard?"

Mr. Jackson laughed. "We had to call him something. He only talks about two things. We call him Jonah because the first thing he started talking about was getting swallowed up in the belly of a fire-breathing dragon. We call him Blackbeard 'cause he claims he fought off a ship on the ocean."

Mother stopped at the back door. The man went through and I could hear him say, "Jonah, you awake? Come on, Jonah, you got visitors."

Mother opened the screen door and stood on the back porch. I walked out behind her.

There were eight or nine men in the backyard, and they looked like a collection of thrown-out rag dolls. Long skinny arms were flopped into their laps, heads hung like they had no neck bones, and legs were crossed or dangling from the arms of chairs like they were filled with sawdust.

Mr. Jackson's words about Joe Louis had me thinking about that horrible fight. If anyone painted a picture about how Gary,

Indiana, felt after Joe Louis got beat, this backyard of poor men in Lansing, Michigan, would be it.

Mr. Jackson went to one of the men who had his back turned to us. He was wrapped in a yellow-stained sheet so that only his head was showing.

"Jonah, are you all right?"

The man's head was slumped to the side.

"Jonah?"

Mr. Jackson looked at us and shrugged.

Mother stepped off the porch. I was too afraid to follow.

She walked to the man's chair. Her hand went to her mouth and she softly asked, "Roscoe?"

The head came up. And slowly twisted to look at her. After a second the man's bony hands covered his face.

And, just like Mother said, we *know* Roscoe Malone.

It seems like if you had nearly a year to concentrate on something and wonder about it and dream and worry about it day and night, that with all that time you'd be able to get at least part of it right if it ever came true. But not one thing I'd imagined happened.

I didn't rush to Father and hug him and scold him and cry on his chest.

I didn't tell him how much I'd missed him.

I didn't gut-punch him for being gone.

I didn't talk or even move.

Mother knelt and put her left hand out. "Roscoe? Sweetheart?"

The man brought his hands down and a skinny arm came

from under the sheet and trembled as it reached toward Mother's hand. Father said, "Peg?"

Their shaking fingers joined together like something Mrs. Henderson had knitted. They stared at each other before Father turned Mother's hand to look at her fingers. "Peg? Your ring?"

Mother wiped her eyes and pulled the string from around her neck.

"Here, Roscoe, it's right here. And I could ask you the same thing."

Father's claw of a hand went to his neck. He pulled out a tired string that had his wedding band on it.

"I knew you'd never give up on me, Peg."

"Never, Roscoe Malone, never." She patted his beard. "How could I give up on you? How could I give up on my whole life?"

Father said, "You found me. How? I thought I'd never see you again."

"Sweetheart"—Mother held her face against Father's—"do you know I've spent the last year writing to every police station and hospital, every boardinghouse and funeral home, and even every morgue between Gary and Flint? I know you, Roscoe. I knew if you were alive and all right there was no way you'd not write. I knew something had gone horribly wrong. Why didn't you write, dear? Why didn't you let us know you were here?"

"Peg, Peg, Peg. I never even made it to Flint, I woke up in the hospital again. It was too much. I thought I was dying. I couldn't figure out who I was for the longest time. Once things started clearing up I *did* write. The letters all came back."

He put his hands back over his face. "I'm so sorry. When I couldn't get in touch with you, when I thought I'd lost you and the kids, I just didn't care anymore. I'm afraid I gave up, Peg."

Mother sighed. "Sweetheart, you're coming home. We have a lot to talk about, Mr. Malone."

"Yes, we do. How're the babies?"

"Why don't you ask her?"

He shifted in the chair to look at me.

His hair was long and dirty and snarled, he had a twisted beard that had bits of food in it, and his eyes burned at me. He sobbed and smiled his jack-o'-lantern smile.

And he was still the handsomest man I'd ever seen.

I rushed to hug him and could feel his shoulder blades poking from beneath the sheet. I fell into his open arms.

"The Mighty Miss Malone."

I could hear how hard his heart hit against his ribs.

There was so much I wanted to say. But everything I'd rehearsed for this moment was forgotten. The only thing I could think of, the thing I wanted to tell him most of all, was "Look, Father, Jimmie got my teeth fixed." I wanted him to know he didn't have to breathe out of his mouth when he was near me.

He choked and covered his mouth with his hand.

"Oh, sweetheart. My Darling Daughter Deza. I'm so happy. It's so good to see you."

Father twisted to look at the house. "Where's Jimmie?"

"He's doing real good, Father, he's all grown up now, you're not going to believe—"

Mother snapped at Mr. Jackson, "How dare you? How dare

you treat any human being like this? Do you know who this man is?"

"Mrs. Blackbeard, look, I—"

"Don't be ridiculous, my name is Mrs. *Malone*, and this is Roscoe Malone. My husband! Her father! How can you allow someone to wallow in their own filth like this? Get me some soap, a washcloth, a towel, some scissors, a razor, a toothbrush, baking soda and Vaseline."

"Ma'am, we do the best we can on what we have, there's barely money to feed the men."

Mother calmed down. "I'm sorry, Mr. Jackson. Is there a pharmacy around here? Deza, write this list down."

Mr. Jackson said, "Hold on, Mrs. Malone, I've got some of my own things you can use to clean him up."

Mother said, "Thank you very much. Could you help me get him to a bathroom?"

I started to help Father up and the sheet fell away from his legs. They were nothing but bones covered in tight, ashy-brown skin.

Mother covered him and said, "Deza, take a dollar from my purse and tell the cabdriver he needs to wait another hour before we go back. Then go wait in the cab to make sure he doesn't leave."

"But, Mother, I want to—"

"Deza!"

* * *

I sat in the taxicab. I was happy Mother had shooed me off, it would've been really hard to watch Father being led around like a baby. Plus sitting like this gave me time to figure some things out.

Like the letters.

Mother was right, I think I *did* know they couldn't have been from Father, but they were real and they were there and it was like Mother says, "Any port in a storm."

Father never would've forgotten to put Jimmie's name on the letters, that should've been my first clue.

But who would send the Malones that much money every two weeks, who was that kind? And that rich?

Mrs. Needham? She has a wonderful heart and a good character. But she's a teacher, and teachers are poor as church mice.

My heart skipped a beat. Dr. Bracy made a whole lot more sense!

She was a doctor, had a telephone right in her house and baked pies all of the time, she must be very, very rich. And she had been very kind!

But that didn't make sense either, how would she know to send letters to us at general delivery in Flint?

I was stumped.

Then a epiphany hit me in the head as hard as Dolly Peaches had!

It was Jimmie! No one else could have known where to write us, no one else would have cared enough to do it, no one else was making that much money. And most of all, no one else would have forgotten to put their own name on the letters!

That was why he didn't get excited when I told him Father was OK.

I cried so hard the cabdriver said, "I told you I'd wait, miss, don't cry."

I said, "I'm not crying for that, I'm crying because I have the best brother in the world and I am so proud of him that I could bust."

* * *

The door of the horrible-smelling house came open and Mother and Mr. Jackson slowly walked Father to the taxicab. I opened the back door for them.

I thought he looked skinny before, but now, with his hair cut short and his beard shaved off and his hideous sheet traded for a white set of clothes like Mr. Jackson's, it looked like they'd cut thirty more pounds off of him.

Mr. Jackson said, "Hold on, Mrs. Malone, there's something of his in the office."

Me and Mother helped Father into the seat between us. He smiled, then shut his eyes and leaned his head on Mother's shoulder.

Mr. Jackson came back holding a shoe box.

He said, "These are the letters he sent. After the first five or so came back marked 'Return to Sender' we stopped mailing them for him. We didn't tell him, but there just wasn't money for stamps. I apologize, Mrs. Malone. When you wrote me, your name should've rung a bell, but it didn't. There are so many people in and out of here that I just didn't put two and two together. When these letters started coming back, I do remember asking him who the Malones were, and he'd never answer."

"Thank you." Mother handed me the box.

Mr. Jackson said, "I'm so glad something good finally happened to one of the men, Mrs. Malone. This place is the end of the road for so many dreams."

He tapped the top of the cab. "Drive safe."

We began the ride back to Gary. Father fell right to sleep.

It was so hard to look at him. He seemed so tiny.

I pulled the lid off of the shoe box. It was filled with envelopes. The first one I pulled out was addressed:

Mrs. Margaret Malone, Master James Malone and Miss Deza Malone

Someone had stamped on the envelope in big blue letters:

RETURN TO SENDER. ADDRESSEE UNKNOWN.

The next five envelopes were marked the same way. Every envelope afterward just had Father's handwriting, no big blue stamp and no postage stamps.

I saw why none of the letters had gotten through. Father had put the wrong address on them. They all were sent to 4309 North Street, Flint, Michigan.

"Mother, Father sent them all to the wrong place."

I showed her one of the envelopes.

"He was confused, Deza. This is our old apartment in Flint, where we lived when we were first married."

I put the lid back on the box. I would never read these letters. Never. They would be filled with nothing but pain.

Mother laid her arm on Father's chest and cuddled him to her. He looked terrible, like all the strength and happiness had been drained out of him.

"Mother? Is he going to be all right?"

"Deza, we don't know how this is going to turn out. You

have to be prepared. You have to look at this clearly. We've got him back and no one can care for him like we will. But this will be hard. He might be very different."

"He's coming home, I don't care."

She squeezed my cheek. "I don't care either, dear."

As we drove, Father would wake up every once in a while, see me or Mother and smile, then go back to sleep.

We were a hour past Lansing and Father had been awake for a while when I said, "Look, Mother, Burma-Shave signs! Have you ever seen these, Father?"

I read to her and Father,

"Ol' Franky Jones ran and drove really fast,
Known as a true football hero.
Challenged a tree at sixty miles per hour—
Final score: maple, one; Franky, zero!"

Me, the taxicab driver, and Mother yelled out the last sign, "*Burma-Shave!*"

There were two more sets of signs and they got a smile out of Father.

He fell back asleep until about twenty miles outside of Gary.

His eyes came open and he pointed his bony finger out the window and said, "Look, more signs!"

We were passing a field. There were no signs, only a fence and fat white-and-black cows.

Mother pulled his hand down and said, "Why don't you try to sleep, dear?"

Father pointed again. "No, don't you see them? Deza, how 'bout you?"

My heart sank. I lied, "Yes, Father, I see them."

His eyes sparkled when he said, "Great! Read them with me."

I looked at Mother. Her 1-1-1 lines were back. She gave me a sad smile.

Before I could say anything, Father cleared his throat and started reading the signs only he could see:

"He had heard that hope has wings
But never believed such lofty things.
It took time to set him straight,
To learn hope was an open gate.
Try as he might, he didn't see
That hope lived in his family.
He had learned that hope has wings . . ."

Father pulled his bony hand down and grabbed mine and Mother's in both of his and finished,

"And now he'll live by these joyous things."

The car was silent as me and Mother stared at the sly smile on Father's face.

He weakly waved his arms and half-shouted, "*Burma-Shave!*"

For the first time in a million years Mother, Father and me exploded in laughter. Together.

But Father didn't get everything right. That last invisible sign really read, "*Next stop . . . back on the road to Wonderful!*"

Afterword

Today it is hard for us to imagine the importance of the Joe Louis–Max Schmeling fights of 1936 and 1938; there is nothing comparable. We could take the excitement over the World Cup; the Super Bowl; the World Series; and the NBA, WNBA, NASCAR and NHL championships and put them together, and they would not reach the level of excitement that these two fights generated.

In the 1930s, boxing was really the only game in town, and the Joe Louis–Max Schmeling bouts brought together a perfect storm of many elements of history.

There was the racial aspect: many African Americans pinned their dreams on Joe's shoulders, hoping that he could show our humanity and give us a sense of pride by excelling in this brutal sport. Race played an extremely important role in Schmeling's homeland, Germany, as well. In 1936, before the first fight, the growing Nazi Party proclaimed that white superiority would be proven because no black man could beat a white.

There was the economic aspect: the fights took place at the nadir of the Great Depression. A conservative estimate of

American unemployment was twenty-five percent. Hundreds of thousands of children under twelve years old were homeless or on the road. It was a time when desperate Americans of all races were searching for something, anything, to celebrate. This is one of the reasons why Negro League baseball games were so important, and it wasn't unusual for more than fifteen thousand people to attend a game.

There was also a political aspect to the fights: Louis and Schmeling served as surrogates for two cultures and political doctrines that would soon be at war. Neither man asked for these roles, but these were the parts they had to play.

It was in this atmosphere that on June 19, 1936, a rather nonchalant, heavily favored Joe Louis was handed his head by Max Schmeling. The euphoria in Germany was exceeded only by the absolute despair the result visited upon many Americans, particularly African Americans. Nearly every black person who is old enough to remember the fight has a story of how devastating Joe's loss was. Ask someone in their eighties about the first fight—the horror of what happened is still alive in their retelling.

Flash ahead two years to 1938. While the racial and economic dynamics had not changed much since 1936, the political scene had altered radically. It was becoming increasing clear that Nazi Germany and the group of nations known as the Allies were about to go to war.

Joe Louis took this fight much more seriously. And on June 22, 1938, in New York City, he and Schmeling met for the second time.

My father was often animated when he spoke about

something he felt deeply; when he talked about that second fight he would absolutely light up. Something came into his eyes that wasn't there very often. It was a sense of joy, a sense of pride, a sense of redemption.

I remember him telling me, "Joe hit him so hard in the first round that you could hear Schmeling cry out in pain on the radio above all the screaming. When Schmeling got up, Joe hit him again and broke his back."

Several of Schmeling's vertebrae *were* cracked during the one-round fight, and he was hospitalized for days to recover from the horrific beating. My father told me that the streets of his city, Grand Rapids, Michigan, and every other city across the country were filled with jubilant, crying people of all races. Joe Louis had given all Americans something to cheer about.

As the years went by, for many people the fight became a symbol of certain aspects of the human condition. In particular, it showed that almost nothing falls into well-defined categories of good and evil. While Max Schmeling was reviled at the time, he was, as we all are, a complex person. He never was a member of the Nazi Party, something rare in Germany for someone of his stature and fame, and mostly resisted Hitler's attempts to paint him as an Aryan superman.

Years after the fight, his path and Joe Louis's diverged greatly. Schmeling became wealthy. Louis, after many economic losses and much poor planning, was only able to find work as a greeter at a casino in Las Vegas.

The men developed a true friendship, and Schmeling would make an annual trip from Germany to see Louis. It is believed that Schmeling provided economic help to the struggling Louis as well. Louis respected Schmeling so much that he requested that Schmeling be a pallbearer at his funeral.

Nothing is as obvious as we want to believe it is. There are different shades and interpretations to every story.

Recently, as I watched the news and heard stories of the horrific economic struggles so many people are having right now, I was struck by this fact: even though the Great Depression took place some seventy-five years ago, we haven't come very far. Billie Holiday's line, "Them that's got shall get, them that's not shall lose," is truer than ever. The black and Hispanic middle classes have been nearly wiped out in the past five years; the "wealth gap" between white and black households is an unbelievable twenty to one, the gap between white and Hispanic households eighteen to one. Meaning the average white household is twenty times wealthier than the average black household, eighteen times wealthier than the average Hispanic household.

Those are cold and impersonal statistics, but behind those statistics are the lives of the poor. Often those poor are women and children—mostly children. I am horrified at the immoral, selfish calls to cut the paltry programs that have been set up to aid these young people. Langston Hughes's line "It never was America to me" (as adapted by David Bowie) played over and over in my head while I researched and wrote *The Mighty Miss Malone*.

Even though Deza is a fictional character, many of her woes are based on the lives and struggles of very real children. A particularly rich and heartbreaking source was the collection of letters children sent to President Roosevelt during the Great Depression.

Authors are frequently asked what they want a particular book to accomplish. What I want *The Mighty Miss Malone* to do is, first, to provide an enjoyable read. Second, as with all of my books, I want this to be a springboard for young people to ask questions and do more research on some of the themes the book explores, in this case the Great Depression and poverty in general. And third, I hope that Deza can serve as a voice for the estimated fifteen million American children who are poor, who go to bed hungry and whose parents struggle to make a dignified living to feed and care for them.

After writing that last sentence, I can't help feeling this: the fact that in late 2011 I can write that there are fifteen million poor children in this country is, to quote the Mighty Miss Malone, "A tragedy, a true tragedy."

(Figures are from the National Poverty Center of the University of Michigan Gerald R. Ford School of Public Policy—2009 Poverty Thresholds.)

Acknowledgments

Although only my name appears on the cover of *The Mighty Miss Malone*, this novel is more of a collaboration than most people would believe. It would not have been possible without the insights and suggestions that a few old and new friends and trusted family members have provided. I would like to thank the following people, who, through their careful reading, helped me more fully understand Deza's story: Habon Curtis, Lindsey Curtis, Cydney Curtis, Sarah Curtis, Kimberly Sleet, Hannah Furrow, Annaliese Furrow-Casement, Camden Furrow-Casement, Alexandro DiCosta, Valis Vanderlinden-Casement, Leslie Acevedo, Kathryn Black, Roz Ivey, Coleen Beamish, Carson Prieur-Smith and her grandpa Doug "The Thug" Tenant, Nechole Drake-McClendon, Knicolas McClendon, Steve Mariotti, Traki Taylor, Saundra Patrick, Joli and Anthony Cooper and the incredible Lauren Pankin.

I was also immeasurably helped by my usual crew of readers, Leslie Curtis, Pauletta Bracy, Janet Brown and, most especially, Rose Casement. Thank all of you for your ongoing support and suggestions.

Much of the research for this book was painstakingly done

by Mrs. Leila Shaiya. Thank you so much, Leila, for digging up sites and readings that brought the horrors of the Great Depression to life. Your work added so much to the book and is greatly appreciated.

A special thank-you to Marian Wright Edelman for her continuing struggles on behalf of the real world's Dezas, the mostly forgotten and ignored victims of poverty: the children.

Thank you to Habon and Ayaan Curtis, Jay Kramer and Gail Ganakis for all of your support. Each of you has made my work life much easier.

Thank you, thank you, thank you to my friends at Wendy Lamb Books and Random House who have brought *The Mighty Miss Malone* to life, among them Dana Carey, Caroline Gertler, Sabrina Ricci and Megan Looney. The many hours you spent going over this book and your brilliant ideas and keen insights have been invaluable. Kate Gartner, thank you for your art direction, and the cover. I am grateful to Tamar Schwartz and Tracy Heydweiller for keeping the book on schedule. For their support and hard work on behalf of my book, I also thank Adrienne Waintraub, Tracy Lerner, Lisa Nadel, Alexandra Bracken, Judith Haut, Elizabeth Zajac, John Adamo and Mary Beth Kilkelly and the marketing team; Joan Demayo and her sales team; Chip Gibson and James Perry.

A huge thanks to Barbara Perris. For seventeen years you have given me the freedom to know that when I make a mistake you will gently show me a better way. Now that you're retiring, I'll miss you a great deal.

Let me conclude by saying the world is unfair. If there was a smidgen of justice, the cover of *The Mighty Miss Malone* would say "by Christopher Paul Curtis and Wendy Lamb." Ms. Lamb, I am so grateful that you saw something in *The Watsons Go to Birmingham—1963* those many years ago. You have not only helped give birth to Kenny Watson, Bud Caldwell, Steven Carter, Luther T. Farrell and Deza Malone, you have also helped give birth to Christopher Paul Curtis, author. I can never thank you enough.

About the Author

Christopher Paul Curtis is the bestselling author of *Bud, Not Buddy*, which won the Newbery Medal and the Coretta Scott King Award, among many other honors. His first novel, *The Watsons Go to Birmingham—1963*, was also singled out for many awards, among them a Newbery Honor and a Coretta Scott King Honor. His most recent novels for Random House include *Mr. Chickee's Messy Mission*, *Mr. Chickee's Funny Money*, and *Bucking the Sarge*.

Christopher Paul Curtis grew up in Flint, Michigan. After high school he began working on the assembly line at the Fisher Body Flint Plant No. 1 while attending the Flint branch of the University of Michigan, where he began writing essays and fiction. He is now a full-time writer. Christopher Paul Curtis currently lives in Detroit with his wife, Habon, and their daughter, Ayaan.